Resonating Bodies

By the same author

SAFE HOUSES

Resonating Bodies

Lynne Alexander

First published 1988 by
MACMILLAN LONDON LIMITED
4 Little Essex Street London WC2R 3LF
and Basingstoke

Associated companies in Auckland, Delhi, Dublin, Gaborone, Hamburg, Harare, Hong Kong, Johannesburg, Kuala Lumpur, Lagos, Manzini, Melbourne, Mexico City, Nairobi, New York, Singapore and Tokyo

British Library Cataloguing in Publication Data
Alexander, Lynne, *1943–*
Resonating bodies.
I. Title
823'.54[F]

ISBN 0–333–47031–1

Typeset by Wyvern Typesetting Ltd, Bristol
Printed by Richard Clay Ltd, Bungay, Suffolk

To K.A.O.F

Acknowledgments

Many 'baroque' musicians contributed indirectly to the writing of this book. I am particularly indebted to Wieland Kuijken for the inspiration of his gamba playing; and to Gustav Leonhardt and Frans Brueggen for that of their playing, teaching and writing. I may, unwittingly, have quoted them. I also do not forget the example of my early teachers and colleagues, Jean Nandi and Laurette Goldberg.

I should like to thank Alison Crum for consulting with me on technical details. I chose not to heed her on one point, though, for the purposes of this fiction: Rose's head and neck are *not* a unity as they should in fact have been.

To Michael Latcham I owe the description of an instrument auction.

I should also like to thank Judith Serin, Deborah Rogers, Philippa Harrison and Kate Jones for their helpful suggestions.

When the heart sinks down (as it were) into the Earth, and would be buried there, yea, when it is almost dead, he with the breath of his Musick resuscitates it again.

Samuell Persons, *An Anatomical Lecture of Man, 1664*

Part I

Rose

1

Listen, Master, while I sing to you. Listen to the music that fills my chest and blossoms forth from my rose hole. Rose of the responsive bosom. The music flutters about inside me; the breasts of the tiny birds inlaid on my fingerboard rise and fall with the strains of my song. Close your eyes and hear it, this voice which resembles the human in all its inflexions; in its accents expressive of joy, sadness, gaiety, sweetness, breathiness, languor, excitement and fury; and in its vitality, its tenderness, its consolation, its support. If instruments are prized in proportion as they imitate the voice, then the prize is surely mine: clean and piercing in the treble, caressing in the tenor, ravishing and golden in the bass. The most alluring voice in all Europe, in the most resonant body.

Restrain yourself, Master. I see you would reach out for me yet: the left hand slipping round my neck, the right caressing my polished flanks. I know. But you have had me all your life, it's her turn now. Stay your hands, tuck them safely away. Do not try to embrace me from behind; to echo the slope of your shoulders to mine. Tonight my new mistress plays. As she once belonged to you, so now I belong to her. You are here at Versailles as her guest, to stretch your legs and listen without the pains of playing yourself. Why not enjoy this old abode of mine with its splendid acoustics, Valois tapestries, Lebrun heroics? Forget for the moment whose touch awakens me, and the gap between us. Let my voice reach out and touch you. Do you hear, Master; will you listen?

Good. Although you brought me to life – as surely as Pygmalion roused his lovely statue to breathe and dance – you never knew me: I had a past, you know. Do you suppose I spent my whole existence waiting for you down in that cellar in Bath? You were not the first to play me nor will you be the last – though I admit you were one of the best. I knew all about you, from the time you crawled down to me as a baby, but for all you knew I might have burst full-blown from the head of a violone. *Viola da gamba, anonymous, eighteenth century*. That was all you knew of me; you cheated me of a maker, a history. I cannot let that continue.

Listen, then, while I sing of me: who I am and who I was before you. But how to begin? Shall I open in the self-assured style of the full-blown French *ouverture*, or shall I slide into the matter, wandering in and out of the keys, *au style luthé*, suggesting, tickling and courting the ear, luring you into the drift of my past? No, I shall begin my own unique way, softly – not too softly, for the notes come out flat and the sound decays – but with deftness; searching my way back to the beginning. Bear with me while I compose and recollect myself.

Christophorus Bernardus me fecit, Paris, anno domini 1670. For centuries I wore this inscription inside me like a birthmark. You can still see it if you peer through my rose hole, though the blue-green arabesques are now faded to nothing. Even to me they became unmemorable, like a scale without shape, rhythm or ornament; not like a good melody which one never forgets. Not that you forgot, Master, when I was made or who made me – you simply never knew, for the dissolving curlicues told nothing. There were other clues, of course, for those who would date me by such methods: my face, worn by touch and the corrosive elements of centuries; my body; the glue that held me together, the varnish that covered me like a blanket – all these things spoke for me.

Only they did not tell the whole truth, as you have just heard. You know now that I am older than you guessed by half a century and also that I am no anonymous foundling but a child of Christophe Bernard. Are you surprised, Master? But I would do more than surprise the ear; I would touch your heart with my story. So listen carefully, Master, while I reveal all.

I was created an instrument of love. It was the year of Christophe's marriage; he made me for a wedding present to his bride, Berthe, who was nearly six feet tall. Now you understand why I was built on such a large scale, and why I was more ornate and had more strings than my contemporaries. It was because he wanted me to be more beautiful and more elegant than any instrument ever made. So he studied foreign instruments, incorporating those details he thought appropriate to my emerging personality. I became a composite of all that was wonderful and imaginative: with Flemish flame-shaped sound holes, a glorious oval rose and inlaid birds on my fingerboard, inspired by the English. And because he was also adventurous, he gave me seven strings rather than six – the first of my kind in Paris. My voice was deeper and more resonant than any of the others'.

So much work; the time it took to be made. Think of it, Master, imagine the agony of being half-born, my heart half-carved, my belly in strips, my soul being whittled down to size. And through it all, to have no voice. That was worst, when I tried to believe Christophe's whispered promises that my voice would be like an angel's, though I could not yet imagine sound.

For a whole year he laboured over me before his marriage, but the wedding day came and went and still I was not finished. For nine months more he worked at his conception: inlaying, painting, decorating, glueing, carving, sanding, sealing, oiling, varnishing, and saying his prayers towards the day when I would finally reach my genesis. On that day of mercy and music he would draw the new bow across my strings – so he rehearsed it to himself – and gaze into his wife's lovely eyes; at last she would understand what it was he had been trying to say but could never translate into words. Through me, Christophe would become eloquent.

He was putting the finishing touches to my precisely carved coiffure. It was quiet in the workshop, except for the sound of his breath close by my ear, its large earring sanded and oiled to a pearly smoothness. We heard the scream, but even then he could not be parted from his inspired midwifery. His wife and the baby both died, but I had come into being.

From that moment I looked out through eyes seeingly carved and was seized with pity, and also with the outrage of Job, at the harshness of human life; my voice became tinged with the passions of sorrow and mourning. But there was also a smile on my face whose secret told of pleasures and games which could lighten burdens. I flexed my enchanting sinews – the gut taken from new spring lambs – and found therein the power to charm men's souls and enchant their ears. I wanted to soothe Christophe; to bring celestial harmony into a discordant world; to sing him into love and peacefulness, and away from death. Don't be embarrassed at my arrogance, Master; in my time I have succeeded. You too have played your part in this entertainment.

Conceived in love but born to death. Words are of no use at such times. But as the lost baby would have learned its voice, so I learned mine, and made the silence speak. In my first moments I sounded the passion of sorrow in accents and shadings of tone, in dynamics loud and soft and all the variations in between, in ornaments both tasteful and precious, in swells and sighs which I drew through my soul from the hollow of my resonant body. So it came to me to triumph over death.

Christophe turned to me for comfort. He set me in an alcove opposite the sorry marriage bed. During the day I rested, settling, stretching and relaxing into my new self while he worked below on other instruments. At the end of the day he climbed the steep narrow stairs and crossed the threshold which divided work from pleasure. After a bachelor's meal of bread, cheese and red wine, he washed himself and came to me as to a bride.

He removes his shoes. Tenderly he lifts me by the neck and seats himself at a window. He wraps his legs around me in a soft embrace, my tailpiece well off the floor. He manipulates my ebony tuning pegs with their bone studs until I am in a fine temper. He inserts a forefinger between my strings to remove particles of dust from my fingerboard. He blows this way and that, producing the gentlest of rippling tickles. He moves my frets – this one a hair up, that one a hair down – and readjusts my temperament yet again. He whispers: *We must have perfect thirds*, while I, nearly losing my temper with so much mummery, am impatient for my first pleasuring. Not yet. He fetches a soft rag and polishes my mother-of-pearl inlay. He blows on his hands to warm them, then slides them into his armpits, holding me tightly between the knees. He cleans his fingernails and cracks his knuckles. He fills his chest with so much air that I am pushed away from him, and as he exhales the fingers of his left hand flutter down on my neck with the softness of goosedown. He leans his cheek against mine. Smelling of linseed oil and soap, he thrusts the bow gently across my strings.

He plays dance pieces he has improvised: a lugubrious Prelude, a measured Allemande, a complex Courante, a noble Sarabande. Remembering his widowhood, he stops before the Gigue. The last slow waves of my voice flatten out to nothing. He wipes his brow. There are tears in his eyes. He strokes my newly carved features while his breathing slows, and then he rests his hand on my head – one fits neatly in the ball of the other – and we sit quietly together, composing ourselves.

Nicholas

1

Nicholas Jordan needed time to compose himself. He had managed to dress appropriately, hail a taxi, negotiate getting into and out of it; to make his way with an approximation of dignity across the vast cobbled courtyard and into the Palace building as far as the Hall of Mirrors. There he had been alarmed at the sight of himself repeated *ad nauseam* – an elderly grey bent figure, half-merged into a hazy background (or was that his failing eyesight?) over-extravagantly framed in gold. The setting, he thought, demanded a more dashing, ornate figure, *à la Watteau*, perhaps: one who carried a lute and took up poses against a background of gold and pink.

Nicholas carried no instrument on his person, would pose for no artist. He walked on, trying to look at the ceiling, but that made him dizzy. The mirrors were too revealing, he thought, to a stooped old man still inclined to self-admiration. A good *rondeau* theme, if subtly varied and ornamented in the playing, could be amusingly *reprised* and *petite reprised*, but a procession of identical Nicholas Jordans, all of them depressingly faded, was quite another matter.

In the Music Room, the audience was already waiting, surrounded by TV cameras, lights and electronic sound equipment. The whole of Versailles was on show, audience and interiors as much as musicians and their instruments.

He must not make the mistake, therefore, of wandering on to the platform and making a fool of himself. He must take his seat purposefully amongst the audience, thus breaking the *modus operandi* of a lifetime.

He peered up and down the aisles looking for the seat with his name on it. They had told him where it would be but he had forgotten. He might remember every note of every piece he had ever played or conducted, but everyday facts he seemed to lose. He wandered up and down, pretending to look for his seat, distracting himself from the sight of Rose humped on her side next to the place on stage that should have been his. He heard his voice inside his head, too high-pitched, as if rehearsing for an interview: *Having divested myself of my instrument, I am now effectively retired.* He cleared his throat: *I am quite definitely retired. My successor will play tonight.* And she will play every night hereafter, he thought. And took his seat with as much grace as a stiff old man could manage, without his precious instrument to guide him. I am in need of Hill's lubricant, he decided: *a composition for pegs which have ceased to turn smoothly.*

He was more anxious than he had ever been before a performance of his own. He tried to relax by replaying to himself his own pre-concert routine. He had made it a point never to arrive too early, allowing himself time for some last-minute primping of himself and Rose, and no more. He had fended off the cosseting attentions of individuals who called themselves stage managers, who invariably knew nothing about music, but who wanted to tell him the story of their lives. He had endured it when they fetched him glasses of water, opened the stage door for him as if he were a cripple. Just as they were now doing for Lucy.

Nicholas saw only himself striding across the platform, taking quick measure of the house, bowing, sitting down with Rose between his legs, adjusting the stand, flipping to the first page of the score, scanning his audience quickly but thoroughly. That done, he focuses his entire attention on Rose: tunes her, fits his body to hers, breathes with her. The audience maintained a respectful silence during this ceremony: a mysterious and impressive, if incomprehensible, part of the performance. The delay heightened their anticipated pleasure.

He smiled. Then the smile faded as he remembered where he was – he no longer had the power to cause shock or wonderment, or any other reaction. He looked up. He and Rose were separated by more than the physical distance between them. Her eyes stared through him and her smile mocked him. He had no further claim on her.

It was like an old nightmare. The music was there on its stand but there was no Rose between his legs. He was impeccably dressed, the audience was waiting – and still there was nothing but a gap; no instrument to hold fast, to anchor his body to the seat or his feet to the stage. So they would fly up as if they did not belong to the dignified Nicholas Jordan. He had to brace them with his arms to keep them still.

Surely it had been the right thing to do, to bequeath Rose to the next generation. Sensible not to wait until his fingers could not bend or stretch without pain; to bow out gracefully before the critics and younger players had a chance to pick him to pieces. A well-timed gesture. Lucy, the closest to him of all of them, was the appropriate inheritor to the tradition. He would not be forgotten; Rose would be well served.

But this precious logic did not calm him. He felt disturbed and unsure of himself, which was out of character. Why had he given Rose away – his own creation? He must be mad. It was like a hasty divorce; worse, a premature death. After all, he still had his faculties, the use of his muscles, his brain power. So long as his heart pumped away, however irregularly and feebly, he could have gone on playing up to the last beat. Why had he done it? For applause, approbation? And if so, whose? All he knew was that he had given Rose away and that it could not be undone. He looked up, straight into Lucy's young face. She could use all his support – more than a pasted-on smile – but he had none to give her, for at this moment she was his enemy. She had taken his

Rose. No, wait, he had given Rose to her. But in a sense, she had taken her.

He felt cold in spite of the hot lights. He always felt cold these days, as if his sinews were already exposed to the corroding air. Look what it could do to strings. He pulled his scarf closer around his neck. Lucy pulled Rose closer to her chest. Well she might, if she knew how strong Nicholas's impulse was to grab her back to where she belonged. *See here, young woman, I am her master; you could never in a million years take my place. Do not delude yourself. Just because I gave her to you. . . .* He comforted himself with the thought that if Lucy knew anything at all, it was what he had taught her, or what she had divined from him. But Rose smiled, as if to deny it; as if there might be more to her.

Wood, wooden: lacking resilience, stiff, awkward, clumsy. Ridiculous adjectives which had nothing to do with his Rose, who lived and breathed and resonated, whose warm vital bodily substance responded to the lightest touch. How he loved her, her smooth surface, the hollow depths of her, the delicate contours of her body, the details of her roseate face. No other instrument of her time had been made of such fine wood. No other instrument glowed the way Rose did. But she was vulnerable. If improperly treated she could dry out and crack; improperly played she could indeed become wooden. His eyes filled with tears. Who would recognise the arrogant Nicholas Jordan now? *Well, he's old, you know, can hardly play any more, feeling sorry for himself. It's a shame, but that was a jolly fine thing he did, handing over that magnificent gamba. You have to admire that.*

I don't want the next generation to take over, he thought. I won't let go; this Lucy shan't take my place. But it was too late: she had. He felt too tired to fight. Perhaps not ready to lie down yet but to sit, yes, and rest. And calm himself. And listen.

When the music started, he fell back. He was roused. Her tone had grown stronger, more rounded, voluptuous. Like her. Listening to Rose warmed him. He allowed himself to be soothed, though he noted she would not stay in tune under the hot lights. It was hardly surprising. The old are not easy, he thought; they do not cooperate in the productions of the young. But if audiences wanted to hear what an original instrument sounded like, they would have to put up with its susceptibilities – to heat, light, bodies, dampness, cold. Rose's exquisite, well-tuned voice made it all worth while.

Always stationed behind her, he had envied his audiences the one pleasure he'd been denied – of watching her. Now he did not take his eyes off Rose: that smile again, which seemed to change with the frequency of her mood, and that voice, with the power to move him so deeply. He listened and she sang to him, as tenderly as if she were putting him to bed. He let her woo him and stroke him. He was a child again, hearing music for the first time. He let himself go, safe in her sound, as round and firm as a pair of cradling arms.

Rose

2

Let yourself go, Master; let me hold you with my voice as you once held me in your arms. Let the wide berth of my strings support and sustain you. Listen and you will not weep or shake. Do not think of losing me, yet. Live for this moment, as I do. Do not waste it, for it will never come back in the same way. It is your moment of grace. I too remember the feel of your hands and of your body wrapped round mine; it was that which distinguished you, not your countenance. I knew you from the intimate feel of your limbs, by the warmth of your breath in my ear and coursing down my strings, from the tactus of your heart against my back. I knew your face too, but only details gleaned during the intimacy of tuning. I loved it when you twirled me round, loosening and tightening my pegs and plucking my strings, your face inches from mine. Sometimes you leaned me away for better leverage, then brought me close again, chest to chest, stroking my temples, searching my eyes. Yours were enormous and blue close up. I believed the pores of your skin were open, like ears, to drink in my sound.

Now your features are indistinct from the other adoring faces gazing up at me. You are one of them; I must play to all of you, pitching my voice to the farthest seat in the house. (The performance of music, as you know, must be more than a *tête-à-tête* between lovers.) I am a public creature; my voice, naturally small and tending to vanish like vapour, grows and fills the room by sheer will and not a little magic. I am not your private creature, Nicholas, nor your creation. As you hear, I am no longer yours alone.

You sit here, my old Master, listening to the voice you know so well, too well perhaps. You want it to do your bidding still. You clench your fists and tuck them away beneath you. You cannot acknowledge our separation. Listen: another plays upon me. I have a new voice you hardly recognise. The bond is broken.

But wait, do not run from me yet. Where are you going? Ah, a stroll in the gardens – yes, perhaps it is a good idea. Let the cool night air calm you. Be reminded of the wondrous concord of our time together; let the symmetry of the gardens comfort you in the wake of our dissolution. You know that all marriages must come eventually to an end – at least ours did so sweetly and naturally. Music consists in the agreement of things, remember that, Nicholas. We never quarrelled or disagreed, even about how the end should go. We played it with grace.

Meanwhile – I address those of you in my audience who do not know me – allow me to introduce myself formally. I am Rose, Viola da Gamba, of the family Viols, noble in size and shape. Like the cello, I am held between the legs: *da gamba*. Unlike the cello, however, which often has a metal tail on which it leans (causing unsightly damage to wooden floors), I rest on nothing but the inner calves, and to these I transmit my full sonority. Holding me can be a trial of cramping, muscle tension and dreadful fatigue, and yet pleasure rarely comes without a measure of pain. After a time the legs become strengthened and better able to sustain their burden. In the end there is pleasure.

I am made to speak by the friction of a bow, which passes over my stretched strings and excites them to sound. The vibrations pass through my bridge to my belly, through my sound post – known as my soul – to my back, and circulate within me. Released from my rose hole – which I consider to be my heart – to the open air, they float to your ears as music.

I am four feet two inches tall. As to shape, my back is flat, not bulging like the cello's. My shoulders slope gracefully downwards – for greater ease of playing in the higher positions – whereas the cello's are ungainly and pompous as *Le Roi-Soleil*. My waist, an unbroken curve, allows the bow to move freely across my strings without touching my sides. The bottom part of me, though voluptuous, is not in any way disproportionate. Altogether I am lighter and thinner than the cello, so that my entire body resonates freely. My bridge, being lower, creates less tension in my strings: they vibrate with less amplitude but greater freedom. And lastly, my neck is fretted with bands of fine gut tied round at semitone intervals which, when pressed, produce a sharp, clear quality of tone.

My seven strings are all of gut – but sheep's not cat's as is commonly believed. Some are twisted like rope, some half-spun with silver and some are covered with silver-plated copper, to give a bigger and more resonant – or *woofy* – sound. My top string is particularly mellow.

There was a time when I was called an ancestress of the cello; a primitive antecedent, like the caterpillar to the butterfly. This is absurd. We flourished side by side, the cello and I, for some two centuries. No person of discrimination would consider mistaking us one for the other. I am quieter, more noble, and, though restrained, incisive and passionate. Even among gambas I am exceptional.

Christophe my maker spared no expense in creating me. He used the finest aged woods: bird's-eye maple for my back and ribs, ebony for my fingerboard and tuning pegs. He inlaid squares of mother-of-pearl and ebony in a frame of multiple purfling – three layers of hardwood edged with ivory – to strengthen my contours. My fingerboard he edged with ebony and ivory segments, my tailpiece *en suite*, inlaying a floral design with singing birds. My nut was fashioned in bone, and my bridge, with a heart-shaped cutout, in sycamore. For my sound hole, he carved a parchment rose.

I come at last to the topmost part of me: my head, set atop a pegbox carved with scrolling foliage. Finial, masthead, figurehead, head of an angel – call it what you will. My cheekbones are wide and my nose by now is a trifle flat, having become worn away with much stroking. My chin, once proud as the masthead on a ship, has also become softer and more rounded. A diagonal scar, running from cheekbone to chin (a recent desecration, about which you shall learn more in due course), is unfortunate: it mars, perhaps, but cannot destroy my beauty. My bow-shaped mouth still curves upwards at the corners: I smile perpetually.

My hair is fashioned in shallow waves, a close bun at the nape; not a wisp crawls out of place, even when I am passionately aroused. My ears are flat. Pearl earrings – irresistible to musical thumbs – adorn my lobes. And my eyes? They stare straight ahead. Some masters liked to say I could see into the future; others thought me blind as a Greek statue. Sad, proud, imperious, dowdy, magnificent, witch-like: so I have been variously described down through the centuries.

And you, Nicholas, how do you think of me?

Nicholas

2

How did he think of Rose?

Nicholas closed his eyes and concentrated on the memory of her features, the way people do who love each other. He recalled her slightly protrusive almond eyes with their deeply grooved upper and lower lids; her callipygous bottom – no, certainly not fat; her chin a delightfully chubby orb. He saw her lips – confidently upturned at the corners – that so mobilised her face. She radiated composure and wisdom from that smile: it *was* music. He could feel the curve of the waves in her hair; the darkened varnish in their troughs emphasised their definition, as it did in and around her eyelids and in the small dear creases beside her nostrils. He remembered the shadowy underside of her chin and how the glorious expanse of forehead and cheeks was marred by a slight mottling. Nor could he forget the scar that she had acquired in 1969, or its painful acquisition. The earrings, only just visible beneath the sweep of hair covering her ears – how it hurt not being able to touch them. *I think you magnificent*, he responded, in abject honesty.

He tried to think dispassionately of other headed gambas he had seen. Most were in museums, a small number in private hands. French instruments were on the whole rather plain, Flemish ones modest and simpering, with bowed heads and half-closed eyes, while the Germans tended to fat, with big noses, double chins and disapproving mouths.

How could such faces inspire music; on the one hand self-effacing, on the other monarchic?

He opened his eyes and saw her again as a shrivelled crone, the prominent planes of her skull painfully highlighted. How the television lights distorted her fragile beauty! – when in reality, age had made her more beautiful. Her back was still as flat as a youth's, her belly a feast of fine grain in the centre, opening out to broad young grain on her flanks. The scrolling foliage on her pegbox would never die, nor the birds on her fingerboard; nor would her lustrous hair ever turn grey. Only catastrophe would stop her now: earthquake, war, nuclear disaster, motorway crash, revolution. He listened closely. How much we need the old, he thought, to enrich our vapid modern world. And how much the young need the old world's instruments to bring harmony to their disagreeable lives.

Time had not been kind to Nicholas as it had been to Rose. It had wrinkled his skin, thinned his hair, weakened his eyes, thrown his heart into rhythmic confusion, bent his back and stiffened and contorted his hands, so that his facility had been broken, his touch affected. A gamba player who could not play was a bad joke, and he did not want to be the butt of it. His last concert had been no disaster, but he had begun to notice an almost imperceptible loss of control. Rose would have felt it: the sweat on his palms and between his thighs, the wayward heart that she had always counted on. For the first time in his life, he had taken a safe, slow tempo in the Bach D Major. It was his cue to leave.

Not yet an old man, but on his way out. He saw that he could do nothing more for Rose; Lucy must do it for him. The truth was – he saw it now – that the old also needed the young. Only they could re-create the past; he could not. The old got stuck in their own traditions. Lucy would do new things; she would infect that post-modernist world of hers with the spirit of Rose. Not his world any longer. They must do without him.

Yet he hated her for stealing his Rose.

He thought of all the other thieves: other hands that had cupped her perfect head, covered her eyes, nostrils, lips, fingered and stroked her strings. Like Christophe Bernard, her fine young maker; her fashioner, her sculptor, her Pygmalion; he her hero, and she the masterpiece of his career; snuggling in his lap, his oily, leathery hand resting on her head. Nicholas felt suddenly short of breath, as if the patriarchal hand had come down over his own nose and mouth. The smell of linseed oil gagged him. He would sooner not know about the proprietary pats and smothering caresses, rather not picture her transported to passion by anyone but him. Rather not hear.

Rose

3

And yet you *shall* hear. Though it distresses you, you will lend yourself to my past; picture Christophe passing his hands over the coif of calm waves he has carved. His eyes are closed as if praying, to retrieve some of the harmony he has given them. His forehead is scored with the parallel lines of the stave, but it is misery's brand not music's. In giving voice to music, my maker has suffered human loss.

I bear witness to his pain. The burden is heavy, for he expects me to be everything to him, to console him and replace the pleasures he has lost. His precious creature: wife, daughter, mistress of perfect harmony crafted into one. He twirls me round and round, peering into the egg-shaped eyes he has carved for me, hoping to see therein a human soul. He holds me by my broad neck and lays his lips on mine: perhaps he fancies that I am his dead wife come back to him.

I do not respond to his husbandly advances. My body does not grow warm and I do not vibrate contentedly against his shaking legs. My voice is that of a *poissarde* and not a bride. He applies extra coatings of rosin, but the hairs of my bow become clotted, the frog with its pearl eyes clouded over. My voice scratches and grates. I stare out over the Parisian rooftops, bored and frustrated, as he wipes off the excess rosin with a spirit rag and tries again; and again and again, he plays this repetitive prelude.

Why am I so wooden? Why do I not yield to my maker, my father who loves me and loves to play upon me and for whom I am sole consolation? Surely love, even without ease, can transport? But I am not moved: the masterbuilder is no musician. He is too awkward, too greedy; his incestuous love produces friction and pain. Each time he embraces me – gripping harder and harder – I fear that the ribs he whittled so lovingly will crack. I long for release from his wounding touch. I would be unbound from him and his dead family. He is my father; he created me. But now he should let me go.

So you see, Nicholas, you are wrong to torture yourself over our transports of delight. It was true he gave me love – too much, as you did, so there was nothing left for others – but there was no return on my side. I felt like a servant-daughter, forever escaping in her dreams. Oh, I loved my maker Christophe, I owed my existence to him, but he did not satisfy me: his playing was not equal to his craftsmanship. The more he sought me out, the more my heart, strings and soul became hardened against him. I did not want to be a memorial to the dead. So I sang my own lament and dreamed my own dreams, which were out of time and tune with Christophe's remorseful fingerings.

He was not a fool, my maker; one who would live forever unaware of my discontent. He blamed himself for poor musicianship, for lack of virtuosity, for having craftsman's fingers too hardened to respond to my sensitive strings. He felt himself trapped between ability and desire, unable to follow through with either. The act of creating me had left him depleted. He put life and death into my voice and that could not be repeated. Still only a boy, he had reached his climax; and what was he to do then? It was like exhausting your repertoire after the first concert, Master. There was no ladder of success to scale; only the awkward slow climb down. After me, he made indifferent instruments with weak glue joints, which, like his name, did not survive the century. He oversaw work in his studio, but it did not engage him. Only I could do that. Yet he knew he could not harness me to him for ever. Eventually, when it became too unprofitable and embarrassing to keep me, he would let me go to one of the great players of Europe. It was my destiny.

He too would forget. He begins to visit the house of a widow who plays the lute. They play duets together in the minor mode, gazing lugubriously at one another, sipping wine in the hazy summer evening light. Feeling a sense of release, I relax and sing out. But I do not please the widow – she would replace me with a violin. The treble voice, she says, lightens the spirit. Besides, where is his business sense? Does he not see the waste and the extravagance in keeping me? Knowing she is right, he nods but does not reply. She could hardly be expected to understand. The first Mme Bernard and I are bound together like wound gut. He cannot yet sell a part of himself.

Eventually he will forget, he tells her; enjoy life, look to the future, replace his mournful creation with live babies and fiddles. He puts his new violin to his chin but his bow arm hangs limply at his side. He cannot make it dip and swoon as she would have him do, to the accompaniment of her lute and lilting voice. Hearing our old voices, still bound by death and memory, he can play no jolly tune.

I think he is too much in love with his own creations, both the dead and the living. That is vanity; also it is selfish. The widow is right, he should let me go.

Many famous musicians visit the Bernard studio, hoping to play upon me. Tales of my beauty augment. Many come just to gaze up at me. One of them even writes a piece, alas lost, called *Apotheosis of the Bernard Viol*. Yet Christophe himself guards me jealously. He would have me hang for ever on a silken cord, like another of his crucifixes. From time to time someone is permitted to finger and bow me, but only briefly. What supreme artist has created such an instrument? they enquire, and he replies, glaring: *I made her*; daring them to take me away. They try to soften him with compliments: *such beauty, such precious decoration*; but he is unmoved. The price on my head is beyond the purse of even the most famous musician. So they thrum me, and leave me vibrating with the thrill of their touch.

I do not know the sound of my voice. It hangs in the air

around me, teasing me; my strings pick up other voices and resonate sympathetically with them. The urge to be played overwhelms me, yet I can no more choose my first master than the crucifix can claim its believers. I must be patient, and hang here, waiting to be touched.

Nicholas

3

Nicholas wanted very much to touch Rose. His palms were wet, his heart pounded, his arm hurt. He wanted to forget Lucy flaunting her not twenty feet away from him, to slip back to the seventeenth-century Paris workshop where she hung newly crafted, guarded by the incompetent Christophe. How he could gloat! How much scope there was for invention! He imagined himself breaking in the wonderful new instrument, with such consummate skill that Christophe would give up his possessive vigil. Take her, take her, she is yours, he would say, thrusting the virgin at him. Nicholas instinctively prepared for the play: his shoulders drooped, his bow arm dropped in a downward curve, his fingers opened to welcome her neck.

The woman to his left turned to glare at him; the man to his right shifted further away. Nicholas gave them each a reassuring smile and folded his hands in his lap. He must control himself. He listened. No tone from the high treble, middle register disagreeable; the bass stifled, no woof. Lucy was forcing her. *One must not be harsh with the instrument, which requires to be treated much as one treats a horse; for if it is forced too much it takes the bit between its teeth and does not obey, on the contrary, if it is excited with moderation, one draws from it all the service one can wish.* Nicholas wasn't altogether comfortable with Rousseau's horse imagery, but he liked 'excited with moderation': it expressed perfectly the baroque predilection, which was Rose's, for extravagance checked by restraint.

Lucy's *inégal* was too predictable; she paused too long between the cadential trill and the final note. Whose mannerism was that? And why was she twitching her eyebrows and revolving her lips like a monkey? Such physical gestures were so unnecessary, so hideous. He saw himself sitting in her place, with the expressionless face that he was convinced he presented to the world. But recently he had overheard otherwise; that in fact he made some very odd faces indeed. Could they be as repulsive as Lucy's? He mobilised his features in time with the music, to see if it felt familiar. Again people looked at him. Was she parodying him; exaggerating his gestures to make her audience laugh at him? He was tempted to leap on the stage and take the bow from her. *Look, this is how it's done: effortlessly. Excited with moderation. Let the weight of the arm give the bow a strong spring and then let go*. Impossible to teach. Only after she had played Rose as long as he had would she be able to do it. Eventually Rose would become a part of her. Then she too would find herself superseded.

He wished he could leave; he had had enough. But he feared collapse. He recalled playing a concert during which a woman suffered a stroke. He had glared at her, outraged by her rude snores. He managed to keep playing – it would have been most unprofessional to stop – but his concentration was broken. How could one person's puny demonstration of mortality compete with his performance? And why hadn't the music, if not his playing, had the power to stop her blood vessels bursting? *Wait, don't go, get back to your seat, quit that hideous snoring; don't die until the music is over*.

But she didn't wait. Nicholas went on playing and the audience closed up around the empty place as if nothing had happened. He played the rest of the concert excited by a sense of fury which heightened his listeners' pleasure. By the end he'd forgotten about the woman completely, as had the audience, to judge by their enthusiasm. (Had she died, recovered, come back for the second half? He never found out.)

No one must die while the music plays. Nicholas calmed himself, determined not to be the offender tonight. He tried to concentrate on Rose, but hated the sight of her between Lucy's legs, with the long skirt draping her flanks and Lucy's limp hair brushing her dark cheek; no less the sound of her stifled voice. He wanted to see her precious purfling outlined against the sharpness of his trouser crease.

No more; the whole spectacle disgusted him. What was the meaning of that dancer, flapping her wrists like a goose in heat? Visual fluff for the benefit of the television cameras; a sellout. It was so superfluous, when Rose could speak for herself. No more suites, couplets, variations; no more recapitulations, reprises. He didn't want to hear about Rose's obsessive maker, the master she longed for; as if life could repeat itself the way music could. He wanted none of it. All he knew was that he wanted Rose again, now. He was a boy again; fifty years had not intervened. He longed for her, lacked the forbearance to stay his urges. The old and the young Nicholas Jordan merged into one.

Young Nicholas's mother had forbidden him to play. She had packed him off to boarding school, like a lovesick damsel on a voyage of forgetting. How could she think he would forget? It made the longing worse, and the resentment. Why deny him Rose? Surely the sooner he learned how to play her the better. His mother ought to be proud of him – encourage, not stifle him. She was either mad or wicked. She was also foolish, because the more he was deprived of Rose, the more his need to play her grew.

He had gone with his father, first to the viewing, then to the auction proper. At the viewing, Rose lay on her back alone on a green-clothed table. On another table were the violins, and at the other end of the room were a late chittarone, a pearwood bassoon and an early twentieth-century saxophone. The smaller instruments and their bows were being freely handled, plucked and pulled apart. Rose's table, he recalled with some distress, had served as leaning post, desk and coat rack for the viewers, including one who had the indelicacy to place his bowler over Rose's head. Happily, a young man said to him, 'If you don't mind, I have come to play this instrument,' and plucked off the hat, unburdened instrument and table of astrakhan coats, umbrellas, catalogues and paraphernalia. The young man removed his jacket, called for a chair, tuned, played a few scales, an improvised prelude, began the Allemande from the C major cello suite by Bach. 'It's a pity,' he said, breaking off after only a few measures, 'but it's not really a very good cello.' Others poked and prodded her, shook their heads and passed on to pristine instruments. Only Harry Jordan was undaunted, because he thought her beautiful and knew nothing of the devastating effects of a botched-up conversion.

The 'cello' was taken off to the auction room and strung up under her chin to dangle against a partition wall. Others, less beautiful but evidently more valuable, were strung up beside her, like moles on a farmer's gate. A young woman with a drawing board across her knee was sketching the auctioneer behind his pulpit, with his great moustaches, and the rows of bidders in shirtsleeves and waistcoats. She turned to draw the headed beauty with the little boy guarding her. 'I'm going to play one day,' he told her. She said she believed him and gave him the sketch to prove it. There was an upper gallery and a stage, like a concert hall; yet it was really more like a circus, with the assistants in frock coats balancing woodwinds on their palms, as if they would juggle them.

Nicholas's Rose was known as Lot 80 [An unusual Violoncello of Original Bass Viola da Gamba Form, anonymous maker, eighteenth century]. Bidding started and stayed low since word of her condition had already gone round: the collectors were feeling nervous and the musicians couldn't afford an unplayable instrument. But Harry Jordan jumped in, and doubled his only competition. 'Well done, Mr Jordan,' said the auctioneer, knocking his gavel and going on to Lot 81, a rare eighteenth-century nail violin. The Jordans and their bargain left together, Nicholas in one hand, Lot 80 in the other. Nicholas had been proud of his father then.

Harry Jordan deluded himself that his wife could be taught to appreciate The Beautiful Things In Life. On the way home, he confided to Nicholas that he hoped she might learn to play the new instrument. But Nicholas knew otherwise. At the age of ten he knew more about his mother's likes and dislikes than his father did. The pride he had only just felt turned to contempt. 'You know she hates old things; she thinks they're ugly. But it doesn't matter,' he added, 'because I should like to learn to play myself.' And he put a protective hand on Lot 80's battered case.

His mother's reaction had been more violent than usual. She picked up the nearest fist-sized object – a jade vase – and threw it somewhere between her husband's and Lot 80's head, fortunately missing both, though destroying the vase. She launched into a stream of invective on the subject of antiques which she claimed to have been bottling up for years. So far as she was concerned, his collection of so-called objects d'art, or whatever he called them, were ugly, repulsive, hideous, ungainly, barbaric and dirty, and she was sick to death of the whole bloody lot of them. She didn't care if it was art, she was sure this monster with the grinning head would give her nightmares, and besides she hated classical music, or baroque, or whatever he called it – she didn't care. Furthermore, if she ever did take up an instrument, it would be the piano, and she would play dance pieces and music-hall songs; something with some spunk in it. She certainly didn't fancy holding one of those decrepit old things between her legs.

Taste was a subject dear to Harry Jordan's heart. He ignored his wife's tirade and later preached to Nicholas with a convert's passion (his father had been a steelworker) on the value of what he called high art. A taste for culture, the beautiful things on this earth: what else was life all about? Music especially civilised us, educated us, developed our minds and feelings – but not the tawdry stuff his wife was talking about; no, not cheap music, that he could not allow in his tasteful house.

Nicholas claimed the instrument for his own, naming her Rose because of her deep rose-coloured varnish and the rose – or what was left of it – decorating her chest. It seemed the best name. His father agreed. But his mother refused to cooperate. Giving 'it' a name, she told Harry, would only encourage the boy in his folly. Over her dead body would the boy play 'it'. If he was going to love any female at this stage in his life, then it should be her and not that misshapen harpy. She feared for his mental health, and his normal sexual development. The instrument must be sold or put downstairs.

They say the woodworm is not fond of music, yet Nicholas's Rose became riddled with it. While he was away at school his mother banished her to the basement along with the other freakish antiques: the cracked mirrors, toys, staring statues, the carousel horse with the grimacing whinny. She stood amongst them, only half-protected by her hard case, with the dampness oozing in. Pieces of mother-of-pearl inlay worked loose, her strings oxidised, her lovely head lolled.

Nicholas wrote to his father, begging him to save Rose from further damage, and not give in to his mother's demands to sell her. He wanted her himself. Bring her to me, he wrote; sneak her out, if necessary. Harry Jordan wrote back to say he was doing his best about the damp, but he couldn't guarantee she would be there for ever. He could not go against his wife's wishes; Nicholas's deception was unthinkable. 'I'm sorry,' he added, 'I should like you to be able to play.'

She haunted him at school. He saw her face in his books and on the blackboards. In chapel he went down on his knees to his madonna holed up in less than all her glory. He heard her voice echoing in the corridors: *If thou longst so much to learne (sweet boy) what 'tis to love, Do but fixe thy thought on mee, and thou shalt quickly prove*. He fixed his thoughts on her in the darkness; saw her smiling and heard her singing in a voice he could only intuit. He huddled beneath blankets, dreaming of her while boys did things to themselves and each other. But all Nicholas wanted was to gather his Rose into his arms and make her sing.

Rose

4

I wanted to sing. I wanted to hear the sound of my own voice; for it to be awakened with fresh skill. I wanted someone young, handsome and touched with musical genius to enfold me; a conjurer in the circle of the ear. Someone like you, Nicholas, who as a boy huddled in his bed dreaming of me; who when he saw me hanging on my silken cord in Christophe's studio would go down on his knees; who would swoon with delight when he heard my voice; who would love, honour, cherish and most of all obey my commands. You see, my daydreams were quite unoriginal. I was a foolish virgin, dressed and waiting for love to strike at an open window; longing for the *opéra* of marriage but taking no account of the price of servitude. I was the passive vessel waiting in silence to be filled with pleasure. How different it is today: women wait for nothing. Lucy, for one, who takes me between her sturdy jogger's legs, gripping and bowing with such confidence. Alas, I shall never be like her; it is my nature to be played upon.

I was certain that my first new owner would satisfy me. I did not think my expectations unreasonable. I knew from the many compliments I had received, the admiring looks, the hordes of gifted musicians, that I was invaluable. Many, I was sure, had beggared themselves to raise the price on my pretty head, but even so Christophe would not sell. What was he waiting for: a prince, a king, a Couperin?

A Graswinkel. A Dutchman the colour of dried catgut, or Dr Tulp's cadaver. A man whose musicianship was as elusive as the blood in his veins. How could my maker do this to me? How could he betray me so? If I cannot have her myself, he perhaps thought, no one else of any substance shall. It will be just as if she had never been made; let the North Sea swallow her up. Was such perversity possible, such jealousy, such selfishness? Out of sight, out of mind, Christophe, but out of ear? Impossible. Or had his new wife swayed him, greedy for gold?

His gold coins and the tip of his nose were all of Graswinkel that shone. His hair was thin and grey, stretched across his skull on top and hanging in dry wisps round the sides. His modest black weeds were those of the Puritan, but the look in his eyes was not pure. He thought himself dignified, elegant and devout in his emaciation. He posed, one hand propped on his hip, the other placed across his shrunken chest. His lips were elongated; he made humphing noises followed by blasts of wind and smacking sounds (*um ja, um ja, zo zo, ja ja*) – and his eyes, which were red and glistening, bulged. I was put in mind of a giant insect.

Govert Cornelis Graswinkel sniffs at me with his proboscis. The reek of herrings makes my strings curl. He plucks me from the wall, as if I were a ripe pear. I recoil at the proximity of him, feel his indecency envelop and overwhelm me. I am not prepared for such a ravishment; I understand at this moment how women feel at the hands of beastly men. He lays me down on my back to finger me. His little red eyes gleam in the sawdusty dimness. His hand descends from his dented chest to his protrusive belly, and revolves; his tongue flops out from between his teeth. He leers down at me, then lays me in my travelling case. I will do nicely, *ja*.

I lay on my back. Gone were the lovely scents from my maker's studio – the fresh wood shavings, the rabbit glue, the burgundy wine, Christophe's soap. Directly above me was a brass chandelier. I saw myself reflected in its central globe, my belly as swollen as that of the wife of Arnolfini. The floor was covered with black and white marble tiles set at a diagonal to the windows, which were low and heavily leaded. The room was bare and stark but for a bench under the window and the long oak table on which I lay. A single painting hung on the wall, of objects from the Virgin's bedroom, painted in tones of white: lilies in a vase, a neatly folded towel, a basin and ewer.

As you know, Master, no painting of this period was without its symbolism, so preoccupied were the Dutch with fear of Death and Vanitas. I noticed a great clock (its face also black and white) and thought, ah, there ticks away time, and here too am I with my dying strings. All we lack for the allegory of 'Life the Fugitive' is a little boy blowing bubbles. But these people were even more obsessed with sin. I could well be the focus of a still-life: Interior With Viola da Gamba – a composition of shocking contrast, between that barren colourless room and my splendid self, reclining on my back, the near-animate representation of vain sensuality.

There are no sweet preliminaries. He manoeuvres me between his vice-like knees, where I rock uncomfortably against the knobbly bones. He cranks my pegs in a crude approximation of tuning. Taking up my bow, he accompanies himself in the singing of the psalm, 'Behold how good and pleasant it is to dwell together in unity'. My voice is nasal, like a diplomat's. That is good, modesty and chastity are what he likes. The angels do not sing out above their master's voice. Nor shall I. My belly contracts and my pitch goes sharp. I am as cold as the tiled floor and as frigid as the bony fingers fretting me.

Oh, but I want to be played, to sing out, to blossom, to embrace the entire room with my sound; to send liquid cries of joy to my heavenly master, Apollo. How my sound would thrive in such a room, were it encouraged. Played by a real master, how it would swell, to fill the room with round, velvety tones. But it is crushed, gagged, deadened by the scarecrow's fingers. My voice comes squeaking through in that austere room with the church pew, whose scalloped curves make shadows on the floor, in the shaft of weak northern light. Graswinkel squeezes my neck harder with his cruel talons, bleeding music from me drop by drop. In the name of religion. *Musica dei donum*.

Nicholas

4

Nicholas pictured Graswinkel's waxy, gut-coloured hand curling around Rose's fair stem, and shuddered. God's gift indeed. It recalled the abomination of his own childhood, when Matron's stump came to rest on the back of his neck. 'You see,' she said, grinning like a Bosch monster and thrusting the stump into his face, 'you see here a hand that will never play music. A blank; a blunt instrument; none of your fine cellist's fingers attached to *that*.' She told him the story (each boy got a different one, he later learned) of how her father had caught her stealing from him – to save up for piano lessons – and cut it off with an axe. It was a most improbable story, composed for gullible little boys learning to play soaring violins and moaning cellos. Better an absent father than an evil one, was the suspect moral, which Nicholas, in any case, disbelieved. He ignored the stump; vowed to harden himself so that the next blow, and the next, would strike in him only dead notes. His performer's nerves would see him through for life.

Rose's neck was wide and inviting. He knew by heart the way the grain parted and curled, the length of that smooth long elegance which was so tempting to stroke. Boys' necks were soft, indented at the back, and covered in peach fuzz. That was where Matron had put her stump, rubbing it up and down, over and over again. But boys' necks were not as fragile as old men's, with their articulated veins and sinews.

Articulation, the magic word, which he taught his students, to remind them that music, like language, had its own punctuation. Even Lucy had pasted a large sticker across Rose's case with the command, 'Articulate!'

Rose, as he first knew her, had looked quite grotesque, with her cello neck uncomfortably married to her gamba body. It was like grafting a giraffe's neck on a human torso. She had been made protean and had become outlandish; an hermaphrodite, a hippogriff. Monsters like that could hardly sing. Before delivering her to Nicholas, Harry Jordan had had her 'seen to' by a Bath furniture restorer, who cleaned her up (she was begrimed with dirt and old varnish, riddled with woodworm, stringless, with a hole for a heart and her soul jutting up through her belly), treated her for parasites, fitted her with a new rosette made of a round of wood from the punched seat of a Victorian kitchen chair, and repositioned her soul and sealed the crack where it pushed through her belly. Finally he gave her a set of four fat wire strings.

It was quite wrong – even Nicholas in his youthful ignorance knew that. But how to redeem her? He tried to educate himself by reading articles and looking at illustrations of 'old' instruments, even when they were freakish curiosities, like the *lyra da braccio*, with the head of a man carved into its back, fully bearded and moustached; or a tiny five-stringed *pardessus de viole* with a sad clown's head. He snipped out a reproduction of a painting of Marin Marais, a French gamba player, holding a large seven-stringed instrument across his knee. He carried it in his wallet for years.

He compared Rose with other 'specimens' of bass gambas in museum cases, and found that she was larger, on the whole, but that her body exactly matched theirs. It was clearly her bridge, her neck and her stringing that were wrong. She should have had frets: he pictured them wrapped round her neck like so many necklaces. He imagined the plump of his fingers against them and the clean, ringing tone they would produce. He made sketches of her with a shorter neck, with at least six strings, and sometimes seven, like the Marais gamba. He practised bowing her underhand, and imagined her lovely resistance. He dreamed of restoring her properly; of saving her from monstrous abuse.

Rose

5

It was sweet of you – the boy Nicholas – to want to save me. I am grateful that it was you and not another Dryasdust: I had no wish to be encapsulated again. To be restored, yes, that I wished for, but to be played was my necessity.

There was another, before your time, who also saved me – not with his music but with his art. Johannes Vermeer. He worked his brush in short caressing strokes. Into my world without music, he brought the harmony of colour and the air of vision. He observed me smiling bravely in Graswinkel's grip and frowned, tensing his great frame. He said nothing, but his painting was more eloquent than words.

The theme of beauty contrasted with ugliness is not a new one. He paints me so that I glow. He gives me such eyes that move and search, and a pair of lips that are more like roses than rosewood, and a bosom that curves with passions within. Like 'The Girl with the Red Hat' (whose eyes, lips, earrings, hat, even the tip of her nose are wet for the large gentle artist who paints her portrait), my form dominates the canvas; Graswinkel crouches behind like an evil troll leering out of the darkness, unclearly delineated like many another seducer and ravisher.

Vermeer is the champion of women. Take, for example, 'The Glass of Wine', in which the cloaked, moustached *mijnheer* smirks sinisterly as the demure *demoiselle* downs the devil's draught. Or 'The Soldier with Laughing Girl' – again, primed with wine, as he prepares to pounce. His face may be hidden but his design is as clear as the map on the wall above their heads. It is an old old story. In 'The Procuress', she is bought with wine and gold; the man holds her from behind; his hand, as wide as a goblet, envelops her left breast. When he draws it away, there will be a stain on her yellow satin dress.

We do not forget. I still feel the clutch of the raptor Graswinkel after these three hundred years. Those red lights in recording studios, Master, they never stopped reminding me of his eyes. Do you deny it? Do you defend the man and blame the procuress? There you are wrong, Nicky. Look to the picture for your instruction and do not improvise. Listen to what Vermeer has to say and you will be the wiser. What do you see? Not one man but three, all in shadow; guilty, weak men egging each other on to darker and darker deeds. And one woman bathed in light from an unknown source. He was an artist who above all things was moved by the sight of luminous innocence in the clutches of the tenebrous.

Ah revenge. Vermeer, who was not averse to painting on Sundays, understood its sweetness. I sat for him while the six different tunes of the Carillons of Delft sounded simultaneously at six different pitches. Everywhere, from his studio, those towers shot up into the sky. Sunday, Graswinkel's day for atonement; mine for love.

Seduction by music is an old theme, Nicholas. Notice how the 'Lady Seated at a Virginal' awaits the player of the viol for their assignation. Metsu's 'Lady Playing the Viola da Gamba' sits, elegantly dressed in her bedroom, again awaiting her accompanist. She gazes toward the bed; her little dog – ah, *symbolique*! – stands on his hind legs.

He was a handsome man, Vermeer. As tall as you, Master, but more powerfully built; impressive with his long brown tresses, large features and flowing artist's robes. All those muscles harnessed to a tiny paintbrush: how moving it was, like the oboist with his powerful lungs, playing *pianissimo*. The strong arm trembles with its tiny brush poised, the dots of colour find their place on the canvas, the dark world of the passions is illuminated with reason, form, harmony, brilliance. My cheeks, my earrings glow. He enlivens me with his points of pearly paint, another liquid-eyed waiting girl. I am as eloquent as the pregnant woman in blue reading a letter. It is the most musical of silences.

His vision restored me: I saw who I was. More than the instrument of seduction, I knew I had been created to light the world with my voice. My notes would die, but I would always speak again. My succession of masters – loathsome, inadequate, worthy and magnificent – each in his turn would die, but I would persist, rising out of their time like the legendary Phoenix, singing my boldest air.

Nicholas

5

Loathsome, inadequate, worthy and magnificent: which was *he*? Ten or twenty years ago, Nicholas would have assumed magnificence, wasted no time in speculation; now he hesitated. The point was not what he thought of himself, but what Rose thought of him.

Graswinkel had surely been the most loathsome, while Christophe, as player, had been quite inept. How many others had owned her? Worthies enough, but how many magnificents? How would he compare with the whole of history? No, he must stop this fanciful nonsense, attend to the concert. For the moment, Rose's voice was generous and agreeable; but he was still not comforted by it. He was competing not just against past masters, but against the future. Who would Rose play him off against after he was dead, and how would he measure up? How even against his own glamorous protegée, Lucy, when she was his age? It seemed that wherever he transposed himself, backward or forward in time, he found only the threat of defeat.

He wanted her ultimate praise. *Of all my masters, you were, and will always be, the most magnificent.* . . . But it was impossible. There was no such thing as absolute magnificence; he would always be valued in relation to other players, as single notes were against one another. The most he could hope for was temporary glory. She would not – could not – reassure him.

Perhaps it was the wrong quest, this best of the best competition. Was he not, after all, *incomparable*? In a category of his own – the only one she loved? Even if he were not the quintessential master, was their relationship not based on a special bond? But she could not reassure him here either. The past, with its revelation of colourful characters, was becoming gradually more threatening. Rose, in her youth, had enjoyed the admiration of great men like Vermeer. Perhaps he should take up painting as a hobby in his old age. He tried to imagine painting Rose's portrait, brushing with deft fingerings. He dwelt on her features, picking out the highlights in rows of creamy dots. No, he could never be a Vermeer. He was a musician; if he painted it would be merely a time-killer, a way of keeping Rose with him until it was all over.

Had there really been such a painting? Perhaps it was still extant, mistakenly attributed to Frans van Mieris the Elder. From now on he would have to haunt the galleries and junk shops looking for it: the lost Vermeer, the Lost Rose.

Now she fugued away from him, his voice chasing after hers, *dux et comes*. His would never catch up; would simply stop while hers carried on. Tonight was proof. He tried to think how to express the measurement of one ordinary man against an immortal instrument, but gave it up as fatuous.

Lost paintings, lost instruments, lost people. One could spend one's life hunting them down. Nicholas, who had harboured the belief that one day his father would turn up to hear his famous son, began one day – and continued to do so for the rest of his performing life – to scan his audience, row by row, before starting to play. It was an unfortunate habit. The delay made audiences fidget. His agent begged him especially not to do it in Japan, where it was considered quite rude. But he had been unable to stop himself, even there, where the chance of Harry Jordan turning up was fabulously small.

It was one of the things critics liked to speculate about. Was Jordan hypnotising his audience, practising some kind of yoga or religion, demonstrating his contempt . . .? They also noted that students – bizarrely – imitated his behaviour. 'You can always tell a Jordan student,' wrote a German reviewer, 'by the rather uncomfortable searching they give to their audiences before playing, as if they were looking for someone, perhaps a lost lover. It may be that Mr Jordan himself does this for good reason, but I doubt that his students do. There can only be one original.'

His father's disappearance had been quite unexpected; it had also been exquisitely, if perversely, timed. Without warning, Harry Jordan had turned up one day at Nicholas's school, handed Rose over to him, along with a deed to her ownership, and left for good. He simply disappeared. Nicholas later discovered that this was a common occurrence, and there were many such cases in police files. But at the time, it left him with a confused sense of responsibility for the defection; as if by demanding Rose – and succeeding in getting her – he had prompted Harry Jordan to defy his wife, and then, for his next act, to do the vanishing trick. In his childish egotism, Nicholas had given himself monumental powers. He saw now that he had merely provided his father with an elegant way of leaving his wife.

But what about leaving his son? Nicholas would never know what this had cost his father; presumably it was the price he reckoned to pay for his freedom. Or perhaps it cost him nothing. This was difficult to imagine, even now, but he could see his father making a detached calculation: freedom for himself against servitude to his family – including Nicholas.

He hadn't known how to feel about the trade-off. Had he gained an unplayable instrument and lost an irreplaceable father; or lost a feckless father but gained a priceless viola da gamba? But he did not waste many hours in solving this riddle, though he sometimes thought his lack of filial feeling unnatural; and he blamed Rose too for her bad influence. If he were to give her away, he sometimes wondered, would his father come back, his mother forgive him? Rose's smile mocked and teased him. He fell under her spell; totally seduced, he stopped asking schoolboy questions and gave himself up to her. He had no need of father or mother. He had Rose. If there were any gaps to fill, she would fill them.

He thought of his mother, how she had tried to keep him from Rose, and lost both husband and son in the process. Was it worth it? Later, Nicholas tried to make it up to her by playing private concerts for her and her friends, but she always found the music boring. She never came to a public concert, though she accepted without hesitation a regular payment from his agent. After a time – there seemed so little point to his visits – he stopped going to see her. He stopped thinking about her, too, except to wonder how his father had thought to marry her in the first place.

But for all his indifference, he never stopped looking for his father. He looked around for him now, for a man who would have been one hundred and five years old. After all, he saw, it was too easy – dishonest – to say he hadn't missed him; the evidence of his obsessive behaviour proved otherwise. It was really quite a terrible thing for a father to have done to a small boy. Still, some of his confusion and guilt had nothing to do with his father and everything to do with him – a gangly, pseudo-religious adolescent. If he had perceived Rose's smile as lewd, her decoration as gaudy and indecent, her rose hole as sexual – then that had been his mire, from which he had to find his own way out.

She had been virtually unplayable, as both cello and gamba, but he could still hold her, caress her, practise in mime. He recalled silently gripping her around the neck as if trying to choke the smile off her face; mentally abusing her for being too suggestive – with her dipped waist, sloping shoulders, smooth flanks – of the female form. When his musical urges made him seek her out, he held her, singing to himself and blubbering against the urges of his all-too-human flesh. How confusing for a boy of fifteen.

It was also confusing, and disturbing, for a man of sixty. Had Rose regarded him as just another Graswinkel?

Rose

6

No, Master, you were no Graswinkel. How could you compare the desperate urges of a boy with the detestable scrapings of an old man? Nonsense. He was obscene; you were . . . merely experimental. I felt the purrings of your body as if they were my own; perhaps they were. Inadequate as I was, and inexperienced as you were, yet ours was an harmonious union. How good we were!

Graswinkel was not good for me. To him I was the Devil's strumpet and advocate, who tempted him to play His works – madrigals, *villanelles, chansons*, variations, even Latin motets (Marian antiphons no less!) – while He looked on and laughed. Meanwhile Graswinkel fingered his library of secret scores and argued with his God. *To be sure, the harmony of the spheres transcends contentious differences between Rome and Geneva; therefore one need not limit one's repertory to the Calvinist liturgy*, etc. etc. . . . More and more the Devil laughed, since He knew He was winning. But I did not, for Graswinkel's kindled appetite for secular music – music I should have loved – was my undoing.

He lights a single candle and stands over me, the cadaverous face lit grotesquely from below. He covers my face with his palm as if to spare himself the sight of me, hissing, *See where you have led me, harlot*! I am glad, in my turn, to be spared the sight of him, but I fear the flames he conjures will destroy us both. Inside I remain cold, violently cold, untouched by the guilty fires that burn in his blood. He rubs his hands together under his cloak; his breath is audible and visible in that freezing dank chamber. But we are allowed no warmth, for to create warmth is to conjure the Devil. Besides, it puts fire in the blood, and that leads straight to the bowels of Hell. But, I feel it, Graswinkel's blood is already fired.

He drinks the Devil's draught and curses me: that too is my doing. Another and another he swills: I am transformed into a siren, come to tempt him with my voice and person. The hollow vessel that I am winks at him; the over-rhythmical scores which he slips from hiding crackle with excitement at his touch. He is lost. He sinks to his knees. Against his pure and good will, alas, he is forced to indulge in musical intercourse. God help us.

The tempo of his breath is fast, his eyes glow like hot coals and he approaches – closer, closer – until he is drooling from the mouth down the back of my neck, pinching my gently dipping waist, staring transfixed, as at a vision, at my back, whispering nonsense in illiterate French and incomprehensible Dutch. The dirty business is at hand. He plops himself down, buttons open ('for comfort, my dear, to give ease to the stroke'). He licks his swollen lips and sways gently. Tonight's titbit is an Italian *canzonetta* called 'Kisses' – a harmless piece of nonsense which he regards as deliciously compromising. *Shall we, mmmmmm*? he murmurs into my ear. He runs his left index finger up and down my strings, clumsily poking my frets, then tears into me with his bow, humping himself against me. Scraping and sawing and wailing – ending in a cadential swoon – he thus relieves himself of his dirty passion, befouling the names of religion and music together.

God's gift or the Devil's? Which am I? Do I cause this lubricious transformation? Do I lure him to play works which lead him to sinful ecstasy? It cannot be; I am not fooled by him. Others do not misuse music so. I know how he pretends to saintliness in other spheres, but just as he beats sense into his wife, so does he beat music into me. As he levies taxes on honest importers, so he nearly bursts my sides with squeezing. As he refuses subsidies for local almshouses, so he denies me the soft stroke which is life to me. And as he charges prostitutes with devilry, so does he charge me also, most foully, this hypocrite and trader in slaves.

My guts rumble and my belly thunders. Would that my hair could uncoil from its tidy knot and wrap him about like the snakes of gorgons, squeezing his life out of him. Then I should laugh in victory, singing, *I, beloved of heaven and earth, shall destroy this whoremaster among men*. Yet I smiled and bowed my shoulders in disgrace. The scales fell from my eyes and I saw our unharmonious world, ever irredeemable, and my helplessness before it. I might move men, arouse their passions, affect their spirits, fill them with a sense of limitless possibility, and their minds with wonder, create a world outside the confines of ordinary time and space – but I could not alter the dull, metronomic progression of evil disguised as innocence. I might divert them momentarily from madness, but in the end they would wreak their own havoc, cause discord and chaos. I could not heal differences, nor could I create love where it did not exist. I was as impotent as Graswinkel. I was like the defiled Mary whose soul remains untouched; but my pure voice, emanating from my lovely bosom, singing of peace, concord and harmony, was as foolish and useless a cry as any infant's in the night.

Nicholas

6

Nicholas longed to hold Rose in his arms and comfort her; to rub her gently with oils; to cradle her in his lap *à la Marais* and rock her as he once had his infant child; to dry her tears; to play away her troubles. He longed to press his body against hers, protecting her from loathsome Graswinkels. He wanted to save her from self-derision, preserve her clarity and composure.

He hardly recognised her quavering voice, those panicky notes. He grew nervous for them both, instrument and player, thought he must take charge; one last embrace, an old experienced hand to steady the flutterings. But he knew they must do without him; he without them.

He gulped some pills to stop the pain in his chest. There was nothing else to do but wait and listen. Useless: how he hated the word. If Rose was useless, he was doubly so, sitting here droning to himself about nothing in particular. Of course she was useless: of less use even than a chair, a clock or a knife. One could not sit on her, tell time by her (except in a manner of speaking), or cut with her. She had not cured his emphysema or his failed marriage; she could not right the wrongs of the world.

He listened. Lucy recovered; there was a new edge to her playing that he had not heard before. She lightened her bow, and the weakness and self-doubt passed from Rose; her brow cleared, her smile shone again. Useless, unquestionably, but an excellent companion. How grim his life would have been without her, he thought: listening to clocks, sitting in chairs, using his many eating implements. Rose added the ornament of her voice to its bareness. She offered him joy and pain. She made him laugh and smile. She gave him pleasure, moved him to tears. What more could one hope for in this world?

He wiped his brow: foolish Nicholas. Rose was no one's infant; no need for him to bleed when she cried. She flourished under Lucy, who guided her smoothly to the end of the E minor Sonata. She did not need his help. Graswinkel's slimy touch had been expunged. Rose, free of him, smiled. Free of her latest master too: Nicholas Jordan. He listened to the Telemann quartet: she was the bass, the support of the group; he was the weak one. He should not have come, to tease himself. His father had been right to avoid the sight of his family thriving without him. She was in excellent voice now, Graswinkel forgotten, her despair evaporated *en l'air*. Only his remained.

Enough. Why should he pity Rose for her centuries-old misfortunes, when it was he who had been used and thrown away, as each of her masters had been and would continue to be? Time with Rose meant time organised into magnificent parcels; flashes through the brain to the bow, delightful, irresistible moments. A bow, a burst of applause, then nothing. What did it signify but another way of passing time until the end?

Rose

7

Of passing time until the end. Is that how you think of me, my dear? Has it come to that? Has my voice lost its magic, or is the failure yours? Is it that, no longer playing me, you forget – how my voice lingers in the air, in your ears, your blood? No, you are wrong. It does not 'die away' (as it may do for others), but wraps you round like a cloak, a secret perfume. Employ what image you will, but do not dismiss it. Those 'magnificent parcels of sound', as you so eloquently put it, do not *pass* the time but *create* it. There is no end to music, Nicholas, only new beginnings.

I mark the end of the *Modérément* neatly and lightly. Yet even as I lay down the last note, I am thinking of the next *Vite*. Before its sound dies away, I am setting the pulse of the new movement. The end for you, Nicholas, is another matter. It is a finality I hardly understand. You must practise patience for it; it will come soon enough and with little surprise or deception in the cadence, and no movement shall follow.

Listen, old Master. I do not desert you, I merely change hands. Think of your own stages of development, as you went from youth to young manhood, to adulthood, to old age. You learned to live without your father; you left uncounted lovers. Letting go was easy for you, perhaps too easy. You make it harder for yourself with me; why? With me it is more an endless cycle of variations; each new master brings new surprises. Graswinkel, for instance, was the key of F minor – a wretched key for me. You were my D major. Of course, I never knew beforehand if my next master would sit easy with me, or not. So often I was disappointed, but then there were moments of exquisite gratification. As with you, my dear.

There is no end for me, as there is for you. Sometimes I wish there were. How pleasant it would be to be buried beside you, your treasured mistress, as Abel's instrument was with him in St Pancras. An idle thought – and not my fate, alas. At every *finis*, I make my *da capo*. However much rocketing and plummeting, however many flourishes and double rhythms, however many moments of rhetorical eloquence – as there were with you – the end of one piece inevitably signals the beginning of another.

I was joyous when Graswinkel's end came. Still young and resilient, I continued to hope for a master who would make me forget. The widow Graswinkel set her root-vegetable features, like one scrubbed and waiting for the heavenly Pot, and allowed me to be played by musicians who lusted after me. Gradually she let it be known that I could be had for a handsome price. Brother Benedictus a Sancto Josepho (whom Sam vulgarly called Brother Buns) passed on the news to his dear friend, Constantijn Huygens. Huygens in turn – tempted to buy me himself, but alas too old – passed word of my availability to his diplomatic contact in London, Francis North, who in turn informed his brother Roger. And that is how I came to England.

Life, I told myself (in a thin but lilting voice), will be peaceful in rural England. Nursed by a retired gentleman, I shall recover my temper. I shall enjoy an old man's soothing stroke, and grow out of my adolescent dream of a master with youth and vigour. We shall be friends in the name of music. I shall become a country instrument, relaxed and grown expansive with rosy healthfulness; my pitch will drop and my voice grow deep and rich, nourished by the rich loam of Norfolk; and the last remnants of Graswinkel's slimeful touch will be washed away. I shall become an English rose. I shall pour golden melodies into my Master Roger's ears, and reap the reward of his adoration.

Nicholas

7

Impossible. No one could have adored her more than Nicholas. He had put mother, father, students, lovers, wife and child second to her in his affections. He had devoted his life to her restoration and her pleasure. He had plied her with virtuosic love; had cut himself off from human intercourse in order to become one with her. He had immersed himself in her; lived and breathed her. She had become his better self, speaking for him and shielding him. In return for her protection, he had given her his life. Who could match him in worshipfulness?

He could not bear the thought of that countrified twit Roger, at his altar of adoration, bowing and scraping with equal enthusiasm over his Brussel sprouts and Corelli's new violin sonatas. Such a man, scratching away in his notebooks from morning to night, wasted the young Rose. Could he even play her? Nicholas doubted that he could manage anything demanding: at most the simplest consort literature – cozy, friendly music; music for anonymous chests of viols; music for amateurs, collectors, scribes. Music for the likes of Geoffrey Piggott, Nicholas's first teacher.

Piggott (who was given, he reminded himself, to quoting Roger North) also owned a chest of viols – a family of mediocre instruments which he proudly exhibited in size order (like his boys) and which he played equally badly. The instruments, like their owner, exuded an air of middle-class respectability and rigidity worthy of a family out of Chekhov. They had complaining voices. Piggott, baring his teeth, played as if he were braying. The Piggotts and the Norths could never know what it was to have a relationship with an instrument; to go through one's musical life, from beginning to end – even in the faithless episodes one may have had – still with that one voice lodged in one's soul.

He had been responsible, however, for having Rose restored as a viol – though inaccurately, with six strings rather than seven. Still, it was an improvement. Before the restoration she had been a risible freak, part cello, part viol, unspeaking and unspeakable creature. Now, though her potential was still insufficiently realised, she was at least playable. What matter in the scheme of things? Humans could breathe with one lung, walk with nine toes, sing with false teeth. Nicholas could play English and Italian music, most of Bach. . . . It was enough to be going on with. (Only later would he realise the error: how she had been cheated of her thunder and growl, her essential Frenchness.)

The restorers had been recommended by Piggott. Roland and Brock were an ageing couple of well-known but eccentric builders who lived like rare birds in a sanctuary, deep in the Devonshire countryside. Yet they were pragmatists. Though they believed in 'authentic' restoration, they were not bone-boiling revivalists. They had no wish to suffer the hazards and difficulties of eighteenth-century procedures. Why torture the nose with pots of bubbling animal glues when marvellous commercial concoctions are easily available and better to boot? Life is too short, they said.

Brock, the smaller of the two men, shaped like a lute, did most of the talking. He had one of those ruddy complexions, which tended to the neon whenever he grew excited. Rose clearly excited him. He folded his hands over his stomach (which he thrust forward for advantage), and pronounced judgment. 'We conclude, Mr Roland and I, from our study of this splendid instrument, that it was originally a bass viola da gamba. Unquestionably.

Indubitably. Observe those sloping shoulders, the huge size, the elaborate decoration. A gamba of gambas, one of the largest we have seen. German most likely; or English, a Barak Norman, perhaps.'

He was quite over-excited by his speechifying; he wheezed rather than breathed. He collapsed on to a stool, fanning himself with a large wood shaving. 'Perhaps this would be an opportune moment for Mr Roland to prepare the tea.' He pointed his lip at Roland. The good man bowed his elegantly striped head (black and silver, like the back of a lute), removed his leather apron and backed out of the workshop. Nicholas remembered wondering how he could allow himself to be bullied by such an arrogant little beetroot. He was altogether puzzled by the behaviour of certain humans.

He left Rose with them; three months later she was returned to him. Her new neck, strings, pegs, bridge – everything was there of the instrument he had longed to play since he was a child. He locked himself in his room and examined her, touching her lightly all over with his fingertips, like a blind man. It took him some time before he could actually embrace her; longer to put bow to strings. He laid her down on his narrow bed to examine her: her new rosette carved out of layers of parchment, the cicatrix around her neck – which would reveal to future generations what she had been. He lay down next to her and slept with his arm resting lightly on her strings.

But he did not play her well. She was no cello, which was all he had learned to play until now. Her frets, her six strings, the underhand bowing she required, all eluded him that first time. He would have to have lessons with the Pigg. Poor Johann Sebastian. Poor Rose. Solemn in his schoolboy's daycoat and lovesick as a bridegroom, he played and played, trying to break her in, like an inexperienced new husband, pounding his wife with a blunt instrument.

Lessons with Piggott meant developing tense, muscle-bound fingers, a fossilised brain, an ear which could distinguish roughly between sharp and flat, feet which flapped metronomically; and a brain which memorised whole concertos mechanically. Historical accuracy, imagination, humour, sensibility, rhythmic freedom and taste were forbidden.

Like a soldier, Jordan. Discipline. One's left-hand fingers are like a private army; those five digits must be trained, day in and day out, whether they like it or not. Do you imagine soldiers enjoy slipping in mud, fielding fire? No, *but they must learn to move quickly or they are goners. Scales, Jordan, arpeggios, divisions: practise or you will be a goner.*

They called that outrage to musicality technique. What he had gone through: the brain, the ears, the heart frozen, the music falling away in chunks like ice floes. Scales, rhythmic patterns, bowings, chords, ornaments, beats, elevations, backfalls, forefalls, relishes; the slur, the thump, the hold. He had even learned Hume's mad *col legno* – the drumming with the back of the bow – though not when to use it tastefully. Leave it to Piggott to teach every known technique he could dig up, but not to think about its proper application. French style was off-limits. What was the point anyway, when Nicholas was English, as was Rose, with her six strings? No, best to concentrate on the English: *Touch mee Lightly. Tickle mee Quickly.*

He was taught 'the decent posture', which meant stiff as a soldier. (Mace, who recommended 'something plying or yielding to an agile bending', was ignored.) The Pigg demonstrated: nothing could have been more repellent than his thin thighs and dry English touch. The nasal twang; that stiff spine; those pursed or parted lips; that scraping and sawing; that undertaker's touch. *Playing the viol is seventy-five per cent hard work, twenty per cent tuning, and five per cent inspiration.* He smiled, showing yellow teeth.

The metronome: an instrument of torture which Nicholas never again used in his life. His own students learned to establish a freer kind of rhythm, which did not necessarily keep with the clock or the flapping foot. But Piggott would have none of it. *Unacceptable, Jordan; one must not fool around with the beat. Ab-so-lute-ly straight, that is what we strive for. The music must be clean, smooth and perfectly even. None of this off-beat stuff. This isn't jazz, you know. No ripples. Like a bedsheet. Think of hospital corners, Jordan.*

How he'd been manipulated. How they'd tried their best to destroy his musicality with their rote learning. It was a wonder he was able to shake it off. How the Pigg would bend over him – that clichéd failed musician – pulling his limbs into place as if he were a doll, taking hold of his fingers, yanking them this way and that, squashing them on to the strings, stretching them into position, holding his elbow while he tried desperately to free the bow, squaring his head on his shoulders, gripping his chin. Good God, it was appalling how such misfits got away with playing on the vulnerabilities of little boys.

Oh, they had put their backs into it, training his mind as well as his body. He had emerged from that torture chamber of a conservatory able to play the cello with heavy breathing, vibrato and deadly machine-gun precision. Rose he played flatly and drily, without breath, vibrato, dynamics or rhythm. It was a miracle that he was left with any feeling for her at all; that, after he left, he was able to shake off the Pigg's touch and bring himself and Rose alive again; that, delving back into history, he could hear the voices calling to him, and respond.

Now it was time: time for hospital corners, and no way out. He had to sit here and listen to Rose's tale of past masters, which made him one of an assembly line of Graswinkels and Norths. Now there was Lucy, and after her. . . . He'd sworn eternal love, silly boy. How could he possibly have known anything about eternity? He could not love her eternally. But there would always be others ready to arouse her with their century's style, brand her with their personal touch. Geniuses or dullards, what did it matter? Let her amuse herself by teasing him with tales of Roger North.

Rose

8

Calm yourself, Nicholas, you have nothing to fear from Roger. (Since when were you so excitable?) He was a rotund gargoyle with hardly the character or strength to pull his own bow. He had ears: great ears, voracious ears, great jugs which were thirsty to drink their fill of *Our dear Art*. But those great flaps were no more use to me than an elephant's. In his retirement, he was fit only for filling volumes with pompous disquisitions on Musick, and reminiscing on the days when he took his meals, his company, his musical pleasure and his business at his brother Francis's house. Even in bed, I could picture them, two pale moons snoring in perfect harmony. The brother made the man. He conducted his career in the law, and put a tune and a rhythm to his life. He told him what part to play, and how to follow, and counted his measures. And then one day he died, leaving poor Roger in his minority; *sans* brother, *sans* king.

Generous as I was, I would have comforted him; let him wrap me round with his stumpy legs, his stomach bulging to meet my back. I thought we might warm England together. I would let him dream of his brother, if he would, that little man with the prodigious nose and the Great Purse between his legs (he was Keeper of the Privy Seal) and a voice that lifted him to heaven; let all the longing and love Roger felt for him flow out of his fingers and enter me. For I was as cold as dead Francis and I longed for a human touch; even Roger's would do.

You are shocked, Master, to hear me abide by so little. But I was desperate, like the wife who accepts caresses meant for another. At least I hold him in my arms, she reasons, imagining the strokes are for her, and allows herself to be touched, if only briefly. She does not ask for his love or even his affection; she does not want to know from where the inspiration for his passion comes. She is not even sure if she still cares. But she remembers how it was to hear the sweet sound of her own pleasure, and longs to hear it again.

Of course I would have preferred a master wedded only to me, whose fingers were married to my frets and whose bow arm, limp but well-directed, would send strong vibrations up and down the length of my strings. Intensive and exclusively mine: naturally, I should have chosen such a master, for whom there would be no brothers in the world, no mistresses, lovers, mothers, children.

It was too much to ask of poor Roger, who lacked the imagination to love divinely. His world was small, limited by his Norfolk county boundaries. Music was to him an entertainment and a diversion, a pastime for noble families living in the country, a ploy to keep folks away from the drink and from panting after exquisite debauchery. Like Graswinkel, he saw music as a diversion from lust. *Music is a vertuous, or at least harmless, imployment within doors.*

Do not envy me, pity me, for I was merely a trinket amongst trinkets at Rougham Hall.

The organ grins down at me with its revolting ears and beard, and its rows of conical teeth capped in gold. He – the great windbag of perfection – is protected at night by hideously painted wings, while I lie out of my case, at the mercy of dust, bats, birds and heavenly catastrophes. My frets fall sideways like sloppy necklaces and my strings are slack looselips. I am captured and transported, like a rare beast, to bed down amongst the common herd.

Roger makes straight away for the organ bench (from habit rather than neglect of me, I tell myself). He climbs up, wriggling from side to side, places fingers in position on the keyboards, stretches his stumpy legs to the pedals, and lets fly a voluntary to knock my delicate maid's head clear off its neck. I am meant to admire, swoon, wait patient and appreciative (as befits a maiden) and not grow restive as a soprano reduced to chromaticism. Alas, I fail. My gaze burns unstopped through his stunted back. I will him to topple from his growling mate, over the railing and down, down, down to the stone hearth of the Great Hall. There he shall be smashed, as I am from the Great Din.

'Well, and how like you the devine Machine?' he enquires, letting off his raucous improvisation and swinging round his stumps to dangle in my face.

It has a good pair of lungs.

'Now 'tis your turn, my beauty.'

Ah, my beauty, he calls me.

'But first a chair.'

But first a chair. He tries this one and that, measuring himself against it, it against me, and himself against me. Round and round he goes, playing his solo game of musical chairs. None is exactly right; either too padded or not padded enough, a sinker or a leg-sleeper, too high, too low, too sloped, too. . . . Stop! Enough! When shall there be music?

And now (having found a chair which will do), there follows a session of poking and prodding, Roger's great nose sniffing the widow Graswinkel's furniture polish as if it were the finest French perfume. He wraps his legs about me as best he can, but he is too small to envelop me with ease. I do not rest comfortably, am not properly centred and weighted; I am not in balance. His legs shake like a tambourine. I am too precarious to sing out, my voice is tight and stifled. I fear any moment my bouts will crack with the hardness (a substitute for sureness) of his grip. He thrusts the bow this way and that, but I feel nothing – no sound throbs in my body.

Yet these matters are the least to forgive. Eventually he

learns to hold me tolerably well, and to propel his bow at some speed; even to play with a small or a larger bow, and to make some distinction between loud and soft, slow and fast, and add a sprinkling of ornaments. (Though he still plays too far from the bridge and so catches at my waist.) But what he can never learn are the secret lessons of the ear, the mind and the heart. His playing is good-natured, sweet, undramatic, unpunctuated, unstylish, unimaginative and uninspired. It is humdrum, moderate and harmonious, suited to the limited ability of an English country gentleman. It is sober and dry; it does not make the mouth water nor the eyes tear. It scrapes the belly more than it makes the heart sing. It fails to declaim, laugh, cry, soothe, question, leap about in merry-making or madness. In short, Roger North is a man better suited to push his pen than to pull my bow.

I had come to a prison of hobbyists and well-meaning bunglers; to the estate of a man who would rather fill reams with pompous disquisitions than me with song. He would even discourse on the benefits of spring gut, when lambs are younger and therefore the strings have more spring. And I would weep for the lambs, that they should be sacrificed to such an end. I wanted a Purcell and what I got was an ass. I was created for the highest art and was subjected to the middlingest fiddling.

Take pity on me, Nicholas. Consider how it was for me with the dilettante. Worse than the boredom was the waste. Purcell was dead; Francis North too, he of the sublime voice. Who else in England would cherish me? Use your imagination, stretch it back beyond your time; you are good at that. Sympathise with me. With how I came too late to England, so there was none to play me as I would be played. I was history's wastrel.

The potential for music is like the potential for love. It lurks deep inside, waiting for the touch that will swell it and bring it forth to blossom. But it did not come; resistance was but vain. I had no choice but to serve Roger as a housewife serves her husband and paymaster, the while roaming hither and yon on staves of my own devising; thinking to myself how clever are we females in the ways of escape, if only fancy-wise. And no wonder so many look to their ceilings and pray, or dream, or sing themselves to sleep while their so-called masters play upon them.

Oh, where was the high-prized noise to make a man's ears glow and fill his brain full of frisks or his eyes full of tears? I would be played, not for the sake of virtue or harmless employment, but for passion's sake. There must be danger in it, or I am not worth my weight in wood. I am no cushion for damping the resonance of the soul, but a sounding box for its amplification. My purpose to Graswinkel was to anaesthetise the passions and elevate the soul to goodness (though he was notably unsuccessful in both). To Roger I was an antidote to boredom, old age and incest. And what did that make me, but the rosy harlot of Puritans and amateurs; the Whore of Harmony?

Nicholas

8

The Whore of Harmony. Nicholas considered Rose thus: the beguiling voice, enticing smile – services promiscuously available to any who would embrace her. And himself: her willing, eager client. But he had paid, so he'd been told, with his humanness. 'Sometimes I'd swear you were some kind of ghoul,' accused Sam, his California paramour. 'The only time you show any emotion is when you're playing. Otherwise you could be dead.' He had laughed, because he knew his coldness attracted her. There was no incentive to change. Later it was too late. His wife claimed it was inhuman to be obsessed by an instrument, and that it made her crazy to be married to a man who showed no feeling for people, by which she meant herself. He dismissed this as delusional, exaggerated.

What if she was right? What if he had traded his soul for a good bowing arm, practised himself into idiocy when it came to dealing with people – women, to be precise? He had certainly learned the artful ways of being with an instrument, but ladies, it seemed, could not be played so easily. He had manipulated, tuned, waited patiently for them to smile and respond. When they didn't, he took offence. (A decently crafted instrument, after all, should respond in predictable ways.) Their anger puzzled him, their crude, prosaic voices stung, and their distorted faces gave him pain. He longed for

Rose's poetry, her song, her sweet smile. He wanted life – love – to be as easy as music.

It had been so, briefly, with his landlady Hannah, in Vienna. (He had gone there after several unprofitable years performing in London.) Nicholas pictured her in the kitchen, with the garden beyond. Her correct milieu, he'd learned, was the outdoors – forest, dunes, mountain tops – but a mental portrait of her as he'd first seen her persisted. He'd come in the front door: she stood at the far end of a long stretch of hallway, whipping hot milk for coffee with a Norwegian twig-stirrer. He focused on the brightness of her at the end of that dark tunnel. 'Who-wee,' she called out to him, 'you want some?'

The house, like its row-mates, had a grim façade, and carried its gloom nearly throughout. But Hannah had rescued its back half, transforming the two light and airy garden rooms into cheerfully modern open spaces, which, for Nicholas, undermined the claustrophobic minor mode of the house. Hannah, when not at work, lived either in the garden or in the kitchen or in her special half of the drawing room, where she grew parlour maples in troughs. (He had seen such plants since – once at Kew, often in Berkeley – their drooping yellow and red blossoms made him think knee-jerkingly of her.) She seemed profoundly uncomfortable in other parts of the house, which was stuffed with her husband's antiques, painted dark green and grey, its windows hung with heavy velvet drapes; even during the day, lights were required. She did not belong in it any more than her plants; would have withered and grown dim. She was like a tree, with broad feet to balance her big square body, yet she moved without heaviness, her tartan plaid skirt swinging in one direction, her grey-streaked hair in another.

Nicholas saw himself, an actor in an old movie, walking jerkily down the hallway towards her. She put her hands on her hips and arched herself backwards from the waist up. A characteristic gesture; another was standing on one leg like a large water bird. She smiled, beckoned him towards her – now he was in slow motion, taking for ever to reach her.

'Come. Come in, I don't bite you. Perhaps you would like to drink coffee with me today. Mrs Lenschmidt has not come today, her usual day, she is ill, and I miss someone to have a chat. I think something very special has happened to you today. You have had a wonderful lesson, or perhaps you have fallen in love? Am I right?' As she smiled, her lips stretched, making parenthetical creases around her generous mouth. 'In a manner of speaking,' he had conceded, rather ungenerously, at which Hannah laughed, throwing her head back, her hands still on her hips. 'You are so very English, Nicky – may I call you Nicky? *In a manner of speaking . . .*' She mocked him with her chin against her chest. 'Come, tell me what makes you so happy; I am curious today to sniff out my secretive musician.'

Nicholas explained about Rose and her restoration following a history of disasters. She had just had her seventh string added in a new, and this time competent, restoration. 'You will understand, from your husband's business,' he told her, 'what it means to return a valuable piece to its original condition.' Again she laughed, at the same time pulling a long face. She shook her head, whipping her cheeks with her hair. 'No, I do not understand my husband's antiques, not at all; they do not interest me, they make me cold. I see only objects which do not live, they only stand in one place and grow dust. How can you compare a musical instrument with an oak table? Never. A musical instrument lives, the table just sits. Your instrument – how do you call her, viola da gamba? – with the name of a flower, that I understand. You know, I am a biologist. I like it very much that things should live. I understand playing such an instrument must be like being in love.

'Of course I hear you practise every day – such a strange beautiful sound like nothing I have ever heard before. Yes, I stop to listen. But I have no idea she looks like this, with such a face.' She sucked in her breath – a sort of 'yah' sound, which he came to love. Nicholas had, rather prosaically, pointed out the hairline join at the base of Rose's head where the new neck had been attached; gingerly tested her new string. 'Shall you play something for me?' she asked.

He played a short Marais prelude, very free and improvisatory. The new string made anything possible. 'Do you know,' said Hannah, 'I have never heard such music in my life. I don't understand it but it brings tears to my eyes. I am very moved by your Rose. Being so close, I think her whole body is alive; she is a real person, singing to me. It sounds silly, I know, but I see her face, she smiles as she sings, and her eyes, it is as if they are looking at me. See, I am having gooseflesh. She makes me smile too.'

Nicholas watched her as she turned and went down to the wine cellar. From the back, except for the greying hair, she looked like a great strapping girl but with a boy's thin hips. She wore knee socks and penny loafers and a fuzzy green sweater. Her big shoulders were like moss-covered rock, her large breasts soft outcrops of heather to nestle one's head between. He smiled at her back. Champagne; her husband's champagne. 'It is my husband's but he will not miss it too much.' She put two bottles on the kitchen table, then went out into the garden and came back with a dark cerise rose. 'Belle de Crécy,' she said, threading the flower through Rose's tuning pegs: Rose with a rose behind her ear: a mysterious rose with an elusive smell. Hannah laughed at her own temerity. 'Do you think she minds?'

Nicholas was not bothered, for once, about Rose's wishes. All his attention was focused on Hannah. She was not young, but her face shone with intelligence and feeling; it was no pretty mask like his. The skin was weatherbeaten, with a network of fine veins in her cheeks. Her eyes were a luminous grey. She had a large mouth with thin lips that stretched when she smiled. He didn't mind that it was a worn old face; rather, it moved him. Her body was still quite youthful.

Naked, it was as lean and strong as he'd imagined. Somehow, the champagne contributed, they'd found themselves – quite the drunken trio – lurching up the stairs, Nicholas in the middle between Hannah and Rose. They'd ended up in the attic room scrunched into one of the old alcove box beds, Rose on the floor beside them.

He let her lead him; rehearse his moves, conduct their

progress. *Slowly, wait, stop, more, more, yes, no wait, not yet, stop, breathe, good.*

NICHOLAS: You remind me of a cello.

HANNAH: How do you mean?

N: Big shoulders and breasts.

H: Does the cello have big breasts?

N: Oh yes, very. Most people can't see them, but they're there. That's what makes such a rich sound.

H: Perhaps you don't like such a sound. This is why you play the gamba. I think you must prefer a lady with flat chests.

N: No, I prefer you.

H: I used to play the cello, you know.

N: So did I. I still teach it sometimes, to horrible small children. Do you still play?

H: No, it's too heavy. I have been very heavy in my life, now I feel like being light.

N: The harpsichord, a cheerful instrument. You could learn to accompany me.

H: Shshhhhh. I accompany you now, can't you feel it? Be quiet. The best duet of all.

Quite so. Perhaps he'd enjoyed the contrast, women with full breasts and husky voices, of human females quite unlike his Rose. Straddling Hannah, he'd expressed himself more forcefully. His fastidiousness was subsumed, his compunctions drowned by her own enjoyment. His playing of Rose subsequently improved too, becoming freer, warmer. He'd discovered a painless preparatory exercise.

Their affair had about it, in the beginning, a playful quality: Hannah remembered the word *scherzando* from her cello-playing days; characteristically, she did not remember *pesante*. Light, like her garden room, like the attic where they made love, like Nicky's eyes. Looking back, Nicholas saw it had all been a great defence against depression: heaviness and darkness as she called it. If she let its shadow so much as fall on her she would be undone. Like the alcoholic's one drink. She was her own censor: no newspapers, 'heavy' books, films, paintings, no memories of war, forecasts of disasters; she even avoided heavy foods in case they should weigh down her spirit. She lived on salads, fasted one day a week, practised yoga, communed with her garden, birds, the sky, the trees. She had no use for the city. She loved music – so long as it was light. Mozart's flute concertos were her favourites. She also liked popular vocal music because it was new, young and lighthearted. She endured the bitter-sweetness because the bitter, she said, never got the better of the sweet.

Nicholas chose carefully what to play for her: rondeaus by Couperin and Marais, tuneful English variations. She listened critically, piping up at once when his stroke became heavy. She argued that even when the music turned serious or sad, there was an inherent lightness in its lilting beats, alternating accented and unaccented notes. She developed a sophisticated taste for the 'new' baroque music Nicholas was bent on reviving (he was discovering new manuscripts all the time). She became spoiled for the lugubrious renditions of Bach and Rameau on old records played by the famous German conductors. They made her laugh now. They were, of course, Hubert's – her husband's – favourites.

If Nicholas influenced Hannah's taste in music, then she influenced his in nature. Several times a week she would get up before dawn to drive out to the country. Nicholas, when he could rouse himself, would go with her. At first he'd looked around stupidly, not seeing or hearing anything, feeling nothing but the cold and damp. He'd lagged behind her as she loped along with her pack (containing binoculars, apples, raisins, rain gear), cursing himself for following her to such dreary places. Then gradually the world had come alive. She would stop, put her finger to her lips and point or hand him the glasses. Then he would see birds – dipper, heron, slow-flapping owl; a family of bounding deer. She made him kneel down to examine a minute star-shaped wildflower; stand in silence while the sun rose. But for the fact that she loved his music (because she loved him?), she would have caused him to question the unnaturalness of his own life.

Sex she coded musically. She would pass notes under his bedroom door. 'I am in the mood for a free prelude.' Or

'Let's make a gigue.' Or, 'Shall we fugue?' She had a capacity for silliness which in anyone else (for example, Sam) would have seemed crude. They continued to make love in the spare attic room, either on the floor if they wanted to stretch out, or in one of the box beds. It was remote from the rest of the house, safe from Hubert. Once they had even made love while he was working in his study, two storeys below. One afternoon they burst into the attic and found Hubert sitting on the floor in his underwear, in the lotus position. 'And what may I ask is so funny?' demanded the furious flower. 'I am doing my yoga exercises. It is extremely therapeutic. And what are the two of you doing up here, may I ask?' Hannah explained she was just showing Nicholas the picturesque old room. But from that moment on Hubert had it in for Nicholas; for catching him undressed, ridiculous without his tweeds and checks, his fat hands in the prayer posture.

Hubert the fake. Nicholas remembered him as he sat in state at the head of his antique oak refectory table, by the light of two candles in their enormous brass church candlesticks, in the gloomy dining room Hannah hated, overseen by a bronze brass of his uncle somebody-or-other. Nicholas had been invited to join them for dinner. Hubert wore his lounging clothes, ceremonially bought on antique-buying trips to London: checked Viyella shirt, twill Yorkshire pantaloons, tweedy Scottish jacket and matching woollen socks, Bond Street shoes. The cartoon German: big, slow, thickset and red-faced. His shoes squeaked, his face shone, his cowlick stood on end. One of Nicholas's greatest pleasures was telling him how German he looked; next best was correcting his English, preferably when it was perfectly correct. Once he had asked Nicholas's advice about a musical instrument he was considering bidding for. 'Advice or advices, which?' he demanded. 'Advices, of course,' Nicholas said, trying hard not to twitch or look at Hannah, who disapproved of his teasing. From then on the ludicrous Hubert said, 'And now I must ask your advices.'

But he was not laughing that night, only watching how Hubert sat there, picking his nose, while Hannah ran back and forth serving. 'Why is it you never think of helping? Do you like having a servant?' Hubert said, 'She is my wife; that is what I pay her to do.' Nicholas winced. 'But that's ludicrous. Hannah is distinguished in her field, she probably earns more than you do, or at least as much. You "pay" her nothing!' Hubert looked around to his uncle's bust for support. 'I am sorry for you,' he sighed. 'One day you will understand how to treat a woman. Besides,' he said, more pompously than ever, 'the exercise will do her good. Did I ever tell you how fat and ugly she was when I married her?' Hannah, who had returned to the room, heard but said nothing. How could she take it? How could she live with such a man? Nicholas tried to defend her but it was impossible.

She claimed it was true – she had been fat and ugly. 'That's not the point,' he'd shouted, losing patience with both of them. 'One doesn't talk about one's wife like that to strangers. It's indecent.' 'But you are not a stranger. You are one of the family.' Hubert slapped him on the back. Nicholas, disgusted, lost his temper. 'Look, it doesn't matter who your audience is. Can't you understand? It doesn't impress; it's revolting, sitting there eating your wife's food and insulting her. At least get off your fat arse and wash a dish.' Hubert grinned and puffed out his chest even further. 'But I have never washed a dish in my life and I do not propose to begin now. Before I met Hannah my mother washed them. It is not a job for a man.' He brushed at his front with a napkin and marched off, blowing his nose into one of Hannah's beautifully laundered handkerchiefs, whistling a Mozart flute concerto, hideously out-of-tune.

Like the discovery of music, innocent and easy before the complications and the hard work set in, a relationship with a married woman had its difficulties. Hannah, to Nicholas's bemusement, had been more upset on Hubert's behalf than her own: she hurt when he hurt (or ought to have hurt but was too thick to feel anything). 'He's so weak, like a child. He needs me. He would die without me,' she explained. Nicholas had not understood. He thought him, and said so, absolutely witless and unworthy of her – but she didn't want to hear it; especially she didn't want Nicholas laughing at him. Nor could she bear their arguments. As soon as she heard a raised voice, she ran out into the garden with the clippers, or to the kitchen sink.

Involvement with Hannah had its price; with Rose, it had felt relatively free. She was his to play when he chose: his exclusively. But she too, in the past, had belonged to others. Christophe Bernard, Graswinkel, Roger North – how many other pairs of legs had she lain between? Had she always worn a bored smile, as she wore with Roger; or a look of disgust, as for Graswinkel; impatience, as with her maker Christophe? Nicholas didn't want to know, yet couldn't help himself picturing them, one after the other, in lurid detail: faces, limbs, fingers placed so, and so. Too late; she too was already married – and not to one, but to at least three and possibly hundreds of husbands. He was not the first, nor would he be the last; was merely another of her clients who paid dearly for his pleasure.

Why torture himself with these revelations? Better not to know where she came from or where she was going; not to dwell on the grosser parts of English country gents who had held her; far better to fool himself that divine providence had sent her direct to him; that before him, she had belonged to the corrosive air alone.

Nicholas, beguiled, leant back and stretched his long legs under the front seat. He allowed himself to be soothed. For a few bars, he lost his train of thought – about infidelity, the pains of human love. Rose's voice slid its way into his body and warmed his blood, like a good claret. He felt her old power over him and the advantage of its comfort. Why withhold his affection now, when he was too old and spoiled by his years with her to love anyone else? Anger drained from him, and the odalisque still smiled. Never mind who preceded him – let her be his mistress again – still; let him bask in her warmth; let her play upon him. For this moment, no one else existed. The memory of Hannah was gone; it was as if he held Rose in his arms again. No Christophe, no Graswinkel, no Roger, no Lucy. Only

Nicholas Jordan, for whom she would sing for ever and ever.

Except that she would not. She did not even belong to him any more. He thought, I am a self-deceiving fool. When she is straddled by other legs, she will tell how my feet were too big or my rhythm too wayward, or that I over-used the *flattement*. Faithless Rose, Comtesse de Boufflers of the twentieth century, what have you done to me? Taken my heart and locked it away in your chest box, to beat next to yours and only yours; convinced me I was *La Jordan, ou La Superbe* – and then left me to die, merely Nicholas Jordan. I am abused by your flattery. Slave to the Whore of Harmony.

Who was it she dreamed of now, behind that inscrutable smile? Was it Christophe in leather apron, a besmocked Vermeer, Francis North of the sublime voice and the sequined Privy Seal? Or Nicholas himself? Or had she forgotten all of them, quite content to pass into the hands of her new mistress Lucy? Was she so disloyal, so perfidious, that she knew pleasure only when it held her from behind and dallied with her? It was her nature, Nicholas reminded himself, to live in the present, and to go from master to master; or mistress, as the case may be.

Would she ever tire – be exhausted by – the never-ending *batterie*? Over and over again, she was trained to respond to different pokes and prods – like an animal at a circus. Strict, free, eccentric styles; good, bad, indifferent techniques. Decapitated, stripped of frets, soul and bridge in one generation, restored of them in the next. A half-century later, the same process reversed, one piece of unnecessary surgery after another. Each time killed a little. How could she endure it? Did any of them make it worth while? Did any, except for him, play her uniquely? Love her uniquely?

Rose

9

Ah yes, Nicholas, yes; there was another who played me, who loved me as well as you. He was unique, yes, that is the word; he stood out from the others, he was my prize. The brilliant match was mine at last (and after Graswinkel and Roger, did I not deserve it?). Yet shall you know? In all delicacy, I hesitate to call him Master before you. Yet he was masterly; the *ne plus ultra* of my career.

Forgive me, Nicholas, the indelicacy of my excitement; I must draw breath. I do not forget you, but the memory of him transports me, causes me to forget the present. The two become intertwined, for it was in this very Salon d'Apollon where you and I now sit that I made his brief acquaintance.

But again I hesitate. My revelation is stopped, my effusions restrained. It is you, Nicholas, who cause this stuttering articulation. You do not want to know, do you? I feel the vibrations of your disapproval, the threat of your unstringing. You will not have me bursting with lyricism for another. It is unseemly.

Yet it must be. You know it is the natural sequence and the rhythm of my life to be handed from master to master. A pity, perhaps; for, yes, I am often exhausted and unprepared, without the necessary *rite de passage*, to go from one to the other – but so it is. When one master declines, another takes his place, and after him another takes *his* place, and so on and so on; the pattern repeats through succeeding decades and centuries. Masters, masters galore; a mistress or two from time to time to refresh and for variety: glorious lovers, indifferent spouses, husbands in harmony – a never-ending suite *à deux*. Yet do not judge me, Nicholas; it is my nature. You would not blame a wild animal for killing predictably and sequentially. It is my nature to be played upon. And what is more, be warned: if you call me whore, then take also the name of whoremaster for yourself.

I disallow your jealousy. Who are you to complain of me? It is I, thinking of Hannah, who am in almost mortal pain, for you loved her in that entirely human way I can never know. You describe my face as with you always, yet for that time in Vienna who was I, the vertical virgin, to compare with your horizontal lover? Her swoonings went to your head; my voice was mere accompaniment.

I too remember that first time with her; how she played on you; how she conducted your strokes, and afterwards taught you to touch her as if she too were an instrument. She made you laugh, by giving names to the strokes, as in 'the French pluck'. Even I smiled at that. You were lovely together – I admit it. And afterwards you included me in your celebrations. For a time, taking me up again, you even forgot her. Having been taught by her, you discovered how to arouse me; how to put into practice the instructions of the old theorists. Suddenly there was air – life – in your bowing. I remember how she bent over us and kissed both our foreheads. She said, 'I love your new stroke.' But you were already lost to her, in me. She taught you how to play me; she was your best teacher. How could I be jealous of her?

My dear, I visit the panorama of my own life upon you not to hurt you but to open your eyes; to bring you peace. It is a privilege. I have made you my witness, just as you have made me yours. Do not spurn my gift: spare me your wanton jealousy, your gratuitous gall. They will only alienate my affections, and never get me back.

Why not give yourself a final hour or two of pleasure with me? Lie back and let me caress you, transport you from care, divert you from your dirgeful dread. Let me sustain you with my airs of rejoicing, ravish you with florid sweetness. Let me touch you in your most receptive parts, fill your veins with my warm fluid, penetrate your delicate openings (so unlike Roger's gross yet useless appendages), arouse you with my song and the pulse of my rhythm, until you are mine again – if only for this hour.

As I was Marais'.

Now you are tempered, let me introduce him to you. *Mesdames et Messieurs: Marin Marais, Ordinaire de la chambre du Roi pour la viole.* He enters the room – this very room, two hundred and seventy years ago – leaning on the arm of his servant. He is carelessly dressed, in loose leggings and bedroom slippers. He has been ill, they say, hardly recovered from an operation, on the subject of which he has composed a piece which he will play tonight. I too am placed in a position of honour, in the niche just opposite the entrance, so that on coming in and raising his head, he sees not the Duke and Duchess or young Louis, but me. He makes his way, shuffling across the room to my side. 'Would you play the new royal instrument?' asks *La Régent.* Marais nods: before he dies, he would play on the most beautiful bass viol in the world. Please, a favour for an old man. The Duchess is so delighted with his modesty, she presents me to him as a gift, that he may enjoy me for the duration of his life, which is not long.

He gathers me up and takes his seat. Smiling like a Buddha – lips pursed, eyebrows raised, cheeks dimpled – he holds me horizontally across his lap: it is wide and comforting. (You have seen the famous Bouys portrait of him, Nicholas, with his instrument *comme ça*; I believe it is now in the Louvre.) How strange it is to be held so! My body is well supported, but the back of my neck is susceptible as I gaze up at Apollo with his lyre. But the lap is warm and comforting; Marais' soft, wrinkled face comes close to mine, studying, loving, with its cloudy eyes, learning my sound as I dwell in his touch. Now I could rest here for ever, with this man who makes a concert of consorting.

I rest sideways on his thigh like a lute, while he supports

my neck with his left hand. As he strums me, the vibrations of the chords pass from my back to his stomach; our souls are one. The feel of his fingers – adjusting my frets, tightening and loosening my pegs, plucking my strings, as if the preparation were as important as the act of playing itself – reminds me of my maker Christophe. I am in a fine temper. He pulls me still closer to him, encircling me with his arms. The sleeves of his costume brush my flanks. He searches me out, finds me.

We are ready. Now I am vertical, *comme d'habitude*, between his soft but strong old knees. The carriage of his hand is more graceful and facile than any that has ever played me. This is the master I have been waiting for – not a dashing young swain, but this old father who comforts me like a babe in arms. He is also a thief – one who steals the hearts and ears of those who listen to him; and a doctor, who cuts away worry and care from the body, like gallstones.

The Surgical Table. . . . A dreadful E minor chord rolls around inside my chest. *Tremors upon seeing it*. . . . My heart beats: boom, boom, boom, boom, boom. Will he survive the shock of so much pain? My own body is poised for it. *Resolves to climb upon it*. . . . I help him raise his old body on to the slab: up, up. But how heavy he is, how old. He is raised up. *The apparatus is lowered*. . . . The gruesome and evil-smelling equipment is coming, coming to invade his body. He is awake. He trembles – how he trembles! – together we quake as it approaches: lower, lower, down, until he faints a moment with fear. *Serious reflections*. . . . He is becalmed by serious thoughts, of life, as well as his gallstones, leaving him. Sweet sweet resolution of the major third. Sweet peace. But suddenly he wakes. . . . *The tying down of arms and legs with silken cords* . . . and, without warning, *The incision is made, the pincers are inserted, the stone is removed*. . . . Oh higher, higher, higher. I cannot endure it, help me – I am wracked with pain; the pitch of my hysteria is so great, I can barely speak, my high C is . . . nothing. Silence; I rest and breathe. And now. . . . *Blood flows*. . . . Mercy. Oh, my voice flows, as his blood flows, bow smooth and strokes unchanging, in a great release of pain, until the blood and the music stop, and. . . . *He is carried off to bed. . . .*

So they laughed at him: poor Marais and his gallstones. But let them laugh, he did not mind. Angels like Marais do not make parodies, unless gentle insinuations, or jokes of which they are the butt, can be turned into music. Music, glorious music; pure music without bitterness to corrupt it. Music which, unlike men, cannot be tortured or pricked by the devil's haired bow. Music which soars above insult and mockery. Music, the divine medicine that soothes and bathes away the diseases and sores of combat.

He nods to the theorbo player who accompanies us, and we begin again: a piece he calls *Les Voix humaines*. It is transparent; nearly immaterial. Sad and ghostly, the theme returns, each time made subtly different by his middle finger, pressing and relaxing on the hairs of my bow; again and again. This is the Marais I have dreamed about, the Marais of whom I shall always dream. His touch is so soft, I moan my pleasure. We are in the silence which comes only after midnight. Barely audible: Marais saying goodbye: to the old style, to our golden age, to life, to me.

Weep with me for the loss of Marais, and do not revile me. Though it was brief, it was no infatuation. My love for him was as deep as any you have known. You knew loss yourself; then you shall know mine. Feel for me, Nicholas; consider the unmarked passing of the great man who was your teacher too. (Do you not acknowledge it?)

Even after two centuries, it angers me that he was so little celebrated at the end of his life; that there were those who dishonoured him at the same time as they pretended to esteem him. There should have sounded a chorus of sobs throughout Paris, reverberating like the great bells of St Geneviève du Mont. Yet only a silence was heard, perhaps even a sigh of relief that the old man – old-fashioned man – was dead. He had paid homage to his mentors, in music which moves more than any other, yet his followers failed to honour him. Not all generosity is repaid. So many were threatened by his simple genius.

Listen to the *tombeau* I sing for my Master Marais: my *exprimés jettés*, my *enflés*; how the tension of my grief mounts in me until it would burst. I should not like to lose my composure. Rest, silence. How empty is the universe without him. I panic, I feel a wrenching of the heart, a chromatic cry wells up from my bosom. I descend the scale, one chord after another, further and further down with each step, slowing to nothing; my voice disappears into duskiness. I am buried with him, my dear dear Marais, one more step unto final quietus.

In his old age he took me with him to his teaching studio in the Saint-André-des-Arts. He owned nothing – not even me – though he had nineteen children to support. He was a prolific man. Three years before he died, he surrendered his honourable title of *Musicien ordinaire du Roi* to his son Vincent. How happy he was! No rancour, no jealousy did he feel for the next generation (unlike some I might name), not even for the teenage son of Forqueray, whom some said surpassed him. The old veteran was not troubled. He did not mind Couperin's *La Superbe ou La Forqueray* (no *La Supérieur ou La Marais* was ever written for him). His only wish was that their 'modern' music – he found it so unpoetic – would not encroach on him before his death.

He was not suited to the new style; only consider his soft round face, the expression of trust for all he knew. He was content with what God gave him; why look to Italy for inspiration? He was not without his experiments – works like *Le Labyrinthe*, with its melodic tritones, its register shifts, the labyrinthine progression through the keys – but he suffered no need for fashion. Forqueray with his adopted Italian clichés, Couperin with his '*goûts réunis*' – these were not for him. He was no copyist, nor a compromiser. He was entirely himself. His music and I were wedded. We were too French to change.

His one sad secret he entrusted to me – his love for Mlle Roland. How ill-suited they were, he the *petit innocent*, she the adventuress. He gave himself away from the beginning, in the dedication to his *Pièces en trio*. He praised her delicacy and skill in singing and playing, her penetration of mind, keenness of ear, grace in the dance, and so on. And then he called her his muse, and even his only incentive; whatsoever was valuable in his work was due to her – etc. etc. And it may indeed have been so: he wrote music which especially touched the heart. But after this first avowal, he was silent. Perhaps his wife reproached him for spreading her shame about Paris. Only in his old age did I stir him to pour out his regret and his unspent passion into me. I understood; I treated his secret tenderly; his longing became mine. *Pauvre* Marais, he could restrain himself no longer. He titled his Allemande, in his last book of pieces, *La Marie-Anne. L'adorable* Roland, now Marquise de Saint-Génie, was at last revealed to all the hungry ears as the object of his lifelong passion. Poor innocent, to be so beguiled by love.

Nicholas

9

Innocent, indeed. At last Nicholas had the satisfaction of mocking Marais: the uxorious father of nineteen children, beguiled by a lady of doubtful repute. He saw the fat little man as the anti-hero of – ah, yes – a tragi-comic pastorale with machines. He holds his heart, bumbles about on a stage, set with mountain grotto and trees. He laments the absence of his *adorable* Marie-Anne, creates a fictitious passion to replace the gruesome reality of a boring wife and nineteen –! – children. He teaches, he writes, he suffers; he plays the professional angel to another man's devil. Above the summit of the mountain his tragic muse floats on a cloud, and the Sun dashes about in horse-drawn chariot. To underscore his bathetic nature, the thwarted hero is accompanied by viola da gamba, playing Alberti bass patterns interspersed with awkward leaps, as in Rameau's comic cantata *Les Amants trahis*. Yes, even Rose would laugh at her vainglorious Master Marais, reduced to the antics of a *buffo*.

Not even she – blind as a *viola d'amore* – could raise the ridiculous to the sublime. (At least Nicholas had had the good taste to stop at one child.) Or could she? Was it really possible that she admired Marais, even in the extreme of his *amour fou*? Yes; she would elevate him to a hero of *tragédie lyrique*. She found his vulnerability not ridiculous but endearing; his capacity for loving, hugely and foolishly, moved her. Nicholas's own capacity for human love was by comparison pitiable.

And his playing too? Cursed Marais! Cursed Rose! He damned their co-existence at Versailles; the choreography of their union; the unspeakable perfection of their time together, too brief to become out of tune. He hated the thought of Marais mastering her before him; to have been anticipated by him was most dreadful. Rose would never describe him as lovingly. *This is the Marais I have dreamed about, the Marais I shall always dream of.* . . . Such a contest he could never win; no one could.

And yet he must. Such beautiful music could not lie; their union must not be turned to farce. How could a life together compare with a one-night stand? There had been no time for Marais and Rose to become familiar; for him to discover the ins and outs of her; for her to learn his cues, or the hidden messages in his touch. Whereas he and Rose were virtually married. Let her not belittle their time together; belittle him.

What was it about Marais? That he had nineteen children, clearly not; but that he loved immensely, romantically – this she approved. It was the theme of her time. *Élégance, propriété, préciosité* – yes, they were all there, but so was also love. Proper love, passionate love, sublimated love, heroic, even hopeless love, like Marais'. Love in all its guises fascinated the golden age. Lully, Couperin, Rameau and Gluck, for each of them love was the premier operatic subject. Pastoral, courtly, godly love; passions that smouldered and ignited; *affaires de coeur* that were furtive, avowed, hopeful, doomed, erotic and venereal, spontaneous or manipulated by the gods – all their music was love. Lovers languished, sighed, mourned, yearned, doted, seduced, enchanted, even killed for love – and all to the most glorious accompaniments in the world.

Had he, like his eighteenth-century counterpart, succumbed to human love? For a time, yes. Surely he had loved Hannah for the time he lived with her. She was his first, and arguably last, love. After her, there was nothing, no one, only Sam.

'Amour, que veux-tu de moi?' he had sung: his pompous Lullian theme. He had allowed himself to 'fall in love' with Sam, but there was little passion in it, and less of love. He enjoyed flirting and sleeping with her; found the lightness and frivolity of their affair quite in keeping with his so-called eighteenth-century world view. One's behaviour, he had reasoned, should be as authentic as one's instrument.

Sam and he had parted. It was sad but not tragic: he had toyed with her, and she with him. But something was surely missing. He had denied himself and Sam. Poor risible Sam, he made nothing of her. Undoubtedly, she had what it took to be a Mlle Roland – only he could not be her Marais. He pictured her bright teeth, black twinkling eyes, smooth dark skin, head thrown back. Laughing at him.

Hannah too had laughed, though not so lightly. They sat opposite one another at the kitchen table, with the fruit bowl, inscribed 'Comfort Me With Apples' between them. He told her about the position he'd been offered at the Paris Conservatoire. (It was a wonderful opportunity to teach, to earn a steady income, to further his reputation.) Again, as in the beginning, they sipped champagne. 'To your future.' 'To yours.' They drank to each other. And then, 'To Rose.' 'To Rose.' They lifted their glasses to Rose, who sat between them, out of her case, one of their trio. Hannah – gay, claiming to be pleased for him – asked his plans.

He had said, 'I'm going to Paris,' but he had not meant the 'I' literally. Of course she must come too, as Rose must; leave Hubert. But she shook her head.

'I can't. He wouldn't survive without me.'

'Don't be absurd, of course he would. Besides, what about me?'

She raised an eyebrow. 'What about you? You are already married – to Rose. I would be your old chaperone; your ungainly goose. I would not be happy trailing behind you, quite unnecessary to your life. I might even become jealous, and this is not becoming in an old woman with skinny legs and fat breasts. It would be a bad timing; as a musician, you would soon despise me. No, I must not go – it is my fate to remain here. We are together already a long time, Hubert and I. It is not so easy to end these things. Some day you will perhaps understand.'

'I won't. It doesn't make sense. You don't love him, do you?'

'In my own way.'

'He uses you.'

'He needs me.'

'So do I.'

'No, this is not true. Only Rose you need; perhaps you want me too, but that is different. You can't have everything you want, spoiled boy. Hubert needs me more.'

'But what about you; what do you want?'

'Don't make it worse. Just go now.'

He would not beg. He must accept her decision, whatever her reasons. But, perhaps because he could not understand them, he found himself judging her harshly, not respecting her, even suspecting her. He felt contemptuous of her mothering of Hubert; her denying herself. Or perhaps she hadn't. The thought crossed his mind that she had seduced other students who had lived with her, and would continue to do so; that he was simply one of a succession of boys; that it had nothing to do with love. It was even possible Hubert knew all about it and – repulsive thought – found it titillating.

Then he actively blamed her: for allowing herself to be badly treated by her husband, by her colleagues at work; for not having the children she so much wanted. He found her guilty of cowardice, of an unwillingness to fight for what she really wanted. For all her 'lightness' he began to feel a heaviness in her presence; to feel weighed down by her misfortunes while his own life and career were bearing him up. Her soft, yielding smile annoyed him, her large breasts repelled him. He did not want someone entirely soft; receptive, yes, but not entirely squashable. Rose was his ideal: yielding but braced with wood.

Perhaps, after all, she was right: Rose was his wife; she was sufficient to him. She was his odalisque, also his shield. She went before him, she comforted him, she sang to him.

So the young baroque *poseur* left Vienna and what he

called 'this love business' (which was, after all, so consuming of his precious, limited time). What was the point, finally, in trying to possess another human being? He proved Hannah right: leaving her was hardly a blow to him, for he had his Rose.

He saw the flaw now. He was no eighteenth-century gentleman, but a man of his own time; the product – or was it victim? – of a civilisation that has forgotten how to adore. He had wasted the chance to transform his life into something romantic. He had denied Hannah, too.

Hannah laughed. Sam laughed. Rose laughed. Lucy laughed. All laughed at him – for Marais had surpassed Nicholas in loving, as he had in musical skill. He was, after all, no *buffo* for loving; only Nicholas was, in failing to love.

Rose

10

I do not laugh, Master – you did not fail me. Does our grand passion not count, simply because it was not human love? It was as physical, as passionate; it was more musical than most couplings. No other doted as you did; not even Marais adored me so. To him I was merely an instrument, though superior; but I could never compete with his Marie-Anne. You made me human. I was sublime with you. Our intimacy was exemplary, our closeness unparalleled. Nor did we tire of one another after fifty years. It was the marriage of melody with harmony: enduring, perfect.

It is just as well you did not love Hannah enough. What if you had? Do not forget, it was the continuation of our *affaire* too, and I was equally demanding of your attentions. I was unused to such desuetude – the two of you together whenever Hubert was away. I was the one to be dropped first. 'To Rose,' you drank, but it was not me you toasted. Perhaps 'To Rose' was the code for what you could not bring yourselves to say to one another.

Then let me say it for you, Nicholas. There was love between you. I felt its vibrations. These things I pick up, in sympathy, as you know.

But there were other matters – confusions, uncertainties, questions of suitability, issues more of logic than of the heart – which caused you to hesitate. Perhaps that was when you lost her. She, like me, was sensible to those wavering oscillations in you. She knew, as I did, that it was wrong for her to go with you. That split second's hesitation, that supposed mistake – '*I* am going to Paris' – these things exposed you: they revealed you in your moment of withdrawal.

I saw, or, should I say, I felt it. You loved her, Nicholas, but you betrayed her with your sobriety, your self-enquiries. *How can I be a successful conductor with a woman fifteen years older tying me down? What will it be like with a middle-aged housewife – no, she'll never find work in Paris. . . .* And so forth. You were not wrong to think such disquieting thoughts. I did not blame you, I merely remind you of them. You intended all along to go to Paris, but not with an unsuitable, short-term lover. You were going with me.

I was your second body, without whose supporting rhythms your heart would stop its beating. I was more than any mistress. I was *le but* of your life. Without me there would be no Paris.

Poor Master, you were so young, you were distracted by Hannah, and yet, in the end, you knew it was to me, your *épouse*, you would give your heart. You could leave others, even betray them – but never me.

In the beginning you cherished me – indiscreetly, obsessively, extravagantly, dizzyingly, drunkenly. As a child, you dreamed of me, and when once you possessed me, you did not disappoint in your attentions. With Hannah, everything changed. Did I say I loved her? Ah, so I did, and so it was (for, yes, after her, your playing became more lyrical, more lush). But while you were in the clutches of your *symphonie à deux*, I was the loiterer in your midst. For hours, days, you forgot me, or you used me as your prop, your showpiece. I was the observer, the *voyeuse* of your progression. My own development was neglected.

So, you see, it was for the best – even had you the gift of *prévision*. What came to pass for Hannah was not of your doing: remember her unclarity of mind. Afterwards, you did not forget her, you merely went on with your life, not making reference to her. It was understandable, Nicholas, in the circumstances. . . . But we are ahead of ourselves.

Let me return to my own *fin de l'affaire*. You will want to know what became of me after Marais. I shall tell you. After his death, I was returned, a ward of the royal court. The Princesse Henriette-Anne played me for a time, but I never honoured her with the name of mistress. You know her portrait, Nicholas, the one Jean-Marc Nattier painted; it hangs here in the Musée. I seem to remember you used it on the sleeve of our recording, 'Music at Versailles'.

I fear I did not respond to her advances. She played from the simpler suites of Marais, the pleasing *pièces de caractère* of Couperin; she even attempted some Forqueray, but it did not satisfy; for all her royalty, there was no authority, no weight in her bow. Consider her portrait: how she sits, in her blue satin skirts as wide as an organ console, her face sweet, her hair blonde, her smooth forehead open to the world. She was without a care. Perhaps that was why I could not respond to her. Or perhaps it was too shocking: to go from my dear old Marais to this self-satisfied child, with no self-knowledge in her touch. *Petite* Henriette could not rouse me. I needed time to mourn; a transition; a silence in which to forget.

After that I was sent, without mercy, to be mastered by the devil.

He takes me between legs as hard and bowed as the *clavecin*'s. They are strong and I am clamped in their embrace. He has none of Marais' soft womanliness. He lifts my bow, feels its weight, balances it on his palm, screws the hairs a notch tighter. 'I like a tight bow,' he hisses through his teeth, which are round and spaced like the ivory studs on my pegs. As for strings – 'What's this, all gut-strung? Hah, only Marais could be so backward! I must have strings, *strings*!' he shouts, stripping me of my simple gut, though he cannot strip me of my memories. He dresses me in his own eccentric design: first and second plain gut, third twisted gut, fourth twisted gut with a small amount of brass wire, fifth, sixth and seventh twisted gut with silver overwinding. Now I am decked out to shine where before I was quiet and elegant; to resonate and flourish where before I was muted. Gut-strung, I growled, now I bellow. My master's booming mouthpiece; I hardly recognise my own voice. How I miss my Marais.

He returns my smile but there's menace in it. He flicks his lacy wrists, and flexes his fingers *en l'air*, demonstrating his agility. I do not doubt it. They are like tapered, massive talons, capable of such speed that they move in a blur – ready to sweep, dive, pounce, rend. *Wait, wait; never have you felt anything like this before . . . the things I am going to do to you. . . .* I feel the rhythm of his excitement even before he touches me, but my own pulse beats fear – fear that I am to be beaten rather than played; worse, that the claw will close round my neck and squeeze till I am strangled. His victim; played out, not upon; drubbed into silence by his brilliance.

Here are bowstrokes I never dreamed of, with slurs of thirty-six notes; portatos, tremolos, upwards and downwards slides. There is nothing he will not do, forcing me higher and lower than I am willing to go, so that I groan and screech my way through his mad suite, while he bends double over me like a demon, desperate to reach the little neck beyond my frets. Howling, I object, but he crawls down my strings, worming his way to the high C until I am undone. He cackles; he goes where he likes.

Nor can I escape his wild yet disciplined bow. And while he drums on my strings he raves, the words fanning the flames of his distemper. Who shall he beat with his stick today? Ah, he has written a new suite of pieces for me, beginning with a portrait of the Sun King – *La Soleil* – long dead but alive enough to be reviled for his pompous absurdity. Louis the gallant warrior, Louis the charming lover, the benevolent peacemaker, man of consummate virtue in his impenetrable breast-plate and blocked shoes, with bowel and nose twice the size of normal men. Louis, an hilarious joke.

And now, another piece of my master's wit. What have

we here – ah, Lully, Louis' lackey: pederast, libertine, swindler, dissipated idler, loose-living, lewd, evil-minded corrupter of a century. Listen to how he parodies him: the over-dotted *ouverture*, the mocking reprise in imitation of the *vingt-quatre violons*, interspersed with sounds suggestive of elephants and whales from the operas; then the repeated boom-boom-boom of Lully stabbing his own foot with his baton. And a quote from the very *Te Deum* he was conducting for the king. The coda, in mock solemn tones, while he dies of gangrene poisoning. *They called him musical*? shouts my master. *I call it copulation between Music and State*.

The last piece in the suite. *La Marais*. I am tricked by its honeyed sweetness into lapping up its venom: tortuous, old-fashioned, incomprehensible in its lack of melody, rhythm, shape; I am force-fed, like a goose, with ornaments until I am gabbling and sick. Sick of my master's cruel portraits; this one I cannot endure, of his short-lived predecessor I so adored. Adore. Let him mimic the public figures – perhaps they deserve it – but not his dead rival; he does not deserve such mockery. Nor do I. Perhaps his style was a trifle old-fashioned, although he proved himself adventurous enough in his *Tableau* and his *Suitte d'un goût étranger*. Everyone noticed how his latest books were filled with the new Italian style, though he wove it in his own idiom. Perhaps it's true we are ready for a new kind of playing – with more excitement, novelty, exuberance than the old prince had at his disposal. But I cannot transfer my allegiance so soon; the pain of loss is too great. In my dreams I imagine the gentle man still plays me. I am touched by his two-finger vibrato, the quavering *tremblement*, his *pincé*, his fingering without bow. I cannot give him up to ridicule.

No one escapes this man. We are all his victims: Marais, I, his wife; the instruments on which he plays out his spleen. His wife, Henriette-Angélique – another angel for the devil to mortify – sits stiffly at the harpsichord, waiting for his next blow. *Tight-lipped daughter-of-an-organist. Drudge. Niggard. How you play avec les doigts marchantes. Go home to your father, I have no use for you*. And he imitates her, the way she sits at the keyboard with her back straight as a post and her knees pressed firmly together – contrary to the elegant contour on which he always insists (the right foot slightly in front of the left and turned at the ankle). She reminds him of the empty cupboards in their kitchen and the grey skies above, and threatens him with punishment in the next world. But he laughs – there is no hell in his world – only sunshine and gilt, and the golden smiles of his most appreciative, royal, audiences, too stupid to notice his mockery. He pummels her with the back of my bow. Again, he shouts. But however much he fulminates, still she makes those soldiers, her fingers, march noisily up and down the keyboard. I fear for her as I fear for myself. He waves the bow in the air as if to strike her again; but she ducks and shrinks from him, as she has from his embraces, and runs to her father, the organist, with his straight back and knees, for protection. And sues my master for divorce, and violent assault, which he richly deserves. Only his son and I are left to bear the brunt of his frenzy.

You must know by now who he was?

Nicholas

10

What game was she playing? Teasing him with another eminence with whom he could never compete. As he knew perfectly well, it could only be the 'wild, curious and bizarre' Antoine Forqueray – the one who played like the devil (while Marais played like an angel). Marais and Forqueray, Forqueray and Marais, their names had become a detestable litany. That both of them should have been Rose's masters was extraordinary. Nicholas simply could not, or would not, believe it. It was simply too much greatness to live up to.

Yet how different they were. He'd performed them often enough together, exaggerating the gentleness of Marais, the *diablerie* of Forqueray. One moved, the other amazed, yet they complemented one another. One could hardly perform them separately, as if the one had become insufficient without the other: rivals eternally coupled. Marais, of course, could not have cared less, but Forqueray would have been spitting with rage, to be joined inextricably with the hateful, incomparable, angel. Yet both of them had shared *his* Rose.

Nicholas did not wish to know them as people – only as anonymous musical personalities. He particularly didn't care to know how they had practised their devilry and angelry on his Rose, long long before his time. To her, his interpretations of them could be nothing compared to the power of the originals. He suddenly realised that anyone who tried to play both must fail at each. *Less devilish than Forqueray; less angelic than Marais* . . . is that what Le Blanc would have written about him? His critics had called him mannered and extravagant. They had remarked on his 'discontinuous' style; many had denounced him for abandoning what they considered the ideal of baroqueness – the unutterably boring smooth rhythmic line (the fools!). But never had he been drubbed for mediocrity. Now Nicholas saw himself as a poor compromise between the two polarised giants.

Forqueray could arouse audiences to pitches of excitement that no other composer could match. Nicholas had enjoyed letting all stops out while retaining full control; had savoured the technical challenges, the dynamic shifts, the sheer devilry. One never knew, with Forqueray, what was coming next, whereas with Marais. . . . But then Marais, he supposed, surpassed Forqueray in feeling. People seemed more deeply satisfied when he ended with Marais – he could hear the aahs coming from the front rows. Fewer fireworks, yes, but was that all there was to gamba music? Audiences, growing more sophisticated and subtle, changing over the years, had begun to appreciate the difference.

He remembered a concert at St Cecilia's Hall; it was during the Edinburgh Festival, a hot evening in August. The combination of visiting Americans in tartan tam o' shanters, and Scottish ladies in mauve turbans, seemed to make the temperature rise even further. Not to mention the infamous Roland and Brock, Rose's first 'restorers' in the audience, Brock by this time quite ancient, fanning a face which was rubescent against his white hair. Roland, younger and calmer, seemed as always to be in charge. They had come all the way from Sussex for the concert, and sat in the front row like proud parents. Nicholas could see the rise and fall of Brock's chest, practically hear the wheezing.

When would they register their regrettable mistake? 'The French builders,' Brock had pronounced, 'did not care to indulge, perhaps ironically, in such ornate decoration; they left that to the composers. Whereas the Germans went in for just this kind of inlay and head carving. German, certainly German, look at the head, a typical *Fräulein.*' He had rounded off his verdict with a flourish, saying that, in any case, a French seven-stringed instrument was too specialised for a young man like Nicholas. 'This way you will be able to play everything in the repertory, and the instrument will not be too unwieldy. Simpson, Hume, Mace, Morley, Purcell, Telemann, Bach, Buxtehude, the Italians, even Couperin – you shall play anything. It will be an all-purpose instrument. Most practical. Only Marais and Forqueray,' he had added, pointing his lip at Nicholas, 'perhaps you will not be able to play them. But then they are rather difficult and queer, as the French tend to be. You know them, of course?' What would the realisation that the pair had been wrong do to Brock at his age? He might not survive the indignity, might have a stroke (not another!) right in the middle of the 'Gallbladder Operation'.

Heat rose from the polished wood floor to the brass hinges of the fine Taskin harpsichord; was reflected from the sweating foreheads and bald heads, and flashed from pairs of gold-rimmed spectacles, necklaces and earrings. He'd washed his hands over and over again during the interval, while he waited impatiently for the harpsichord to be tuned. In the heat, it took longer than usual: by the time the treble was tuned the bass was out again. Nicholas had had trouble with Rose too. It was the kind of weather when fingers slip off frets. And then there were the strange acoustics of an oval room. Elegant it may have been, but it caused the sound to swoop, bounce, echo, ricochet and even, in the exact mid-point of the hall, to disappear entirely.

He'd started the second half with Forqueray's C minor Suite. *La Rameau*: slow and dignified. Rising chromatic shifts followed downward spirals, the dotted passage grew more and more agitated, then the bass, nice and pompous, rounded things off again. *La Guignon (vivement et détaché)*: a piece that sounded light and easy to play, but was tortuous; it forced one into the lowest and highest positions, even above the seventh fret to the 'little neck', in a chromatic passage which could sound like eloquent ravings or, if he was not careful, the squeals of a stuck pig. That night he'd erred on the side of correctness, because of the heat and the acoustics and the harpsichordist (who tried to take everything at a terrifying clip: he wanted to get home by eleven to hear himself on the BBC), and the annoyances of old age and death (new terrors!) that the ancient Brock had called up. His playing had been reliable and adamantine, over-careful, uninspired. Forqueray would have spat his contempt.

Tonight too was terribly hot. Eighteenth-century Versailles might have been naturally air-conditioned, but now the temperature was distinctly unfriendly to old instruments, not to mention old men. He felt for Brock tonight. He loosened his tie and collar. He hated Forqueray. He pictured him, as in the portrait by Tournières, in his elegant white cravat and lacy shirtsleeves, the pale green coat with the huge cuffs, slightly open to accommodate a comfortable paunch, the sturdy legs, the broad face with the self-satisfied grin on it. The devil. Was his own face as red as Brock's had been in Edinburgh; or was it deathly pale?

Lucy played *La Silva*. It washed the room in a sudden coolness of slow wavelike chords. Forqueray in one of his rare gentle moods, almost sentimental; a portrait of Marie Antoinette's doctor. A piece which often brought tears to the eyes of the more sensitive, or affected, in one's audience. When Nicholas played it in Edinburgh, he noted Roland shedding a discreet tear or two, presumably for his dear Brock, whom he would soon lose. These many years later, Nicholas – pretending to remove an eyelash – dabbed at his own eyes with an unornamented square of English linen. Foolish old men.

Those pieces Forqueray had played on Rose – *La Soleil*, *La Lully*, *La Marais* – where were they? Lost, or suppressed by Forqueray's son? He could well imagine the garbled, close writing in *La Marais*, the doubling back on itself, the salad of ornaments, the tongue-in-cheek *préciosité*. The exaggerated parody would have made Marais affected, tedious, fulsome, when he was actually easy on the ear. Too easy, perhaps, for Forqueray's taste. Why had no one written a parody of him: *La Forqueray ou La Diable*? Nicholas would have enjoyed playing a piece descriptive of the pompous, jealous fiend. But Rose's voice seemed to remind him: who was he to mock jealousy?

Roland and Brock had wandered back to the Russell Collection room afterwards to congratulate him on his splendid performance (it was less than that). 'I see, by the way,' added Brock, rocking on his heels, 'that the instrument has undergone considerable change since our time. French now, seven strings. I seem to remember we decided to do six, on the German model. This suits rather better, I should say, though rather specialised, rather specialised.' They both smiled, in a queenly way, and walked arm in arm past the quiet keyboards. Reprieved for another year, two, six months? Life was too long, one was bound to make mistakes; there was no point in apologising.

Lucy's performance of *La Boisson* was not satisfactory. She produced a rather wretched noise that grabbed him in the ribs. Or was he having an attack? He held his chest and breathed slowly while the pain abated. Mustn't clobber the instrument to death. . . . Nicholas pictured Forqueray beating Rose, his wife, Marais. Was such behaviour excusable in a composer of his limited talent, or could only a Bach have got away with it? Why should even genius be excused from civility? It was one of those curious anomalies – absurd when one thought about it – that people tolerated behaviour in artists which they would not in lesser mortals. Excuses were legion: it was the temperament, the sensitivity, the being highly strung. . . . That did what? That caused them to be selfish, egotistical, egomaniacal, cold, cruel?

Oh, the compunctions of old age. He saw himself hiding behind Rose, playing Forqueray for effect, *becoming* Forqueray: the devilish, baroque he-man; trying to appear cool, to draw his audience's attention away from the sweat which gathered on his upper lip (no one but Rose could feel the dampness through his trousers). A joke now. He would never get away with it today. 'Macho' musicians got hooted off the stage by their female colleagues. Cold resolution was out; 'feeling' was in, 'sharing', 'expressing' oneself. Women – formidable genial amazons like Lucy – expected men to be as gentle as themselves; as 'giving'; as 'warm'; as generous in their affections. The more artistic you were, the gentler you were expected to be.

Nicholas considered how he had looked – how Lucy looked – as she played Rose: the drooping shoulders, the underhanded bowing, the limp wrist – attitudes of peacefulness and love. French music's gentle disposition. Nicholas listened to the Couperin they now played, Lucy accompanying: the hautbois with its mellow and piercing wail; the flutes which sighed so amorously in the tender airs. Perhaps, he thought, the French were never as adventurous or violent in their passions as the Italians (or Forqueray, who copied them!), but perhaps it was to their credit. Those Italian passages: how they instilled terror! One feared they would degenerate into dissonance and ruin, and yet the danger would suddenly pass over, leaving the listener fairly ravished; the thrill was having flirted with destruction. Compared with this, who would not agree with Raguenet that the French were dull and stupefying in their music?

And yet. . . . Nicholas continued to weigh Forqueray against Marais, Marais against Forqueray. He liked the dramatic turns of phrase which Forqueray had borrowed from the Italians, but he decided that gentleness, after all, rather than virtuoso vitality, was the winner. The languishing effects, the weak articulation of a finger – these were the antidotes to violence. The great art of subtlety and restraint was to touch on the passions with exactness, delicacy, neatness, niceness. To suggest rather than beat one's audience about the head. To touch the heart and the ear.

He listened while Lucy played Marais' *Tombeau de Saint Colombe*. Rose wailed her grief, lost substance, became weak and feeble, then recovered and became strident again; sweet, tight, wrenching sounds, one after the other, Lucy produced, the transitions always just right. Endless invention: he was touched.

Had anyone written a *tombeau* like that for him, he might almost die in peace.

Rose

11

But come, you aren't dead yet, Nicholas! One's *tombeau*, as you well know, is written after the event. The others never heard theirs, unless in heaven, nor will you. Yet if you listen, you will hear Lucy's homage to you in life. It is not only Marais who inspires her. You are the one she plays for still, the one whose favour she courts. Playing the instrument you once embraced, she embraces you too; is your lover too. No, Nicholas, there is no apostasy here, only renewal. Trust her; or if not her, then me. At least this hell-bent century can revive and imitate as no others could; for that we must be grateful. We do not deny you; if anything, we sing your hosannas.

You say you would die in peace if I loved only you. Oh, truly you would thrive on such exclusivity. You would prefer it had I no history to taint me: that I had sprung Christophe-crafted into the twentieth century. Yet from where do you suppose the depth of my voice comes, if not from the wear and tear of time and love? Your years gave you maturity and skill (and not a few grey hairs and wrinkles); mine gave me a deeper colour and a sublimely melting voice.

You cannot have it both ways, my dear. If you want my munificence, you must take my past masters: they made me what I am. For all his devilry, I loved *le père*. He drew me out prodigiously. He brought out a side of me I hardly knew existed. In his hands I produced a great guttural noise; I transcended myself; I became vast, booming, magnificently bellicose, dynamic, venturesome. No one else, before or since, has inspired me to such voice. We were justly famous throughout the land.

Yet – mark it well, Nicholas – I loved the son too: Jean-Baptiste Forqueray, *le fils*, the gentle son who had been collecting curses (accompanied by a thrumming of strings and a gnashing of teeth) from his father since he was a boy. The elder Forqueray, if it is any comfort to you, did not die in peace. Such a nature could not. He fought washerwomen and dukes; in due course he defied the Archfiend's emissary. 'Go away,' he cries. 'I shan't die yet. That son of mine will steal my instrument, my soul.' He points a shaky finger, much reduced, in the direction of poor Jean-Baptiste.

Le fils sits with bowed head; in prayer, guilt, sadness, regret, anger. In the quiet intervals of the old man's sleep, he ministers to him: bathes his forehead, changes his soiled nightclothes, even sings to him. The son is by now a man in middle years, still full of life and yet, as ever, afraid of his father, the dying tyrant.

I stand to attention at the foot of his deathbed, dust gathering on my upper lip: Jean-Baptiste cannot bring himself to play me while his father still lives. He is afraid of killing the old man, or of being killed himself with further curses. But the father's wishes are not heeded; his Maker will have him, willy-nilly. *You shall inherit my instrument over my dead body* . . . are his last words to his son.

Over his father's dead body, indeed, Jean-Baptiste Antoine Forqueray, *le fils*, became my new master; and we flourished, after a fashion. He played me for dear life: for his own, for his dead father's. In his devotion to his father's memory, first he published his pieces for gamba, and then – excessively pious – transcribed them for harpsichord, an instrument now more fashionable than I. The once-queen of instruments, I was piteously deposed, as only royalty can be, and my new master knew it. Why else distort those pieces tailored for me to fit the jangle-box? Because I was become obsolete, unmarketable; my music mouldered in the bin, while those transcriptions for the harpsichord sold like *petit pain au chocolat*. Jean-Baptiste may have loved me, but filial piety did not stop him cocking a sharp ear to fashion. It was he who added three rather mawkish pieces of his own to the collection, then wrote my epitaph (the first): 'The viol, in spite of its advantages, has fallen into oblivion.'

So you see, Nicholas, I too know what it means to pass from favour.

I had other champions, of course, but rather unreliable. The absurd Le Blanc, for one, tried to flatter me in his polemical writings, but succeeded only in condemning me to swifter oblivion. In his imagined drama, my adversary, the villain Il Violino, accuses me of asthmatic sighs and weeping distemper. He calls me 'Madame Wigbox': 'Oh you of such ostentatious display and little effect. . . . There is the same proportion between the size of your belly and the sound which comes out of it as that between the mountain in the throes of childbirth and the mouse of which she is delivered.' To which I reply by calling him a pygmy and an abortion, with the voice of a mangy cat whose burred tail is on fire. *Quelle comédie*. It is all nonsensical stuff, and yet its message is serious enough. The violin (and Italian music in general) is suitable for exciting great passions, whereas I (and French music), with my tenderness, am relegated to the pastoral and the out-of-date.

But not yet, not so long as the Queen loves us, and the Duchess, and my master's patron, the Prince de Conti, and especially La Pouplinière, at whose house we play at least once a week. My master Forqueray so far is safe – so long as he has royal support and so long as he has pupils to teach (his prize pupil is the King's daughter, Henriette-Anne) and to admire him. We are employed still at court, at the *Hôtels* where the nobility have rooms, at the Concert Spirituel (when they are not having the Italians), and, as I have said already, at La Pouplinière's. My master is happily in favour, but what will happen next?

Rameau is the leading man of the house; he conducts not only its orchestra, but its musical taste. Diverse elements of society are entertained here: artists, women musicians, men of the world, actresses, *filles de joie*; not to mention the high nobility, the princes of blood and the kings of finance. It is a menagerie, our host a sultan. But, alas, La Pouplinière is a man subject to *ennui*, capricious and restless, in quest of novelty in music as he is in women. He seeks constant distraction from himself, and in this I perceive our danger – my danger.

I feel the rumblings and I know that eventually even Rameau, with his penchant for both experiment and compromise, will be deposed. Too French and yet not French enough. And I shall go with him, and so will my master, and all the other players of outmoded styles and instruments.

Yet for a time we are still in power. The Théâtre des Grandes Écuries is a spectacle of exuberant untidiness. How the crystal lamps sparkle, how the gold glows on columns, how the angels and gods and goddesses float heavenward! Everything is in motion; unbridled and yet symmetrical. The laws of gravity do not hold: shells, fruits, flowers and vines run riot. The heavens appear to have opened, irradiated by a supernatural light. Rameau's glorious music – our music – combines with this architectural magnificence in joyful harmony; and all thoughts of mortality are forgotten.

These royal entertainments! While we play, the Duchess of Burgundy deals cards in her ante-chamber – with the door left open, of course. Others gossip, chew ostentatiously and stroll about. Naturally, I prefer the Chapelle and the Grand Cabinet where the serious concerts are held. Recently, I accompanied Campra's cantata – the one in which Acteon is turned into a stag for spying on the Goddess of the Chase and her playmates as they bathe, and torn apart by his own dogs. I shall never forget the dancer, Acteon, weighed down by his great stag's head; how his poor thin legs buckled, and how valiantly but uselessly he struggled against the attack; crushed and bleeding, his great head half hanging off.

Rameau too they attack like dogs – the *Lullistes* on the one side, the *Buffonistes* on the other. The latter want simple platitudes of Italian *commedia*, like Pergolesi's *La serva padrona*. Rousseau, their spokesman, accuses Rameau and French music altogether of complexity. French singing is one long bark, he writes; quick passages are like a hard angular body rolling over cobbles. And so on. The *Lullistes*, on the other hand, are outraged by Rameau's harmonic speculations and his dramatic freedom, and would return to a 'pure' French idiom. Sniped at from both sides, how can he survive? They spread such horrible stories about his opera *Zoroastre* – and yet one cannot get tickets to see it. The French are capable of such contradictions; they are dogs at work. Already I smell the blood.

Yet at La Pouplinière's everything is as it once was; this is our base, the safe house of *Ramisme*. I reign supreme. Our supporters gather round and listen. Forqueray, at fifty, still as needy as a child, turns for comfort to Rameau, whose thunderous voice and personality echo Forqueray *le père*. With his crabbed bony face, Rameau exerts a ghostly power over him. We are all in thrall, for his music is our enchantment. *La Cupis*: the flute and I make a lullaby of our voices; our thirds, our glissandos in alternating, soaring loveliness, would melt the hardest heart.

But not that of the perfidious La Pouplinière. He gives leave to his mistress to evict Rameau – after so many years in residence – from his house and his payroll. Soon our landlord is seen in the *coin de la Reine* among the *italienisants*. He is no longer Rameau's champion, but his avowed enemy, and we are all of us in the cold. Where shall we play now?

Our world grows smaller. After Rameau dies, my master has no one to follow. He is bereft. He teaches. He engages with Friedrich Wilhelm of Prussia in a great correspondence, in which he reveals all the secrets of my playing, which he learned from his *papa*. He plays in small private gatherings with his wife, but we are less popular than before. We do not play in operas very much – not even Rameau's. The cellos have taken over.

I hear what others cannot hear. That the Italians shall win, with their arias and their melodies like saddles, fit for all horses alike. Stamitz and snuff-boxes will prevail. Gluck will oust me from the orchestra pit, Boccherini from the salons. Jelyotte will plunk-a-plunk at his guitar while the dilettanti drink tea. Couples dressed to the hilt, parading, galloping, mincing, will come in droves to Pergolesi's operas, for the antics of singers trained in Italy. Yet I doubt if they hear the music when they are so busy fluttering behind their fans, jabbering and twittering and winking. Oh they love the spectacle and the gossip and the fireworks; they tap tap tap their programmes in approval and cry out their delight or hoot their disapproval. They are like children let loose after lessons. They must be amused. Soon they will be eating ices throughout the performance. Ah, one could almost remember the airs to sing oneself upon quitting the opera house, if one but had an ear. There was a time when every kitchen maid in France sang the air of Amadis (*Amour, que veux-tu de moi?*) as she picked her endive or threw corn to her chickens. No one hears the courtesans and mesdames singing *Stizzosa mio stizzoso*.

They call the new style more natural – more melodic, dramatic, even revolutionary – but these things do not signify to me, or my master. Young Forqueray retires and I am returned to court where no one plays me. Only the memory remains of Marais' gentle bow passing deliciously over me; of Forqueray *le père*'s exciting thrusts; of *le fils*' agreeable strokes. Now I am departed from such advantages; I fall into nothingness. I am cast out. Where I go (where before I was well received), now I receive a uniform response, admirably concise: I do not know you.

Nicholas

11

I do not know you; this Nicholas recognised. For some time his style had been found wanting, he had been the butt of jokes, of sarcastic reviewers, of young upstarts trying to take his place. He understood there was a cycle to fashion in playing, just as there was in clothes and modes of behaviour, but it was an affront nevertheless to be put aside before his time.

Listen, he told himself, you are not alone. Consider the company you are in: Bach was laughed at, Rameau they called a distiller of baroque chords. According to Diderot, his music was good only for amusing children. Perhaps he was right; perhaps all of us in age are fit only for singing to children.

He imagined Rose, under threat of destruction and, like him, unprepared for death. Would they axe her in her sleep, nothing left but sticks and strings? He entreated her (thinking he cradled her in his arms): *Let us perish with the Baroque, let the Age of Reason continue without us; and good riddance. Since they fail to appreciate us, we are better off buried. We are one, instruments of passion, delight, inconsistency. Yet the rondure of our unreason is lovely, is it not, my Rose . . .?*

But where was he? Where was Rose? He tried to clear the befuddlement of his brain, disentangle his present and her past. It had been comforting, if alarming, to think of them joined together, armed with music and wise philosophy, fighting against the philistines. . . . But it was muddle-headed. Today Rose was under no threat. She was brilliantly alive, assured of continuity. Their situations were reversed. She, at Versailles, was home again, while he, with more than an intimation of his own mortality, slumped in silence.

Was this how Hannah had felt? She had come to Paris unannounced, only weeks after he'd left Vienna. She'd taken an overnight train, checked into an hotel and phoned him. But the brilliant young M. Jordan was out, teaching all day, rehearsing an opera in the evening, and after that, partying. He simply did not know she was there – waiting for him, watching the rain, phoning his room every half hour. Why the desperation? Had she been overwrought from travelling, upset by her own temerity in coming to him? But why had she come so soon? Had she changed her mind about Hubert; finally left him? Perhaps she had confessed to an affair with Nicholas and he had been violent with her. Or had she changed her mind about Rose – decided she was not, after all, enough for Nicholas? Or was it simply that Hannah missed Nicholas too much to wait for a planned rendezvous?

Whatever her reason, she had come – and found him not at home. This she took as a sign that she had been wrong to follow him. The poor trailing goose. By midnight she had despaired, and swallowed enough pills to put a whole orchestra to sleep for ever.

The students had invited him to a party after the rehearsal. He went and enjoyed himself. He thought of Hannah from time to time during the evening: he missed her, but he was not inconsolable. He had enjoyed having a lover – Hannah made him feel manly, competent in more than music. But best was what she did for Rose. Rose, feeling everything, sensed a change in him; which she approved, and to which she responded. Being with Hannah loosened him. He brought his lyricism home to Rose. Now Nicholas stood, with a hand on her case, watching his students disport themselves. He would not trust Rose to the heap of instruments tossed on the bed; she, unlike Hannah, must be with him tonight.

By the time he got home, Hannah was dead in her hotel room; the police had been trying to contact him; his phone number had been crumpled in her hand. Nicholas asked to be left alone with her till morning, and was granted his wish. So he sat with her body, with the evening's music and wine having gone to his head and mingled, and he imagined he was Orpheus.

He takes Rose out of her case and embraces her: warm vibrating Rose, who is for once merely an instrument. He plays, sitting on Hannah's bed, his back turned to her. Her stretched out body practically touches his but he does not turn to look. So long as he does not, and does not reveal the reason, he may recover her. This Cupid has assured him. Nicholas plays a gentle song: the blessed spirits do their slow-paced dance, and there, there – he can feel her stirring behind him – is his wife. Eurydice. Her breath against his neck, her voice, is familiar, German-inflected; it moves him but he doesn't turn. His obedience is his love. But she is displeased. Why won't you look at me? Don't you love me? She begs, she taunts. Without his love she would sooner die; she is in despair. How can he just sit there, his long back a barricade, spurning her for Rose? How indeed? He groans and, betting against death, turns to look on his Eurydice. She is as before, lying on a common hotel bed, quite cold; the music has stopped. He turns back to Rose who is still warm. *Che faro senza Eurydice*? he laments. But when he hears himself sing the name Eurydice, he is appalled. He remembers: this is Hannah! This is real life – death – not opera. Idiot. What did that beautiful music have to do with anything in this seedy room? It was beyond his power, beyond Rose's. His music was less heavenly than Orpheus's. Or twentieth-century gods were harder to buy off with music.

He could manipulate Rose until the rosy-fingered dawn came up, but never win against the gods. He was lucky the Furies didn't tear his head off and cast it in the Seine, still singing. It was all very well charming the birds and the beasts, and audiences far and wide, but to try and seduce Death in a dingy Paris hotel room – he might have gone too far. (God knew what the other hotel guests thought; perhaps that they were in heaven.)

There was a knock on the door. Nicholas rallied. Ah, Apollo – Cupid; another chance, an answer to his prayers! Come to restore his Eurydice, his Hannah, to life.

But it was Hubert, come to take his wife's body back to Vienna.

Dear God.

Had he heard Nicholas playing, singing to the gods? Nicholas switched on the light (it was a dark morning with pink streaks across the sky: ah, Romantic Paris!), laid Rose in a corner and opened the door. Hubert, flown in from Vienna, looked more like an inflated schoolboy than ever, his cowlick at attention. Had he actually clicked his heels? Nicholas remembered some such gesture; perhaps he imagined it; perhaps it was him clucking to Hubert because words were unthinkable; or perhaps it was Hubert clucking back. The two of them in duet: *La Poule*. No threats, no violence, not so much as a raised voice. No tears. Hubert said, 'She was going through the change.'

Rose was right: he had forestalled, he had not entreated, and in the end he had left, blaming Hannah for her own unhappiness. No coaxing, no flattery, no time, no listening. He played Rose with more feeling. Where was human love?

He did not want to know. He had congratulated himself on seeing greater beauty in a lined face than a baby-smooth one – as he had on hearing greater beauty in Rose's tone than in that of a modern copy. But what did he know about the cause of those wrinkles, that premature greying, those worry-lines that he found so intriguing? It did not interest him to speculate. An odd point of view (as others later pointed out) for someone who made it his profession to delve, musically, into the past. But understandable. Human personalities were so much less comprehensible, so very unpredictable.

He had reacted by hating the opera – the entire eighteenth century – for giving birth to a world of fake happy endings. Who was this god of love to revitalise Eurydice and put everything right at the last minute? It was absurd, this ridiculous *catastrofe matrimoniale*, inserted to please the courts and the public. What kind of 'reform opera' was this, with such antiquated nonsense tacked on? He resented the students – singers, musicians, dancers, crew. He was hardly able to get through the final performance.

Of course it was all absurd. The mundane tragedy between himself and Hannah bore no relation to the legend; or only a contorted one. Nicholas leaves Hannah behind in Vienna. She comes after him. When at last he realises she has followed him he turns around, but she is already dead. He plays his glorious gamba Rose all through the night, but Charon laughs at him. No Cupid appears in the morning, only the cuckold husband, Hubert, with his trite and vulgar diagnosis: the menopause. It was almost more funny than tragic.

He was furious; he could bear nothing sweet. Rose, he saw, had come between him and the woman he loved. Though he never stopped playing, he in some way blamed her for Hannah's death. His playing became more aggressive; more Forqueray than Forqueray. He railed, too, against Gluck and his asinine librettist – the so-called great reformers and their banal Hollywood ending – the eighteenth century at its worst. For Hannah, there had been no operatic reprieve, no Cupid's descent from a cloud machine to restore her to life. She had killed herself. She was dead, simply that and nothing more.

He had not known – still did not know – what to do with those terrible words. Then, as now, his clever gambist's hands had been utterly useless: delicate, elegant, dead hands. He had experienced loss as a boy (his father's disappearance), but not this blatant death – death by choice – of someone he had loved; at least cared for very much. And for the first time, Rose could not make things better.

He had gone over and over how it happened, cursed her bad timing, her misunderstanding of events, her private misery. If only she had waited, he would have been overjoyed to see her, they would have had such a good time in Paris. He would have been so proud to have her at the second performance of his Orpheus . . .

Or would he?

The truth was that he had hardly thought of her since leaving Vienna. Part of him had needed to get away from her. He could not seriously imagine himself burdened with her: she was too old, too fragile. It had been an idle, frivolous invitation, and she knew it.

She had come to test him, and he had failed.

Afterwards, Nicholas experienced self-disgust for the first time in his life. He had blamed everyone but himself. Now nothing ever would be the same again. There was no sense to be made of it, no cure for the pain. Reform was not enough: he wanted revolution.

Rose

12

Why then, Master, here it is, the Revolution is on its way. Images are burned, great houses are stormed and sacked; when the troops are called out they are pelted with stones and broken furniture. Over the din there are cries of *Liberty*! What does that word mean to me, who cannot exist without a master; who cannot stand erect without human support; who have no voice but that which my masters provide? And yet I must be free: played upon, yes, but not enslaved. Fraternity, too, I must have.

Am I deceived? Is my hidden purpose to provide the sonic glitter that sugar-coats corruption, hoodwinks foreigners and diverts courtiers? Am I the marionette who, in my innocence, recounts and perpetuates royalty's absolutism? Do I animate a manipulated history, breathe life into an opera of fabulous heroes who are mere disguises for tyrants? Am I their unwitting darling? Poor grinning fool; can the Revolution be right?

Imagine, Master, as you sit here tonight at Versailles in overheated splendour, how it was then. We had such an extravagant display of fireworks that even the Austrian Queen herself was pleased (by then she was known in the streets of Paris as Mme Deficit). Fireworks, there had always been fireworks at Versailles. But this time – though our royal audience wallowed in the elaborate fakery of forgetfulness – they crackled with menace. In gold-embroidered silks and red velvet capes, the images of nobility blazed and were reflected in the pool at their feet, until it became molten. Meanwhile, the governess of the royal children was burning in effigy in the streets of Paris. The gilded bosoms would heave with resentment when they heard about this act of rebelliousness. But for now, only their foreheads and eyes smarted as they listened to me, posing prettily, sighing their appreciation. In a moment of silence between movements, a boat glides into one of the illuminated grottoes and disappears.

I accompanied them in their folly, realising a furious accompaniment to Discord, who sings of her enemy, the King of Love: *Et ne me force pas à m'entendre louer/Un roy qui te déteste*. Another king threatened by discord. Drums: their inexorable accompaniment left no room for doubt. The subtle instrumentation of the *ancien régime* – Campra, Clérambault, Rameau – was coming to an end. These scenes which they were privileged to witness were end-scenes. Let us exercise our noble voices until dawn, I thought, for this music shall not be suffered longer. 'Tremblez, tremblez,' command the placards to the King, while I tremble at Medée's invocation to vengeance:

> *Volez Démons, volez, servez ma colère fatale,*
> *Brûlez, ravagez ce Palais*
> *Que la flamme infernale*
> *Détruise ces lieux pour jamais.*

I sang, yet even I with my wooden eyes, I saw that yesterday – with her love of Love – was already a corpse.

A harness maker enters the house of the manufacturer Reveillon and hurls a Louis Quatorze chair from the window. For this he is shot through the chest; like a killed bird, he falls screaming into the crowded, narrow street. Other retributions follow upon the death of the chair: a scrivener and a pregnant woman are hanged; people are exhibited in stocks alongside the gallows; prisoners are branded with hot irons or sent to the galleys. I hear their cries above our music. Shall I too be broken?

The Versailles streets are strewn with carpets; along them the Estates process: purple and lace first, nodding plumes second, dull black last. To the sound of trumpet, fife and drum, the royal procession paces through the streets, preceded by ranks of palace officials, mounted pages and royal falconers with hooded hawks on their wrists. But only the black-costumed commoners are clapped by the watching crowd. Talk of revolution has been fashionable for years; now the call to arms is urgent.

I stand idle, listening to the peal of the tocsin striking its warnings. Soon the people riot again, ransacking a monastery, the customs ports, more than I can know. A great cry goes up from Desmoulins: *To the Bastille*! The weapons of besiegers and defenders crackle and explode in smoke in the summer air. 'Tis no music to any ear but the patriots', some say. The music here at Versailles, meanwhile, a *comédie larmoyante* by Dalayrac, in which I play but a small part, is marked by an extraordinary boredom. The Queen is nowhere to be seen, though treble tee-hees can be heard from the passageway, while the fat King snores. My bow is too well rosined, like the sentiments of this sticky comedy; meanwhile the blood drips from the severed head of de Launey, paraded through the streets on a pitchfork. I hear their shouts more clearly than the Dalayrac, and I feel not the ineffectual touch of Philidor's ringed fingers but the blows of their fists. I would hold my ears against a young girl's cry for bread, her small hand beating a drum in starved rhythm.

Philidor, my temporary master, hearing of trouble, travels to London for a change of scene and a few rounds of chess, until such time as the air is clear of insurrectionary smoke and cant, as he calls it. I am left behind to cower in corners; to listen in silence and wonder where it will end. In the equation of revolution, the freedom they urge will bring my demise. I am sure of it. Some are marching for food or work, but that is only half the story, for there are others calling for blood and our heads. I retreat deeper into my corner, afraid to show my equable face; my eyes bulge at the truth. There is no place for us: we are doomed together, I and my royal patrons. We are the enemy, unlikely bedfellows though we be: the aristocracy, its servants and its pets, the nobility and their instruments of pleasure. Alas, I am one of them.

The Opéra is closed as a sign of mourning. Paris is one great nightcap, sighs the Comtesse de Seneffe; no balls, no concerts, everyone stays at home in fear and trembling. Yet at Versailles there is a banquet, with eating and drinking and toasting the King and a trampling of Revolutionary cockades. Anyone with ears in his head can hear what is coming, yet they do not listen. Are they such fools? Listen to the chorus of angry women – fishwives and ladies of leisure – they are setting off from Paris this very moment and are headed towards us, to the accompaniment of beating drums under a lowering sky. They scream their libretto of blood-curdling tortures intended for the Queen. This is living *opéra*. I can hear it coming better than the ditties I am forced to play. Yes! They are here! The royal prisoners are led away, the heads of their bodyguards impaled on pikes before them. Then comes the stream of triumphant, dishevelled men and women – the so-called mob. I am left behind.

Philidor returns. He takes me to the opera house, where I sit amongst the cellos for a revival of Rameau's *Castor et Pollux*. The royal couple show themselves in their box and receive a prolonged ovation. Is this still possible? Do the ancient instruments still play; the *ancien régime* still reign? For the moment, I suppose, we are tolerated. We tell a story of love and heroism set in the mythological past; dwell in the old recitatives, revel in elaboration, ornamentation, create certain harmony in an uncertain world. The old forms, I realise, are worth preserving, not for their own sake, but for the beauty of their conception. I savour the details, I indulge in gratuitous meanderings. This is my *raison d'être*. Music is like life; when inflexible and timebound, it loses *la joie*. The King bows to me; Philidor bows back. Yet we will soon topple, all of us; like Rameau himself, like Forqueray, we are all bones.

Here is a scheme I recognise. Life, like music, repeats itself: discord – resolution; crisis – solution. The people rise up and they are shot down. Domergue the cellist has been beheaded at Nîmes. The bass violinist Duport, who turned (said Voltaire) an ox into a nightingale, has left Paris for his safety. Yet his bass (the ox) and I – the beast and beauty – are left, abandoned to our respective corners to await the end. Would that it were as decisive as a clean chop and into the fire with me, as they have done with the harpsichords. It is only right that they should be done with us; that they should rid themselves of their so-called *instruments of oppression*.

Music.

I hear of blood, slaughter, rapine; I have not the vocabulary for such things; I would like to deny them. Music is a liar, a pretender, like the King; like the King, therefore, she must be silenced, for her speech is too fantastical to be believed. The time is come when Truth must be heard, ugly, unpoetical Truth. Will they wave my pretty head on a pike over the roaring crowd? I can sing without a head. I would have them do it, for I am guilty; as guilty as Philidor and the others who have absented themselves from the struggle. I would be played as before, agreeably, with refinement; some heat but not this dreadful burning; with vigour not violence. This Revolution is too extreme for my taste; it is rather Italianate. My voice, you see, cannot compete with their shouts, for it is still unutterably tender: *Les doux plaisirs, jeux charmants*. . . . Ah, how sweet to accompany Venus in her victory over Discord!

Tears of humiliation gather in the King's eyes and course down his fleshy face. He holds out his arms to the people: he has been good, liberal, beneficent. But he has plied one trick too many; the innocent face does not convince. The skeleton shakes its bones in the royal closet; he is done for. Therefore, our heretofore King, prepare yourself. I hear it all. The twenty-four drummers beat their ominous roll (they remind me of the twenty-four violins – of another king of another time, also fat and undoubtedly corrupt; but he kept his head, unlike this one): Brrrrr, Brrrrr, Trrrrrr, Trrrrrr, almost but not quite in unison and of such a din to stop the heart, not rally it. The Furies chant their chorus, egging on the executioner with the boom boom boom of their poles. *Les tricoteuses* never lose a stitch. The priest mouths useless prayers. They have turned tables on the King; the bow becomes the blade, and he is now a fat lute, bowl-belly down on the guillotine without his head. No more: *The King is dead; long live the King*! Now the people cry: *The King is dead; long live the Republic*!

What music now?

Nicholas

12

There was no music; nor form, nor coherence, nor direction; only noise and confusion. Nicholas, in panic, had tried to push through the crowds of students, but stopped, fearing violence – though more against Rose than himself. He stood on the edge of one of thousands of mini-groups and listened to their songs and chants: *Nous sommes un groupuscule, nous sommes un groupuscule, nous sommes un* . . . a repetitious unaccompanied litany for thirty thousand voices in sporadic bursts, one group taking up where another left off, sometimes overlapping in stretto.

Poor Rose; to think that she had lived through two Paris uprisings. Her forebodings in 1968 must have been greater than his. Did she think he would lose his head? Did she fear she would be trampled, burned, desecrated, shoved away for another hundred years? Would she be lost in the tumult?

As he thought of his audience impatiently waiting at the Conservatoire (he was on his way to give a lunch-time recital) he had been irresponsibly pleased. He had not been playing well since Hannah's death. He welcomed distraction, even of the destructive kind; perhaps especially. At least let him toy with danger; prove, like Orpheus, he was not afraid of going where he didn't belong. The risk was not great; this was not 1789. There would be no fearful climax to the chanting, no drum rolls, no Furies' choruses, no heads would roll plop into baskets. This was May, 1968: merely thirty thousand students out for a walk on a fine spring day. This time it would all end in jollity. So he had believed.

They wrote self-admiring graffiti. Nicholas particularly liked: DOWN WITH THE DEADLY RHYTHM OF THE PRODUCTION LINE. They were anarchistic and amusing. Even the older people were enjoying the spectacle. *They're only having fun. They're young, innocent, what's all the fuss? When I was their age. . . .* Sans culottes with Che Guevara beards, furies in leather mini-skirts. *Look, fancy dress. Who cares. Let them be. Let them play their guitars, chant their slogans, wear their beards down to their navals, their skirts up to their crotches. Go on dance, dance, to hell with the authorities. Leave 'em alone. Not a hair on those ravishing heads. . . .*

And if they did touch them? If a truncheon came down crack on a skull? Who would stop them? Would it split open? Not far from Nicholas was a face covered in blood. What's up? Where did the flics come from? Suddenly people had started running and screaming; they ducked inside their windows and doorways, they left the streets to the fighters, those with nowhere to run. Out of levity had come chaos and its gruesome equipment: round shields, square shields, wooden truncheons, black rubber truncheons; rifles, gas grenades, hip guns. New chants could be heard amidst the coughing and crying: *Professeurs pas flics, professeurs pas flics. CRS-SS, CRS-SS.*

The demonstrators were transformed; from innocent partying children playing the game of revolution they had become street fighters. There was no smooth transition. Masking their faces with handkerchiefs, they formed human chains, set fire to cars, attacked fire engines with sticks and stones, braved the water jets, spat, screamed and fought the flailing truncheons. Nicholas watched with admiration, thinking them versatile. Variety, in life as in music, was always desirable so long as the player was in control of his instrument. But Nicholas was not. Having put Rose down long enough to tie a handkerchief over his nose, he found she'd been kicked across the pavement and was in danger of being trampled. He panicked and lunged for her, then ran.

A truncheon blow caught him on the shoulder. It hurt, but was not serious enough to stop him. He took Rose home to safety and returned to the streets. No more concerts, no more lessons. He was angry enough now to join the students' strike. Music, he saw, had no place at a time like this; not Rose's kind. It was a romantic movement and, like romantic music, subject to insufferable maunderings followed by self-indulgent outbursts – like the three bloody Fridays of May. Not exactly the *Journées révolutionnaires* but, to the participants, just as inspiring. Not quite so for Nicholas; the police violence disturbed him, but he still could not bring himself to join the battle; he still had to worry, after all, about his hands.

Cowardly musician? Of course he had been afraid; who in his right mind would not be? Only those who had nothing to lose, or were too young to care, or too impassioned, threw themselves into the fight without hesitation. Nicholas had been caught in the middle: he sympathised with the rebellion, but its style was no more his than Rose's. But he had no other contribution to make. His resulting frustration he took out on Rose, mouthing naïve absurdities. 'You are nothing but the light-headed champagne of the mandarins and bosses. What have you to say to the workers and students of Paris?' Art, the family, religion – they were all in it together. Like Puvis de Chavannes's fresco, Rose should be dipped in plaster and silenced. Music and art, however beautiful, were corrupt, distractions from the true revolutionary purpose. They must be shut away. He locked Rose in her case.

The *petits révolutionnaires* had gone out on the streets, Nicholas among them, in fancy dress plundered from the wardrobes of the Théâtre de France. Roman centurions, the Sun King, Marie Antoinette, they flounced out to play revolution. He might have gone as Forqueray or Marais, with Rose as his prop – a missed opportunity to play himself. But the leadership were not pleased with his group's posturing. 'The occupation of the Theatre is a baroque, unplanned gesture; a flourish on the margin of the Revolution,' they wrote. Still an irrelevance, he found himself on the street, flushed out of the theatre by DDT squads: an aborted revolutionary.

What should his offering be? Art must be available to all. Baroque music could hardly be justified by the tiny minority with a taste for it. But why not make it more accessible? Was there any intrinsic reason why ordinary people could not appreciate it? Of course not; it was merely a matter of convenience and opportunity; perhaps also comfort and familiarity. Ordinary people would not attend concerts in bourgeois concert halls and churches – obviously not! Such places were symbols of repression. They would be out of place in them; they could not afford tickets.

Bach's *St Matthew Passion* in a Renault factory: a brilliant solution! He had mobilised his students from the Conservatoire into a musicians' workforce. Dressed in everyday clothes, they marched to the factory, carrying their instruments. They set up at the far end of the hangar at ground level with the chorus on a platform above. Acoustically it was hopeless; no matter how much they played, or sang out, their voices were lost. But no matter; they would make their point.

But nothing was heard; God's music was lost in the rafters. Music which should have been played in His house before His altarpiece, witnessed by His angels and cherubim, simply evaporated. Bach's genius, Rose's poignant voice, Jesus's Passion – amongst the bedizened metal carcasses, they were reduced to a few pathetic cries in the wilderness. What hope of converting the heathen when they could not hear? Of Nicholas ever attaining revolutionary heaven?

Quelle farce. Bach amongst the primary-coloured metal skeletons. And the people – ah the people! – who were they? University and Conservatoire faculty, students and families, slumming it in their 'workers' weeds. Where were the real people, the workers themselves in their Sunday best? At home in front of their TVs or out at cafés arguing about the strike. They wouldn't dream of returning to the factory at night; especially not for a concert. Not that serious stuff, church music. Save that for Sunday. It was boring enough then.

Nicholas had directed, and also played. Rose's solo aria had been most unnerving, with her voice swallowed before it was out; the strip-lights half a mile above their heads hardly illuminated his score. The bass couldn't hear Rose either. And then the shouting in the street became louder and louder. He kept on playing, determined to finish no matter what. But the cries drowned Rose's sighing refrain, the organ's wheeze, the final Passion. No one cared to listen while He gave up His life.

These were his so-called comrades – yet they had come to break up his performance. They knew not what effort it had cost him, nor apparently did they care. Baroque music – in a manger or a mansion – was yet another convenient symbol. So long as he played, it seemed, he was the enemy. They chanted their slogans, threw bottles through windows, beat on doors. In due course, the police arrived. In the skirmish, Bach was killed.

He lost more than his job over the fiasco. He shed his revolutionary persona, divested himself of his revolutionary conscience. Nicholas Jordan, viola da gamba player and baroque revivalist *par excellence*, was himself revived.

He looked around him, and abandoned the ashes and the tear gas and the burnt-out Renaults – and Hannah's memory with them. Out of the rubble Rose was saved. A miracle. She must be taken away at once, away from the deadly rhythms, the anarchy, the disorder. He thought, *I will fly her to America. To another world where Music shall be welcome.*

Interval

Nicholas

The hardest time. One was between pieces, between times. There was no rhythm to the *pause* except for the mundane activities one filled it with. What did audiences do? Perhaps he ought to get up like the others, have a glass of wine (*gratis* from the English sponsors), mingle, go back-stage and congratulate Lucy – kiss her on both cheeks, as he had learned to do in Vienna, long before she was born. Rose next. He saw himself laying a hand on her head, fondling an earring. How else to greet her? No, best not to get too close to either of them; better to wait it out, not excite himself.

The interval – when one played oneself – was spent going to the lavatory, washing, re-tuning; then one simply sat or walked about. Now Nicholas wandered here and there, nodding to people who still recognised him, but did not stop. He helped himself to wine, and moved on. In his solipsistic world, no splendid milieu existed. Only the *intermission*, the music-less nothingness, to live through; one's past to remember. One looked out, if possible (green-rooms seldom had windows, however). One cleaned one's nails. Finally, one considered one's mistakes: how this piece could have been better played, that passage more wittily phrased, more fluidly fingered. Or one congratulated oneself on a particularly elegant section; whistled it again, savoured it. He would derive little pleasure from a post-mortem on Lucy's playing.

Musicians' lives, he thought, were so much easier

nowadays. Students played for one another, even professionals supported each other. They formed groups, discussed, lived communally; had revolving, open affairs. It seemed a jolly, comradely business, but altogether too public for Nicholas's taste. Music was a rare plant.

Groups and more groups, how they proliferated – like everything else in London. England – backward, unreceptive, insular England – had finally opened up to him and his free 'European' style. They needed him. Harpsichordists and cellists were thick on the ground, but gamba players scarce. He'd been able to distribute his favours amongst the best groups, pick and choose which concerts to play, where to travel, which recording contracts to sign. Many of his colleagues resented him, but he knew it to be *la jalousie de métier*.

It rankled that his own students had been so unutterably lazy. All they had had to do was pick up their bows and play, according to principles he had unearthed and set down for them. Oh, they had a certain amount of talent, quick ears, were not without taste, had a feeling for the period, but they had never immersed themselves in it the way he had done; they were never actually out of place, as he had felt himself to be, in the twentieth century. Not merely studying the past, but living it. He and Rose.

He had done it all for them; then they picked his brain, imitated his style, took his place when he became too enfeebled, and shone in his stead. The next generation, the inheritors of so much work. Lucy on television, live from Versailles, playing an original instrument. His. The once-famous Nicholas Jordan an anonymous member of the audience. Lucy's shadow; Marais' shadow.

Marais had had mentors, royal patrons to support him, all the great musicians of the time to write for him and accompany him. Versailles and the great houses had been his to play in, and all of educated Paris had listened to him. And what did he, Nicholas, have, when he started out? The Pigg. There was no tradition of gamba playing in post-war England. People had never heard of the instrument. It was a wonder that he learned to play at all.

He had gone to university, where he read musicology (one did not play music in those days at university). He studied old manuscripts and laboriously copied them out. These and Rose became his mentors. He experimented on her, until he gradually produced a better sound, with a lightness and a variety of stroke; he even cracked the mystery of the curious French unequal rhythms. Rose led the way, and he followed.

He taught himself to read the old clefs, grew accustomed to the writing of the treatises. Soon the manuscripts, with their irregular, waving, lozenge-shaped notation looked more beautiful than modern printed music, unvarying and without personality. He began to hear the music in his head as he copied it out in the library, in the green glow of the table lamps. When he returned home to play these treasures on Rose, he sprinkled them generously – though not always accurately – with articulations, ornaments, *notes inégales*.

Still, the improvement was extraordinary. He felt as if he'd gotten inside the music, inside Rose. She sang out, resonating more fully than he had ever heard her. No Great Bell of Saint-Germain, perhaps, but not half bad. And he had discovered these secrets for himself.

He had not deserved the inattention he received those first few years in London. Nicholas recalled the freezing church halls, empty but for a few pensioners trying to keep warm; the Holywell Music Rooms in Oxford, where a handful of puzzled-looking students, wearing hats and gloves, listened most politely; the Wigmore, where the sound of Rose's voice bounced up to the ceiling and disappeared before it ever reached the dozen or so intrepid souls who had come, Lord only knew why, to hear a young man play the viola da gamba.

He had invited his young fellow musicians up to his rooms to listen to him. He fed them, poured them wine, woke them up with coffee. Anyone who fell asleep was disinvited. He practised during the night and early morning hours, when other students were learning about love. Occasionally he succumbed himself, letting some particularly keen young woman into his bed, though not into his heart, or wherever it was love was said to dwell. He played his part with cold concentration; his performances were always reliable, if without conviction, his technique impeccable. When it was over, he felt nothing but relief. It was like being back at school, acting the musical robot, moving bits of his body without listening to or feeling what he was doing. *Good show, Jordan. Splendid stuff. Amazing fingerwork....* They rewarded him with encores which exhausted him, after which he showed them out, staring over their tousled heads into the *nonmesuré* future; where Rose awaited him.

Later on – in middle and even old age – there were supposedly (so gossip trickled down to him) still eligible young things ready to die for the magnificent Nicholas Jordan. How the Botticellian flautists tilted their delicate necks in his direction, their fine blonde hair falling languidly over their cheekbones! The violinists drooped, their tones swooned. He could hardly give a lesson without suddenly becoming aware of two moist adoring eyes fixed on the least musically relevant parts of his anatomy.

They had tried to imitate his playing; as if it would please him to hear himself replicated. It did not. Love – if such it was – clouded their brains; stopped their originality. He made it clear that if they wanted his admiration, they would have to develop a style of their own; vision, imagination, wit. They listened, nodding as if they understood, licked their lips, made even bigger liquid eyes and pushed the pads of their soft fingers deeper against the frets. They put their heads down so as not to be distracted by him. They would be good, obedient; if nothing else, pretty and demure; perversely continuing to misunderstand him. He had listened and caressed Rose's worn face. Occasionally he thought of Hannah – the beautiful lines around her mouth and eyes.

Frustrated by his remoteness, the students' fingers, which should have been relaxed, became even tenser claws. What did they have to do to please him? You want to know? he raised an eyebrow at them. *Tell me something I don't already know. I'm bored with my own voice. Give me something different. Don't give me rules, give me love.* Not understanding, they blushed.

The earnest ones, who marched in and out of his studio with metronomic predictability, were more businesslike, though equally joyless. They had learned to get his approval, but not to excite his interest. He sat at the far end of the room, facing them. It was necessary to distance oneself – both musically and otherwise. Also, they must experience the aloneness one felt performing. *I am your audience. I sit in the last row of the Queen Elizabeth Hall. Project to me, do not mumble to yourself. I am not here to hold your hand, like your teachers at home. They gave you little stars, chocolates perhaps. No more. Now you are grown up. . . .* Those hurt looks. What did they want to hear? That they were geniuses? That he adored them passionately? Their excuses for not practising were laughable, their petty problems – finding rooms, speaking English, earning money – bored him.

How embarrassing were the tears, the childish dependency; quite unsuitable in grown-up students. They should have known better than to treat him like this: father, brother, friend, lover rolled into one. He was teacher and no more. The red eyes, shaky bows, soft quivering chins were so tedious. He wanted music; he got sentiment and subservience. Cowed, insulted, dissatisfied, frustrated, lovesick – some fled, wasting most of a year's worth of lessons; others returned, with upper lips newly stiffened, to get on with the music. Some spread petty gossip about him. Why? To punish him for his disinterest? They thought him cold, but had no concept of their own selfishness.

That predatory one. On the pretext of asking him to consult on an instrument being built for her, she drove him to the country, stopped repeatedly for drinks at remote hotels. Over dinner, she confessed her real reason for the abduction – as it turned out to be. Disgusted, he left her at the dining table with the not inconsiderable bill, and took a taxi back to London.

So many arms reaching out to him. Did his music make them drunk; or did his playing not even signify? Talk to me, pay attention to me, love me, care for me, look at me. It was overwhelming. How could he be discreet, keep them at arms' distance, when they clamoured so to get at him? It was a pity to fall from grace so vulgarly, yet the temptations were enormous.

At least he had behaved with seemliness. Lapses could be tolerated if the overall impression was one of control, of a clear distinction between music and sexual attraction; between passion and *the passions*. Still, it was a tricky business. Thank God for Lucy, he thought; at least with her the rules were clear.

Rose

Rules? Do I hear what I hear? My dear, has the wine touched your brain? Up-ended it? Do you calculate the behaviour of note to note, man to woman, student to teacher? Does improvisation give way to prescription; dégagé to dictum; freshness to rigidity? Enough; you have drunk too much wine; it is against the doctor's rules. Ah, there you are again; perhaps it is the theme of your declining years. Rules for music, rules for life – ah, spare me! I know it without hearing it, the exact proportion of long to short, loud to soft – it is not music. And age to youth? Were there rules too for how you treated Lucy? Was the indifference calculated? The callousness? And the tenderness – which the others never knew – was that also formula?

I do not believe it; you are become perverse in your dotage. You say things merely for their sound; meaning flies. The Interval tries you: you are unoccupied; you think of things. It is quite worrying.

How was it with the others – the mere students? You are right, many were more than willing-hearted. But you yourself were not without eagerness on occasion; did not always keep your professional distance. It was, naturally, not the pretty ones caused you pause, but the ones whose playing pleased you. Though it worried you, I remember, that you were vulnerable to their charms. It worried me too.

As for your admiring audiences, they could never have enough of you, their baroque darling. When the halls were full, people overflowed to the stage; they would have filled the aisles if they could. The truly besotted ones followed you from Brussels to London to Edinburgh, from Los Angeles to San Francisco to Vancouver, only to hear the same programme yet again. Quite mad. Was it a compliment to your musicianship; my voice? In some cases, yes. Others came to gape at you, their spectacle, their star, their baroque pin-up, their – in Los Angeles – *hot property*. Even our records sold out. Imagine, Forqueray at the top of the hit parade! The music critics, of course, lost no time in finding their own reason for the amazing success of 'Wild, Curious and Bizarre: The Complete Suites of Antoine Forqueray': namely, a glossy photograph of Nicholas Jordan free with every three-record set. As I remember, it was a heavily airbrushed colour portrait of you, suntanned, wearing a white suit, with your hair blonder than ever. I, dark and handsome, leant against your shoulder. You were utterly bemused by the idea (who would not be?) but had been talked round: a small price to pay to get people to listen to this astonishing music. Do you remember it? You looked half-asleep, with a twisted, supercilious smirk that was read as sexy. Silent, I merely smiled.

I could not understand your popularity. I feared your self-love would diminish me. But you grew unimpressible, insensible to flattery. The little sorceresses lost their provoking magic, and in the end I won the struggle. You returned to me.

We might have been alone in an empty concert hall: just the music and I were enough. You threw no kisses. You smiled rarely, and when you did it was painful to behold. Your stiff bow was hardly a proper obeisance. You gave them no eye-to-eye contact; no satisfaction that you were playing to *them*. You were hard-pressed to answer questions. You insulted interviewers with your cavalier responses. *One must have a strong stomach for this nonsense of a cult*. Do you remember saying that? It outraged your worshippers, who longed to read words of wisdom, rules for brilliance. Instead you gave them a long-trilled malediction.

After performances, they would pounce – invade your green-room, line the corridors of your exit. You took on the hunted look of a rock star: the dark glasses and the quick getaway. There was no need; our audiences were civil, tasteful, reverential. There was no question of torn clothing, obnoxious screams. They wanted merely to engage you in conversation, ask for lessons, compliment you on your playing, ask innocent, tedious questions such as, *Excuse me, Mr Jordan, but how do you do those fantastic flattements*? But you cut them off. *The music must speak for itself*, you said. Amen. Holding me close to your side, you put your head down and butted your way through, mumbling *excuse me*, but giving no excuse. You left not a few puzzled expressions behind. But they almost always came back. Only critics lost patience, saying your playing was too eccentric and your expression too dire: an unholy combination. Do you remember the one who labelled you *difficult, serious, remote, aristocratic* – that absurd necklace of adjectives? And the other, who said you lacked stage presence (which was true) and that you got away with it – audiences forgave you – only because you looked so good. Did the man lack ears? Certainly you looked good, but you sounded even better.

But let us return to our places; the interval is nearly over. Lucy, who is less – how shall I say it? – driven than you, appears to welcome it as a chance to unwind. She fills the time gracefully. Even in her long skirt, she does exercises in yoga: the plough and the cat. Then she sits cross-legged (skirt hitched up in a most unladylike manner) and meditates while everyone else makes a fuss. When she breaks her pose, she is refreshed, and happy to see me. I can tell by the way she tunes me that she is avid for the second half. In good temper myself, I forgive her her indelicate behaviour. After all, times have changed.

Drink up, Nicholas. Take your seat, it is time to listen again. The second half will be shorter and lighter – a common pattern. I favour it myself, for after the interval one does not feel like singing such serious songs. Audiences, too, becoming tired and over-refreshed with alcohol and gossip, cannot be expected to concentrate for ever.

Come, leave off your earnest broodings. Let me transport you from care. Listen, Nicholas, and be easy while I sing to you.

Part II

Nicholas
13

Nicholas could not be easy. Where was he? Where was Rose? Why was Lucy playing her instead of him? Who was leading him back to his seat with such insulting solicitousness, and why? Perhaps he should have left during the interval, but he had promised Lucy he would stay to the end. An obedient old man; his life, his movements, out of his own control. He was disoriented by the unmarked time of the interval, and by the *inégal* of his own heart. He had experienced a sense of his own famousness, but it had soon given way to loss. Was it the wine? Versailles' formidableness? He, like Rose, ought to have felt at home here. Like her, he should be revelling in the moment, cocking his ears to her loveliness, to Lucy's; forgetting his own past. But the present meant only one thing to him: the loss of Rose. And that reminded him of other losses in his life.

July, 1968. He had arrived in California – but Rose had not. He waited for hours at the depot until they told him to go home and check back the next day. To distract himself, he walked the unfamiliar streets of Berkeley and San Francisco. He tried to convince himself that, even without Rose, he was a musician. But they were indivisible; he was incomplete without her. She would soon arrive and all would be well. They would play their American début in Hertz Hall on the Berkeley campus. They would be well – no, ecstatically – received. One had only to notice the conventions of dress and behaviour. These flamboyant individualists would welcome them, adore them. They would think Rose the perfect example of their *Small is Beautiful* ethos. What better standard-bearer than she? Long-haired students, black people, yellow people, people in headbands, beads and caftans; long skirts, short skirts; sandals, bare feet. Soon they would belong to him; to him and Rose.

But presently he felt disoriented, separated from everything familiar to him. It was nothing like England or Germany, or even Paris for that matter. Even there, in the midst of the revolution, there had been a uniformity of purpose more easily comprehensible than this free-for-all, in which there were no rules, no etiquette but *Let it all hang out*. Yet there could be advantage in that: the eighteenth century seen afresh, uncontaminated by history. Let it be revived, white-washed of corruption, profligacy, reaction. Let them consider, without prejudice, its music.

He'd walked and walked, exhausted by picture-postcard views, sun, ice cream, flowers as anarchic as the humans. Like the parlour maples – huge drooping yellow and red blossoms – growing to seven, eight feet tall. Indoors in Vienna, they had grown to two feet at most, even under Hannah's expert care. Monstrous. Must everything be larger than life? Would Rose's aristocratic, tempered voice even be heard?

She was missing. He questioned the airline officials who were dealing with the matter. Did missing mean stolen? *We would not like to say at this point, sir. No sense jumping to conclusions. We're quite confident at this point in time that the item will be recovered.* The item indeed. Another week, and still no Rose. He berated himself for painting VALUABLE MUSICAL INSTRUMENT on her case. How absurd; it was practically an invitation to theft. *We might have to entertain the possibility, sir.*

She was discovered, several nerve-racking days later, in Tokyo, where she had been dumped on a dock. She had spent two weeks in the rain. Nicholas could feel the dampness in his own bones. Water creeping up and seeping in;

oozing round her. Water lapping her chin, filling her lovely belly. Drowned. Decomposing. Washed up on a beach, a bloated rosewood corpse, her ribs water-bleached and jutting out; still smiling. The gruesome image joined him in the night.

In the Customs hall, Nicholas removed her from the damp container. He opened her case in slow motion, afraid to look. Rose's smiling, flat-nosed face greeted him. Ah. He lifted her out, under orders from Customs. No smuggled drugs, see? Only an empty sound chest, joints swelled but miraculously undamaged, waiting to be filled with music.

Rose

13

And yet no music fills me up. I am empty but for a dribble of moisture around my rose hole. Oh, my voice, my voice, where have you gone? What are these blubberstrings? California, land of milk and honey and ice cream; if one could but feed on it till one's voice became round and rich and smooth as the thighs of these tanned blonde girls in shorts. But I alone am starved. First I am soused in Tokyo. Now tropical heat. My strings are slack rubber bands, my glue joints melt. I am a great cooked goose, basted in warm varnish. My master tries to tighten my strings but they will not hold. Seven strings are more than I can support; the tension will break me apart. All this sunshine, noise, brightness; all that living, bouncing, shouting; those giant plants, trees, buildings, refrigerators, people, cars. . . . I am soup.

I am tested and manipulated: they say I am 'in movement'. I am, like the earth itself, unsure of my direction. The experts prescribe quiet and a cool, even temperature. I am encapsulated in an air-conditioned, humidified chamber. The silent cold freezes my soul. Sound needs movement, flexibility; I am stolid. The droplets of moisture turn to ice. White cold a shock to the system after black heat. Contracted. A tight pain. A block of ice in the shape of an hourglass. A frozen smile. I can see the fog and later the sun, but it doesn't reach me now. I might be back in my glass case in the Paris museum, the year 1850.

Down below, in the museum cellar, the tempo of life was *grave*. A museum is not a reflection of life as it is lived but as it has died and been preserved. Not hearing my voice, how could the bored visitors in their free-flowing neckties (bringing with them whiffs of fresh air from the Paris streets above) know me as they strolled past my case? My neighbour the stuffed flamingo – what did they know of him? In my partial view, I saw only a scaly leg, a few dusty feathers, a vitreous eye. In my ignorance of him in life, I only imagined how big were his wings and the great rush of music as they beat the air. Each of us in our state of preservation created discomfort: people whispered, caught our silence. Something was quite wrong. Observing the flamingo's dead eye, my unexplained smile (like an idiot's), they passed on stealthily. Some of the younger ones might press their noses against my glass enclosure and tap tap tap with their fingernails. I did not blame them; my beauty, without voice, is unsound.

The minor mode inspires and paints sadness; it throws a mourning veil over the object it portrays. The ear does not find true repose, the soul cannot but be unsettled as it listens. It longs for transition to the major.

Today it would not be so. Museums are no longer such dead, despairing places; no, they are quite alive with sound and motion. One presses magic buttons; is privy to clocks ticking, whales singing, lions roaring, harpsichords and violas da gamba exercising their voices. Even the mummies speak – or are spoken for. *This is a mummy. Old King Amenophis III, who killed one hundred and two lions in the first ten years of his reign; he built a pleasure lake for his wife Queen Tiy.* . . . All those lions, that dredging of lakes; what a noisy life he must have led. But now – silence.

At the beginning of my stay in the museum I was beautiful as ever to look at. But I was consumed from within by woodworm, caught from the viola pomposa which shared my case. I lost my equilibrium from a too high moisture rate. I played host to families of moulds and fungi, became mantled in powdery green. My strings oxidised and snapped at the nut. My ivory inlay yellowed, my poor head began to wobble. I became attempered, cracked and runnelled with the woodworms' burrowings; blackened, greened and yellowed; without strings, without voice, head lolling. It was an entombed, encapsulated, mummified death; I was quiescent, immobile, benumbed. I crepitated.

What was my fate? Would I, like the other aristocrats, simply disappear for ever? Would I become extinct, *functa officio*? (I was no longer mentioned in the list of instruments.) Should I be unmade, as if I had never been conceived; uninvented, unimagined? Perhaps my colourful visitors in cloaks and velvet jackets would take pity on me, or be inspired, once again, to hear my voice. I doubted it: they treated me as a curiosity. My sixth sense told me they were worshippers of bigness, of opera spectacles, of exotic orchestration. Their hero was hailed as 'King of the Keyboard' and he played on a fortepiano I did not recognise.

I had no place in such a world. I was better off a prisoner and an object for future generations to look upon and study, with admiration for my beauty but also contempt for my misdeeds.

And yet, though I had been dishonoured, I had not been undone: neither ceremonially stripped, buried, thrown into a trunk, nor sold for firewood to heat the Assembly Rooms. I had been withdrawn from the fray, but I had survived.

Nicholas

14

Nicholas too had survived the revolution; it would not have done for him to act the doom-laden Englishman. He was no prisoner, and Rose was returned to him. Yet he felt he was living in a child's painting. Everything was flat, the colours primary, the sounds blatant, the music blaring. Nature, people, objects, lacked subtlety: the trees with their violent spikes, the houses washed in ochres and mauves, the flowers with red and yellow gesticulating pokers; the fictive blue sky. At first the garishness and the immoderateness offended his dignity, and hurt his eyes. But he bought sunglasses and a floppy white hat, and let his dignity fend for itself. Gradually the vibrations slowed, and the voices quieted to his ear.

He saw the world rose-tinted; that is to say, he lived just beside, and overlooking, the Berkeley Rose Garden. From his living-room window, he had a perfect view of the curved, manicured terraces rising up the hillside. He saw young people meditating, taking photographs of the Golden Gate, oohing and aahing over the sunsets (they ignored the smog). After dusk, relationships were consummated, and, in full daylight, their nuptials took place.

What could be more idyllic, with the scent of roses accompanying? Music too was a necessary part of the ritual. Every Saturday there would be a rehearsal; then on Sunday the wedding. Baroque music was deemed especially auspicious, perhaps only because of the fad for harpsichords and recorders, and because people liked 'something different'. The musicians dressed in pseudo-baroque outfits, the wedding guests too. One wedding, in particular, Nicholas remembered for its motley participants. The bride wore a low-cut pink satin gown and roses in her hair, and the groom, whose long blond hair was plaited down his back, wore a velvet jacket with a lacy shirt and cummerbund underneath. The minister was dressed as a Pilgrim Father. The guests wore flowing dresses and shirts of a dazzling variety; many were barefoot. An historically confused couple carried spears. Babies cried and the sun burst hot upon the musicians as they played Georg Phillipp Telemann as if he had invented the sewing machine. Such even stitches! And how impervious to heat, musicians and instruments alike!

But now even Rose languished no longer. With the first rains, after her summer's rest, she regained her voice. His distinguished French beauty, Rose of Paree, sang for him once again, and would soon sing for the descendants of the pioneers of the Wild West.

He had strolled across campus through Faculty Glade, among the redwoods and live oaks, in his patent-leather shoes and full evening dress, with Rose in a piggy-back sling across his shoulders – a rather comfortable way to carry her, he'd discovered – and he could cover his ears when the Campanile bells (a Sienese copy) started their out-of-tune pandemonium. Nicholas imagined all the reproductions of Rose that would inevitably be made in this land of imitation. She would become common property, like a Vermeer and its multitude of prints. Better not to copy, he thought, but to preserve the originals in museums or with particular owners, whose protection would save them from cheap mimicry. (Lucy today would call him a reactionary so-and-so for this view; yet who was she to talk, the heiress of Rose?)

The baroque was very much 'in', the concept of authenticity was trumpeted about, and the eighteenth century was energetically celebrated. He was amused to hear a radio broadcaster cry, 'The harpsichord lives!' as an over-enthusiastic crash announced the opening strains of the Italian Concerto: an advertisement for harpsichord kits – clumsy simplified reproductions of a magnificent Ruckers in Belgium. But no matter, they played. Recorders proliferated. One could so easily pocket one and tootle like a Watteau shepherd up in the hills.

In the midst of all this came Nicholas Jordan: handsome, British, *neat* – and, to top it off, the owner of an *original* viola da gamba. The baroque-niks were ecstatic; Nicholas became an instant hit – even before they heard him play. (Everything here was instant: there was no gradual development.) But after the concert they exalted him; he became a West Coast hero. His dignity was disoffended.

All seats were sold out. Perhaps anyone from Europe drew a crowd, he could not be sure. If so, it was an insult; more like a circus than a concert. But his doubts were assuaged by the applause: when would it stop? Did they gush over every performer like this? Never mind, they were warm and welcoming, in fact surprisingly sophisticated. It was not an easy programme, but they could not get enough.

Three encores later he let them go. He held up his hand, bowed deeply. His sun-bleached hair fell across his forehead; Rose's mother-of-pearl shone. The rest had done her good. He held her up one last time to beam her new-born smile at them: his American Rose.

Rose

14

Rose of the Rose Garden, Rose of Paree, Razzle-Dazzle Rose: what is this foreign dance you lead me? First you expose me to the elements, then you demand that I sing like the *rossignol en amour*. Well, I shall not do it; I am *impuissante*, wilted; my voice is rose-water. Have patience, Master.

You are beginning to resemble me, with your dark face and your hair parted in the middle. Have your eyes become more blue, or is it that everything is brighter here? Do you really thrive in it? To me it is harsh, the light shows every scar and blemish. I fear the exposure of my imperfections. In Europe no one saw or cared, but here. . . . They will want to raise the volume on my sapless voice.

Their voices, those *fortissimo* nasal twangs: *Gee, what a gorgeous instrument. I've never seen anything like it. It must be real old. With a head, too, like a lady – how neat. My God, what a neat place to live, right next to the Rose Garden. Isn't that weird? I mean, what a coincidence. You call your instrument Rose, right, and here you're living next to the Rose Garden. Wow, amazing. Makes you believe in fate or something.* Neat, neat, neat. Only for your sake, Master, do I smile and revivify.

I feel your excited breath rise and fall against my neck; what do you want of me, Master? That I should try again and fail? No, this time I shall reward you; I have languished long enough. You have cared for me, kept me cool, allowed me rest. I know what such restraint has cost you. Now it is time to answer your care. Besides, I feel strong again, capable of holding my tune. I miss your touch, and I am jealous of that modern contraption you have been practising on. Try me, I give you my blessing. Mount me, hold me, string me, tune me; do what you will and I shall do your bidding in return – only gently, Master, gently. *Attends*: I shall be your American Rose – your Los Angeles Beautiful, your Fragrant Cloud, your Touch of Venus, your Amber Queen – only do not expect me to belt out a blues or croon or yodel like a cowman. I can only go so far. There, the best I can do; your reward: the smoothie of the Golden West.

Me, me, me: I cried out and you heard. Charily, you played me in, as if I were new again; like the virgin in Christophe's studio. You touched my strings and I was kissed awake; and this time you were no child.

How good you make me feel, Master, so warm, so stirred, to the depth of my soul; there are sunshine and flowers in your fingertips. Tonight I am plucked and plumped, tickled, bounced upon, and swooped by your bow. Your chords thrill me. Saturated, impregnated, I burst forth with song. I resonate to your every move, you respond in turn to mine; tonight we are divine. I feel our power, Master. I feel your hair, rustling gold leaf, brush the side of my face; your fingers draw the music from me.

You are in love with yourself and me; I too. How shall our hearers not respond? Oh they do, they do, Master: they adore our affair; they are as inspired as we. Let us play the *Suitte d'un goût étranger*. What better choice for outlanders? They feel the slow and quick trills, the arpeggios, the sudden dynamics, the swells. The audience vibrates with affection; their minds and their bodies are ours. *Les Tourbillons*: your bow flies relentlessly over my strings, leaping widely from bass to treble, treble to bass. Now *Le Labyrinthe*: we are almost beyond our listeners; yet they follow through a maze of harmonies and modulations – I go where

I know not next – to our freedom, our pure fancy, our blend of modern and ancient; our sublimity.

We were superb, Nicholas, in our Berkeley début. I could believe, after that, that all things were possible in America. Your playing had become new-spirited, sunshine-intoxicated. And its effect on me . . . I throbbed and tingled and whirled; I was in an ecstasy of febrility. It was an *embarras de richesses*. But you saved me from senselessness; restored us to reason and wit. Reminded of my century's legacy, I regained my poise, my *sang-froid*, my aplomb. For a moment, I thought you were Marais holding me on your lap . . . but no, let me make no invidious comparisons. Yet you were, to me, Marais and Forqueray rolled into one: the most magnificent of all.

There is my endorsement, Nicholas – it is yours at last. Does it make you happy? But words can never suffice; it is the music that carries the message. Take it, Master, and drink it like a tonic. I only return what you gave me.

You gave your heat to me. The others who tried to touch you, you gave rime and frostbite; to them you were *glacé*. Yet in spite of the chill, they would not go away; they saw beauty, they heard music, they were excited. Your posture was a challenge to them, and they persisted, hoping that eventually you would melt like ice cream in the sun. Only once did you *lose your cool*, and then I suffered for it. It was a mistake for us both. You should have sensed danger when Sam threw herself in your way. Or, rather, in mine.

Nicholas

15

'Oh fuck,' said the waitress, tripping over the viola da gamba. That was how it started with Sam: like the beginning of a bad novel; a caricature of bad taste. Nicholas, hitherto innocent of such callowness, was both taken aback and intrigued. She lay on the floor of the restaurant, cursing and laughing in an altogether confusing *quodlibet*, her legs apart and her skirt hitched up. Nicholas failed to see the humour in it, but something about her demeanour made him laugh along with her. Suddenly, perversely, she turned on him. 'What the hell is so funny? You think tripping over somebody's axe and falling flat on my face with my ass in the air is so funny? Now I'll probably get fired for being such a *klutz*.' Nicholas struggled to comprehend. He was amazed that this gauche creature should refer to Rose in such a bizarre manner; she had been mistaken for many things, but never before an axe. It must be local slang; perhaps she would explain it. After all, he was living in America; he ought to learn something of the natives' speech patterns. He helped her up, and offered to intercede on her behalf to the management. It was obviously his fault; she must let him take the blame.

Such gallantry! Good God; Nicholas, some thirty years later, was still shamed by his own actions. Having gotten himself into such a compromising position, why did he not extricate himself? Why on earth had he become further involved with such a creature?

The more estimable, if secondary, reason was that – for all her crudeness – she uncannily resembled Rose: tall, pear-shaped, thick-necked, dark-complexioned, small flattish nose, square jaw, crinkly hair (though Rose's was drawn back in a discreet bun while hers stuck out rather wildly); she even wore the same kind of simple pearl earrings. He remembered calling her *steatopygous*, and her delighted response. When he explained, she put her head to one side and said, 'Pear-shaped. You mean fat ass, huh?' Her smile was less secretive than Rose's: teasing, outgoing, less fragile. The primary attraction – unsuitably, irrationally – was her coarseness.

Berkeley had a clear social-geographical tidiness about it. The higher up in the hills one lived the richer one was, and the more exalted (at the top was Parnassus); the whiter, the more extravagantly housed. People sat out on their west-facing decks, sipping gin-and-tonics, surveying the photogenic bay, the city, the Golden Gate and Mount Tamalpais. Nicholas lived near the foot of the hills; and Sam dwelled unequivocally in the flatlands, about a mile beneath him. Her only view was of other pastel-coloured boxes and a series of front yards filled with tires and junk. Her own patch was tidy, well tended.

Nicholas recalled the little, low house, with its white walls and strips of dark wood panelling. It was filled with plants, several musical instruments which Nicholas took to be guitars, and amplification equipment Nicholas had no familiarity with whatever.

'You play?' he'd asked.

'Not really, I just accompany myself. I'm the lead singer. With a group.'

'You mean an ensemble of some kind?'

'Yeah, a group.'

'Does this group have a name?'

'Uh-huh. "Duck Soup".'

'I'm sorry, but I don't understand.'

'What's to understand? It's the name of my favourite

Marx Brothers movie. Don't tell me you don't know who the Marx Brothers are. . . . My God, you are under-privileged.'

That was when he'd begun to take her jibes seriously: suspect Rose, doubt himself. Suppose he was lacking? Absorbed by Rose, he had eschewed any contact with popular culture. He knew nothing of its music, its films, its art; he shared none of its memories or its ambitions. Steeped – lost – in the eighteenth century, he had bypassed his own kind. He had played himself, with Rose, into oblivion. Only a second childhood would reclaim his life. He could still do it; Sam would show him how.

He asked her to sing something for him. 'Nuh-uh, no way, I don't compete with you classical guys. Not tonight anyway. Besides, I need my backup.' She changed the subject. 'I have a feeling you must be famous if you played in Hertz Hall.'

'Somewhat,' he replied.

'You're being modest, I can tell. What's your name?'

'Nicholas Jordan.'

'I don't believe it!' she shrieked. She fell against a cushion, clapping her hands. 'You're right, now I see the resemblance to your picture. You look even better in real life. Shit. Now I'm really embarrassed.'

Nicholas's current embarrassment – remembering her crudeness – soon abated. Now he was moribund, he could excuse his one mercifully brief fall from grace. His middle-aged rebellion had been unseemly, perhaps, but looking at it philosophically, one could say he'd merely been immature and vulnerable – to a young woman's determination to lead him away from his true purpose. A temporary weakness of character. Quite common. But, unlike many, he had regained his composure, his strength. Rose, fortunately, had not been seriously hurt in the process. He himself came away unscathed.

There was no harm in reviewing the episode.

'Show me your instrument,' she had said. His reply was, 'First wash your hands.'

She sat on the floor, cross-legged, with Rose on her lap.

Nicholas squatted next to her, steeling himself for some flippant remark. It did not come. She was quiet for a full five minutes, busy examining Rose; she touched her face, caressed her as if she was a giant doll. 'I can't believe it, this instrument is so beautiful, I've never seen anything like it. You actually *own* it, I mean, you didn't steal it from a museum or anything?' She peered down into Rose's eyes, traced her features with a finger. She shook her head. 'It's like she's alive, the way she smiles and her skin, almost as if there's a real person trapped inside. She gives me the shivers. Here,' she said, handing Rose back to him, 'play something.'

He repeated all the solo works from that night's programme, while Sam lay on the floor, on her stomach. She listened attentively at first, smiling up at him after each piece, but said nothing. By the end of the programme, she was asleep. He stopped playing and she woke up. She didn't apologise. Her earlier infatuation with Rose had already ended; now she found her weird, the music hard to 'get her mind around'. But it didn't matter what she thought, did it? She knew nothing about 'real' music. Her kind was instinctive, like sex. That she could demonstrate without backup or amplification. Which she did.

In the morning, as they lay in bed talking, she asked him if he liked performing. He said he liked playing but didn't like the public aspect. 'Shit, that's hypocritical. I mean, face it, you're a performer, right? If you weren't you'd fiddle away to the mirror. So if you want people to listen, you better be nice to them. You get paid, right?'

'Handsomely.'

'Then how can you complain? I get paid for my service, you get paid for yours. I smile to the customers at the restaurant even though I hate their greasy guts, but I'd get fired if I didn't; and I wouldn't get any tips. I don't see the difference. It's just something you've got to do, give them something for their money. When I play with "Duck Soup", I give my audience lots of smiles, and we rake it in.'

'Rose smiles for me.'

'That's weird; creepy – like she's some kind of dummy,

with you sitting there behind her making believe she's doing all the running. Uh-uh, face it, you're the performer, so perform. Part of that is conning your audience.'

Nicholas let himself be jeered at, chided, he enjoyed being played upon by her. He needn't take her seriously. She poked him in the chest with her finger; climbed on top of him, made him laugh, tingle. She knew so many variations: right-side up, upside-down, inside-out, crab-wise, pretzel-wise. Never mind what she thought of his playing, his stage manner, his music, his Rose. Never mind anything but Sam's touch.

Rose

15

Sam touched and you vibrated like a string. You were a fine instrument, Nicky, responsive to the push and the pull. Obedient. Versatile. You could be instrument or player at will; at any rate, when she willed. Gripped between the knees – a position familiar to me – trapped, not wanting to move so long as the music be sweet. And it was sweet between Sam's knees, was it not, Nicky? So sweet that I was forgotten.

How foolish of you to exchange the prototype for the copy. You say she resembled me, but I deny it. She was so recent, so burly: those limbs like newly turned bass flutes, the thick waist, the toy breasts, Gorgon's hair, the broad feet with crudely painted toenails. And you dare to compare her to me?

Listen with me, Nicholas, while I rest: the harpsichord plays *La Dangereuse*, an appropriate piece. Lucy has placed me in shadow, like you. The spotlights and the cameras are trained on the soloist, though you will notice that they stray in my direction. Is the television's wandering eye so fascinated by my old face? Tell me, Nicholas, does it turn from me too as I play; even from me?

But no, Sam was no *Dangereuse*. She was no subject for a sarabande; not serious, not central to the suite. At best, she was a tailpiece, one of Couperin's little jokes.

While you drank your coffee, I recollect, she crooned,

hanging over her *ghee-tar*, that wretched degradation of an instrument. But the music did not hold your attention (how could it?); the nape of her neck diverted you. Her head was bent forward and its hair covered her face. You leaned close behind her, in that familiar way, as if preparing to tune her, and nuzzled. The indelicate wench giggled and brushed you off. She was busy with her 'axe', trying to improvise the Andante of the Bach D major. I recognised the harmonies, and nothing else. The rhythm was distorted, the key was changed, the bass line was simplified out of recognition. She lifted her face and serenaded you – I cannot call it singing – with the melody line, and nonsense words. A shocking performance. But you were delighted; you thought it *cute*. For shame, Nicholas.

She cooked omelettes. She said, 'I hope you like 'em nice and gooey.' You did not demur. She sucked on her fingers between mouthfuls. That self-satisfied smile, so unlike my own. Then you too sucked on them.

Worse was to come – but you were open to anything from Sam. I can still feel it. With your kind assistance, she wraps her limbs around me. You spread her legs (remember, she was *au naturel*), shift me until I sit, more or less correctly, between her thighs. Oh my dear procurer, how can you? Sam laughs – 'She's so big' – rolling her eyes and lolling her tongue, fit-like. You pretend disapproval, but by this time she knows, we both know, how to rouse you. She seizes the bow and tries to saw me in half, tapping with her big toe, bobbing her head, rocking me back and forth as if I were one of her *pop* instruments. I refuse to speak, naturally. You pull your chair behind hers, you put your arms around both of us, and direct her stroke. Sam giggles. 'Hey, there, Rosie,' she peers around at me, 'won't you make a sound for me, just a teeny weeny little one?' Rosie? I grunt, I creak, I growl – but do not speak. Not for her, and especially not for you. I am no beast with three backs. No one's Rosie.

You too preferred the duet. The sight of her spread open to me – her pornographic prop – was too titillating. Removing me, you took my place between her knees, with a lack of restraint the eighteenth century knew only in its boudoirs.

Le bon goût. Ah, slippery, slippery notion! A gift of nature, it cannot be learned; it can barely be defined. It is that which sets a fine musician – let us use the example of a singer – apart. If one could explain her especial quality, one could explain good taste. But it cannot be, any more than the working of the tongue and palate. All these are nature's gifts; one cannot correct the defect of mind that leads to ill-formed taste. Sam was a living example of it: the frigid being (I refer here to her soul), who could be neither corrected nor excited to improvement. Excitement for her meant one thing only, about which I do not pretend to know. As for taste, she suffered the example of her country: vast, young, excitable, enamoured of novelty. The mind is cramped, its edge blunted; there is nothing on which to form it. She was like a vessel with a hole in the bottom: you poured and poured your tasteful liquor in, and it only dribbled out.

Nicholas

16

'Bon-goo,' said Sam, turning good taste to poppycock. *Le bon goût*, to her, was like a corset – an instrument of torture, an affront to nature; in her own words – prissy, constipated, real weird. She admitted as good only those things which her undeveloped brain, unsophisticated palate and sensuous body immediately felt as enjoyable. If she had to force herself to like something, it was not, by definition, 'good'. Nicholas's music, for example, was dutiful medicine to her. 'My mother used to tell me classical music was good for me. Like cod liver oil. Yuk.' She believed only in good times. This was as foreign to Nicholas as *le bon goût* was to Sam. So the lessons began, in reverse.

'Taste,' said Sam, slipping a huge pickle into his mouth. 'You've never tasted a dill pickle in your whole life? My God, you're a food virgin.' And indeed, Nicholas had not tasted most of the things she imposed on him: pastrami sandwiches, bagels and lox, Mexican chilis, thirty-six flavours of ice cream, exotic fruits. For such things one could learn the taste, she said, contradicting herself, or perhaps mocking him. 'You're getting there. Just stick with me and you'll be fine.'

Though he failed to recognise it at the time, her double standard was as clear as a two-part fugue. Baroque music was 'a drag', but listening to current popular music was admirable. The one, after all, was remote, irrelevant, inessential to life (as she experienced it), whereas the other expressed and interpreted life in all its contemporaneity. One lived and listened in the present. In this, Nicholas supposed, she was consistent – but in little else. He realised that she had been attracted by the exact qualities in him that she later sought to change: his aloofness, his foreignness. Perhaps the challenge appealed to her. She had certainly done her best to lure, corrupt and mould him in her own – or her juvenile society's – image. Then, once he had shown his willingness to change, she said, 'I can't stand flunkies.'

Confused, he followed her up Mount Tamalpais. 'How can you walk in those hot sweaty things?' She referred – outrageous young woman – to his fine English shoes. He did not attempt to defend them. 'Those toes need to breathe.' She hauled him off to a sandalmaker, who drew his feet in outline on a piece of paper; two weeks later he was the owner of a pair of thonged soles. He was aghast at the feel of strap between his toes, socklessness. But Sam soothed. 'You'll get used to it,' she assured him, and was right. Sandals, cut-offs, flowered shirts, beads, flared trousers. She even gave him a T-shirt screen-printed in lurid letters: VIOLA DA GAMBA POWER.

They traipsed through woods and along hot dusty trails. He was infected by the poison oak plant. For a time he could not bear to touch Sam, or Rose; he had to cancel concerts. 'So what,' she said, 'the break will do you good. Join the real world. Have some fun.' Fun, Sam's philosophy of life. Food, sex, exercise and music should all be fun. Anything else was a drag.

Rose was a drag. 'I mean,' she said, 'the music is so tortured.'

'Perhaps you mean subtle?' Nicholas suggested.

'Yeah, maybe, but so subtle, it's hardly there.'

'Ah,' said Nicholas, with some irony. 'The ultimate inability to call a spade a spade.'

She laughed. 'Who said that?'

'Wilfrid Mellers.'

'I love the guy, whoever he is.'

The attacks, in the guise of consciousness-raising,

worsened. Sam called Rose a freak and a relic, accused him of trying to reconstruct a world better buried. What was the point of all that old stuff? All those people sitting in hot, crowded concert halls, going shush shush so they could hear this one old instrument sigh like a damsel in distress, and maybe a harpsichord go tinkle tinkle.

As for baroque opera (or any opera for that matter), she found it totally ridiculous; divorced from real life. Her kind of music was different. The words were emotionally charged, the tunes were singable, and the rhythms were basic. People relaxed while they listened to it, enjoyed the paltry jokes, messages, puns; or talked simultaneously – it didn't matter. It was fun.

'Just like I say,' said Sam. 'Instruments, you pick them up and strum and pluck and fool around and do your thing and people listen or don't listen, then everybody claps and afterwards you go out and get drunk and eat pizza. Okay, maybe you're in your own world while you're playing a gig but then it's over, snap' – she snapped her fingers in his face – 'and you wake up.'

Yes. Even now, years after all this had happened, Nicholas could revive the spirit of Sam as the finger-snapping critic; could rekindle a frightening distaste, which she had prompted, for the way Rose kept him married to another century. She had controlled him, seduced him into playing only those pieces that suited her. She removed him from everyday life – and for this he had even blessed her. His life laden with history; the past undercutting the present. So easy to project himself into Rose, his own life empty.

Others were still more contemptuous than Sam had been. Just this morning, a Paris paper had referred to *the stinking gangrene of . . . professors, archaeologists, touring guides and antique dealers*. Did the disease include musicians? He thought of his mother and how oppressed she had been by his father's antiques; Hannah by Hubert's. Dead things. Fossils. Dead worlds. Rose beautiful but antediluvian.

He had taken Rose to one of Sam's parties. It had been the usual noisome gathering, with thunderous amplified music. Insistent head-bobbing took the place of civilised conversation, and an anarchic, ape-like style of dance. Nicholas thought of the precise, quick steps and wrist-flicks of baroque dance, the way a body could tilt forty-five degrees in a perfect straight line and hover, then take off again like a skirted bird. But why should they understand? Why should they not value the free more than the stylised; the young over the old? Why, indeed, shouldn't he? It was, after all, the twentieth century. *C'mon, let yourself go, man.* They elbowed him, passing him a joint. He took it and tried to do with it what was required of him. He hoped Sam was watching.

Nicholas admired the prim silver roach clip, but the smoke burned his throat and eyes; he found himself embarrassingly close to tears. Where was Sam? Only the trail of her patchouli oil remained, commingling with the marijuana, the perfumed candles and the incense into a high-churchly brew. The bits of stained glass and string-mandala hanging in the window increased the sense of churchiness. Before Nicholas had worshipped only Rose; now he was ensconced in Sam's joss house. And where was the high priestess herself?

He had a drugged vision of Rose metamorphosed into Sam. She wriggled free from between his legs, turned to laugh at him, stuck out her tongue and ran away. I must go and find her, he thought, thinking of Rose-as-Sam, but his limbs were uncooperative.

A young woman in a sari and halter and many bangles reached out for him: she would pull him up from the floor to dance, but he would not. There was a limit to his participation in Sam's hellish games. He hugged his knees apparently for safety: foetal, innocent, desperate in the enemy's camp; punishment for the spy. The so-called music tortured his teeth, the soles of his feet, the tiny bones connecting his spinal column, the backs of his knees, his testicles. Sam said, erotic, but he thought no, rather as erotic as a trip to the dentist in its buzzing, grinding, sawing, unvarying monotony. Nicholas closed his eyes and squeezing his knees to his chest, tipped himself back and then forward, backwards, forwards, rocking and breathing in tortuous time as others stomped and careened around him. All the philistines in the world whom he had ever frustrated, who could not tap their feet to his, Rose's, free and subtle music, were evidently gathered in this one room. They had trapped him; this was their revenge. This terrifying rhythmic boredom.

The heat and pounding put him in mind of molten gold, the gold of fillings perhaps (more dentistry?), or, more poignantly, water lit fancifully by candles and fireworks to seem molten, as at Versailles on the night Rose and all the other relics of her time were disappeared. Then one image gave way to another, as Nicholas had come to expect with smoking. Go with it, advised Sam when she was around; ride it out. So he went, willy-nilly, to Paris, where the sky after the night's rain was another kind of liquid gold – à la Turner – and the room where Hannah lay was as cold as she was; but Nicholas even so lost sweat that dripped on to Rose's shoulders, that trickled down her front and disappeared into her rose hole. And for all the music that had poured out of him, there was still a corpse on the bed. Then the knock on the door. But what had been a surprisingly diffident tap from Hubert (though it sounded to Nicholas then in the early morning like a godly pounding) was now a crash that might have been a gun, so sobering was it to Nicholas; that almost but was not quite concealed by a saxophone hitting its highest and unmightiest screech and a smash of cymbals that marked the end of the musicians' set. It was the sound of an instrument hitting the floor.

Nicholas moved fast enough to see Sam still spread-eagled on the bed, surrounded by lovers male and female, more than he could count or than the bed could accommodate – even had it not been heaped with ponchos and bags, not to mention one large viola da gamba. If Rose was smashed. . . . He ignored Sam and her dispersing entourage: some of them gathered round in a show of concern; others sloped off. He concentrated on Rose, who had tumbled to the floor, her case gaping. She was revealed miraculously undamaged, except perhaps for her dignity. He soothed her in his arms.

After a time, Nicholas laid her gently down and went outside to look for Sam's lead playmate. He found him sitting on the porch eating a brownie – which Nicholas knocked out of his hand. This produced a look of wounded innocence and the advice to 'cool it, man.' Forget it, Nicholas said, realising that neither Sam nor her friends were to blame; he was himself for his negligence. 'What, is it a valuable axe or something?' asked the *innocente*. Extremely, said Nicholas, unthinking, and went into the kitchen to say good night, or possibly goodbye, to Sam. And then to the bedroom to retrieve Rose.

Rose

16

But you cannot retrieve me because I am already gone. Spirited away from Sam's house; captured, insulted, soon to be disfigured. You dallied too long with Sam, your goodbye strung out, an unbaroque coda. Did you eat her brownies too? Were they good? Did she lead you back into the living room, clear out the other guests and sit you cross-legged while she sang to you, her kindergarten harmonies distracting you from the sound of a window thrown open, the nimble thief making his getaway, driving smoothly with me through the night to another world?

I describe no *opera buffa*, Master.

Shall you hear a synopsis of the first act? I was at the foot of Sam's water bed, the swish and glub of her energetic group exercises slowly dying away. I rode the waves in my case like one in a boat lost at sea. The water bed is not my element; is it yours? I wonder how it is with you and Sam, Master, the riding of the waves. And water in your sleep – does it creep into your bones, give you nightmares of drowning? Or does Sam reassure you with her body?

I am alone in there with Sam's playmate. He sits and I rise up, displaced. Gradually we reach equilibrium, his hand on my case to steady me. I can feel the resonance of your words: *extremely valuable*. They echo dangerously inside me, in time with the slowing oscillations beneath me. This thief will have me, I can feel it; yet there is nothing I can do. I have no voice to protest. The tragedy will happen. Yet your betrayal is the greater wrong. I gave you the gift of my nonage, Master, to give to this young place – and what do you do but throw it away?

I am in Oakland: Oakland, worse than hell. O horrid realm. A ramshackle shingle house near a freeway overpass. The noise is unceasing. A big room under the eaves. Hot. The thief's friends talk in short, *staccato* spurts, a kind of pecking order counterpoint. They sit in tattered armchairs, smoke and drink beer. They sweat. The air is stale. They have no notion how the heat affects me. They could train a heater on me, or float me in a boiling bath; it is just as well. Even so, my strings uncoil. Later, when it cools, I shall tighten again, then weaken, then tighten.

Do the chords of your own throat tighten, Nicholas, to be reminded of my calamity? And for what: Sam's infatuation with your pretty accent, your romantic figure in black tail-coat and white tie? How quickly she stripped you down to the common time of all men! She dressed you in her own image, then whirled you round and round until you were too dizzy to see or hear. She hated me, she denounced me, and you lost faith, seduced by a flash – shirt too short, trousers too low – of her twentieth-century midriff. Does the memory still excite you, even in old age? Foolish Nicholas. Mine is as brown and smooth, and more enduring. Hers by now will be as dry and cracked as Christophe's leather apron, while mine, with its delicate curve, will be firm and silky for ever.

My fall from grace, Sam's apotheosis: it was ill-advised, Nicholas. Listen, we are playing Couperin's *Apothéose de Lully*. Lully was another self-serving rascal, raised up for deification; though at least he wrote fine music, which is more than can be said for Sam. Such wit! Such music! How marvellously we portray the agitation of Lully's contemporaries, in their subterranean murmurs; how we suggest their doleful *plainte*, like the sound of sick cats prowling an echoing alleyway. And the raising of Lully to Parnassus, by counterpoint and hemiola: Apollo be praised! Accursed Sam!

When death comes to claim you, Nicholas, the real death, remember me, not her. She left you untuned; for that I do not forgive her. Nor for her lies and her accusations, calling me humourless and dead. You hear the error now; let me not abuse you more. Our concert is almost over; soon we two shall be divided for ever. Let us say the score is even, and let the end of our time come naturally, and without further recrimination. I did my best to prepare you; Sam was a mere quaver in your life, one of those upwardly tending dots with a waving tail.

But let us return to the scene of the crime. What a coward he is! And such an easy job: no bloodshed, no hysterics, no need to restrain me, blindfold me, drug me, bind my mouth. I do not scream. Yet my smile still infuriates. He would have my head, at least, as recompense for the pointless trouble I have caused him – for it transpires that I am not what he thought I was; I am unbarterable baggage. In his frustration, he turns me to face the wall, says I give him 'the creeps', it's almost as if I am watching, listening. I am. I can hear the click of a weapon behind me.

Perhaps it is the disappointment – I am not the eminently saleable guitar he thought I was – that angers him. He cannot sell me, for I am a marked creature: too valuable, too dangerous in my uniqueness. He is delinquent, not criminal, and were I in a position to pity his frustration, I would. But victims may not pity. He lifts me from my case.

He swings me around on my bottom and holds me by the neck: a stranglehold. When the knife flashes, I cannot defend myself, or even close my eyes. He gouges diagonally from the outside corner of my left eye across my cheek, over my nose and down past the right corner of my smiling mouth. A rose, sadistically pruned. I do not bleed, yet he wipes his weapon with the tail of his shirt. Relieved of his gratuitous gall, he is well satisfied. Only he fails to observe that I still smile. You see, he cannot desecrate me so easily; cut music to pieces and throw it away. He is the pitiful one, the vandal, the deaf and blind one, without music in his soul.

He would be rid of me, for I am of no possible use to him.

He calls Sam, his co-conspirator. She arrives, furious. 'Who in their right mind would steal a hot piece like this?' she says. He answers dolefully, 'I thought it was just a regular guitar. What in hell is it, anyway?' 'Well it ain't, and you better get rid of it before the whole Oakland police force is down on you.' 'You take it,' he says. 'No way. You want to get me into big trouble with the musician? Tell you what, I have an idea. Go dump it somewhere, and I'll tip off the police. That way nobody gets hurt.' 'Where?' he asks. Sam orders, 'Let's go, I'll show you a good place.'

So they abandon me on a hidden beach by the shore of the Oakland Estuary where the pavement runs out to a set of gravel parking lots at the water's edge. I lie on a thin arc of sand abutting the Sea Breeze Yacht Center, looking out across the dark waters of the estuary. It is the middle of the night. I hear the water lapping, the rumble of the freeway in the distance. I am afraid you will not come for me, Master, will not find me down here; in Oakland, worse than hell. What if another finds me first?

My face, I think, is not damaged beyond recognition, but you shall be my mirror; if I see horror in it I will know. Old scarface. But what is a scar between old friends? My voice is feeble but undamaged – as yet. You will come? I am not calm, hearing the waters so close. I can picture the white masts bobbing up and down. In the morning, some sailor will find me; what will become of me then? It must be you. I am your muse, Master, your partner in pleasure and in life. Make no calculations, it will be fatal; do not for a moment hesitate. Come quickly. Hold out your arms to me on my dreadful beach on the other side of Lethe, amidst the howlings of Cerberus.

Allez Orphée, allez, que votre amour extreme
Serve d'exemple à l'Univers.
Il est beau qu'un mortel passe jusqu'aux Enfers
Pour se rejoindre à ce qu'il aime.

Hasten, hasten noble lover.

Nicholas

17

Nicholas dressed quickly in the dark and waited for the police. They had been tipped off during the night, and had immediately phoned him. Did he want to come along? Of course, of course, he said; but where? There was a rest. 'Down on some god-forsaken strip along the Oakland Estuary.'

Nicholas pictured a narrow channel fronted by junked cars, jetsam on the beach, derelicts huddled around a pit fire. Who would get to her first? Already one of the winos might have found her, plunked a few strings and done a jig before smashing her against a steel oil drum and feeding her into the fire. Her smiling, charred face. . . . Dear God, Nicholas prayed, let us be first.

He wondered if he should call Sam, but decided against it. How could he trust her? She might even have masterminded the theft. It was possible; the suspicion alone was devastating enough. But he was most to blame. How could he have left her in the first place, unguarded amongst the Boschian revellers; traded her for a rolling stone, neglected her for a flibbertigibbet? It was his betrayal that had angered the gods and muses. The crash was undoubtedly a warning, but once again he'd left her unchaperoned in the bedroom. This time there was no warning: she was spirited away from him by an angry *deus ex machina*.

He saw it all quite clearly, Rose's enemies divided in style but united in purpose: the revolutionaries and the Sams of this world, all railing against Rose, all shouting for her lovely neck. The French students had made him doubt her, Sam to forget her. Now a common thief had dispatched her. No more. Enter the police screeching up to his front door. For his sins, he would follow Rose to the underworld. And for his life, bring her back.

They were not alone. Sam followed in her yellow VW. Behind her came People to People Television. Nicholas was furious but could do nothing to stop them. Sam, who had bid them come, asked (but did not wait for the answer), 'Aren't you happy to share your good fortune with the world? It's a terrific human interest story.'

They were interviewed on the spot of beach where Rose was found. Sam got in on the act, to lend what she called moral support. What morality did Sam know? She just wanted to see herself on television. Later, watching the news, he acknowledged that her acting was excellent, her timing spot-on. Outrage became her; she was more convincing in her passion than Nicholas in his detachment. But he was not won over; could not forget that it was one of her friends that had stolen and brutally branded Rose. When she offered to go home with him, he thanked her for her support and left her to ooze her sympathy into other ears (and microphones). He concentrated his energy on Rose; Sam should divide them no longer.

Alone with Rose – with the horrendous scar; his guilt, his anger. There was nothing to do but play; to reassure themselves that neither was damaged irretrievably. And that they would never again be parted.

He held her tentatively, conscious that she had survived more than a night outdoors. He oiled and rubbed her down; let her know that Sam had been a mistake, and that it was over now. But she looked sceptical; too much oil beaded her brow. Nicholas wiped it off, and turned her from him. He would play; by his touch she would know.

The first note was hardly audible, but it grew in tone, as if she were saying *ah, I remember you*. But did she forgive? It was still an *adagio* of hesitant triplets, of a catching in the throat, of uncertainty, dislocation, crying lost. But Nicholas persisted, and with Bach's help they reached the higher register. *Welcome, Master*, said Rose, with her old familiar voice. And then they returned to the home key together: to the sweet snatch of melody with which they had begun.

Rose

17

Oh rescue; oh freedom! How my master cradles me in his arms! Never has there been such a reunion, our joyful fortunate moment. I am his comfort and he is mine. He presses me to his bosom, smoothes my troubled brow, drinks in my odour. At first, he is unsure of me, as I am of him, but soon love sings to us: an instant of bliss shall recompense an age of pain. Bach's G minor Adagio heralds the celebration of the lovers reunited. I was never away, we were never parted, never did a Sam come between us, nor an outlaw ever drive me indecently to the underworld of Oakland. I am come back, to the Rose Garden – Rose's garden – scarred but otherwise intact.

You would hold out your arms to me, Nicholas. But disremember the present; take what comfort you can from the past. This was California: I might have lain smashed in the gravel, my ribs mingled with old bones. But the gods and goddesses were with me. The police found me. You rushed to my side and gathered me up.

You carried me to the car and held me on your lap. I could hear the pounding of your heart – or was it mine? You sat for some time, recovering, not daring to look. Perhaps you feared trickery; that I had metamorphosed into a guitar. But at last you opened my case and peered in. The scar made you catch your breath; you said, 'Dear God.'

But for that, I came away undamaged. Of course it took

time to regain my composure, my trust, my temper, now I saw what a dangerous place I was in. How they chained down the café tables in the street, how children were stolen in the dot of a note. Why not me? Especially if you continued to leave me alone during your escapades with Sam. But perhaps you had learned your lesson.

Sam learned hers, but too late. Did you know, Nicholas – I think not – that her change of heart came from love? That in spite of her easy manner, she panicked at the thought of losing you? Oh yes, after what happened, she realised you held her the enemy. She tried to win you over by defending me in public, but you felt her insincerity – as I did – if not her panic. It was like heaping ornaments on a badly played melody. You would not let her ooze her way back in. You saw reason: for this I am grateful.

How strangely you look at me today, Nicholas. Is it the scar or is it something else which cuts deeper? Can it be that Sam's accusations still rankle; in reliving the time, you feel them keenly once more? Am I tainted? Must I defend myself, even now, against the Sams of this world? Must I remind you of my worth? How shall I convince you? Not by words, never by words, only by sounds.

Ah listen, Nicholas, to these delightful, meaningless sounds that pursue one another, clash with one another, imitate one another; that caress, mingle and absorb one another. These are the magic spirits of the air and the quintessence of me. Words by comparison are empty and clumsy; the bowstroke to the thick flapping tongue, a hummingbird.

Did not Pan summon Echo on his reed pipe without either words or gestures; was not Apollo, with his lyre, the progenitor of all the choruses of the Muses; did not Orpheus move Charon by the eloquence of his lute; and did not Bach venerate the Divine Being in his Passions in such form as no preacher could have imitated? I tell you that beauty captivates not by what it has to say but by the form and manner in which it is said. Just as a lover rejoices to hear his beloved speak, so bewitched by her voice that he is oblivious of her meaning, so music enchants by its very existence, and by the union of melody and harmony which resonates in our innermost being.

Enough, you must love me for what I am, and if that is not enough, then admit you have wasted your life. But I shall deny it. You created beauty; and pleasure in the beautiful resembles unselfish love. In playing me, you transcended yourself. Your audiences too, in listening, thought not of themselves but of me. Hear the order and purity of my voice. Does it not cure you, if not of old age and illness, at least of self-doubt? I have shown you a mirror in order that you may admire, not reject. Look, Nicholas, you are still a man of music.

I depend on you; on your appreciation, your contemplation, on your body which resonates in tune with mine, your heart which beats in sympathy with my rhythms and your mind which fosters me. Without you I am past history.

Nicholas
18

Without Rose Nicholas was nothing; no human could replace her. Neither Sam nor 'Duck Soup', after a predictably brief time, could satisfy him. He had been excited and flattered by Sam; soon he was bored. He saw his reconstructed self as ludicrous; a nearly middle-aged man playing hippie, fleeing his own life. It was a narrow escape for him; a knife-cut for Rose. The scar was the permanent mark of his negligence.

Sam, the chameleon, had turned up at the airport. She claimed a change of heart since Rose's misadventure, swore sympathy with his cause, with Rose. Now she wanted to learn about baroque music; she wanted Nicholas to take her with him, guide her to the right teachers. She would take proper singing lessons; they could even – unlikely story – perform together. She was unctuously, and implausibly, contrite. He was tempted, but the sight of her perfect nose concentrated his mind. It would always remind him of Rose's disfigurement. Besides, how did he know that she meant what she said? Doubtless she was fed up with living in Berkeley, saw Europe as glamorous, Nicholas as an easy ride. He studied her loose easy gestures, the professional twinkle. Even goodbyes were a time of brilliance for Sam: the shining face as predictable and irrepressible as the sun. She would never make a baroque musician. Shades and sandals, brown as a cello; Rousseau's child loved the world too much.

But perhaps Rose was right: Sam had panicked at the thought of losing him. This he had not considered. It was possible that when she saw the damage to Rose, and Nicholas's sudden backing off, she did a quick *volte-face*. Suddenly, Rose was worth defending; Nicholas, *qua* Nicholas, worth cultivating. But if so, it was a lucky escape. The thought of Sam hanging possessively on his arm, vying with Rose for his attention, was still an alarming thought.

Rose hung at his side in her new travelling case – designed especially for her by Brief Cases of California, Inc., a farewell present from Sam. She squatted next to Rose. 'Rose, bee-ew-tee-ful Rose, I'm really gonna miss you, babe.' Then she stood up and threw her arms around Nicholas. It was a trying moment. She shrugged, told him he didn't know what he was missing. Then she ran back to her yellow bug without looking back – just like in the movies – and drove off in a cloud of black smoke and a trail of rude explosions.

Nicholas boarded his plane, put Rose in the seat next to his (he would never again risk air freight with his precious baggage), and carefully strapped her in. He closed his eyes; others had done likewise. It was like the sleeping scene from *Armide*. During take-off, he put a protective hand across her middle. Some malevolent force, after all, if not another personal evil-wisher, might want to do her in.

Rose

18

As we took off, I felt the shield of your body. It was an eloquent gesture, Nicholas. It soothed me, even through my case; even the rumble and roar of the aeroplane could not hurt me. Nothing could hurt me now. No one questioned my existence, my purpose, my efficacy. I was in first class, in a seat of my own. You were beside me, Sam was left behind. I was your pride; no one was between us. We made our accordance amidst the sonic vibrations. I felt safe there, in the sky; far above harm. I loved my somnolent fellow passengers.

How good to be going back with you; to be leaving the country that, even though it loved me, had also reviled me. How can one sing amongst evil-wishers? How does one play ungrounded? No, we could not go on in that brash, threatening place. It was too large, too confusing: it would kidnap us or buy us. There was only one solution: that we return to Europe, where we belonged: old, weathered, armoured England. Home, Nicholas.

England was not my home, but I had been there before: this journey was in fact my third. The first, as you know, was with Roger North, at the end of the seventeenth century. The second, two hundred years later, was with a diminutive Belgian collector by the name of Arnold Dolmetsch. He had found me – to fill in my history – languishing between a *chaise-longue* and a ridiculous suit of armour in the window of a Paris antique shop. As I presently discovered, he never missed a chance to poke about in junkshops and salerooms, where a sharp eye could still find miracles. (Instruments such as I were not so much the prey of collectors as we are today.) And what a bargain I was, even in the year 1893. I returned with him to England's protected shores.

Arnold Dolmetsch needs no *ouverture*. He is known today as the first revivalist of early music in Britain. He with the *lamps of genius* (I quote his third wife, who was referring to his eyes) and mounds of hair, who dressed in lace ruffles, velvet and silver, according to the pre-Raphaelite style; he who attracted attention if nothing else; whose heavily accented orations brought the sound of the lute, the gamba, the harpsichord (decorated by Mr William Morris) to audiences of Bohemians and Bloomsberrians (who were invited to partake themselves of *petits fours* lest the music fail to please); in short, he who acted as musical barker to the people of England was my very own elfin deliverer. But for his hair, we were the same height.

Having liberated me from my *oubliette*, he brings me back to England, to a house in Haslemere which is already synonymous with viol consorts and sandals. Arnold himself proves even less of a gamba player than Roger North (remember his size, Nicholas; he could easier cradle a bowl-bellied lute in his arms than accommodate me between his miniature *gambe*). But unlike Roger, he recognises his own failing, and once he has boasted all over London of his good fortune in landing me, he hands me over to his daughter, Helene, with no lack of ceremony. In due course, however, the question of my ownership shall be hotly disputed.

I wish you could have seen her, Nicholas; she was so beautiful. Like him, she would hardly have reached to your chest, yet somehow she managed to encircle me in her tiny limbs, though it was the only thing she did with confidence; for the rest, she succumbed to the unbalancing forces around her. She was too frail, too resonant inside that alarmingly thin skin.

She carried the burden of her parents' differences. Intelligent as her father, dutiful like her mother, she was as divided in her loyalties as a bipartite gigue, hopping a nervous dance between them. While Arnold called his wife unmusical, unteachable and unbeautiful (all of which, I regret, were true), she accused him of being a proselytiser of queer early music; of falsely representing himself to her as a teacher of the violin – and therefore dashing her ambitions to bits. She claimed, too, that the inseparable duo of father and precious daughter (people said they breathed together musically) excluded her. She could not compete with the beautiful child prodigy. The bits and pieces of dismembered instruments scattered over her kitchen reminded her of her invaded and fragmented life, and only the instruments were ever put back together again.

While they quarrel, young Helene cowers behind her bedroom door, trying not to listen, shivering, even biting her own thin hand to stop herself screaming. There are times she shakes so much she cannot control the bow and her trembling becomes mine, like the *vox humana* of the dreadful Victorian house organ. But I am her deliverer: the one she trusts to release her from discord, through whom madness becomes music; as beautiful as herself, with a smile that comforts even if it cannot cure.

She learned to play me, not magnificently, not even correctly – dominated as she was by her father's teachings – but in a way I shall always remember. She was my first mistress. You must remember that I had been under the bow of men for over two hundred years. It was not a matter of instant liberation. Change in certain circumstances comes slower than in others; you should know, Nicholas. I leaned hesitantly against that fragile bosom.

It is so different now. Your women gambists are no longer amateurs or daughters of the court; your favoured students, of whom there are now more females than males, are more brilliant than their male counterparts (viz. my new mistress Lucy). They are as strong, as definite in their strokes; they do not wilt and fade like delicate flowers; they do not have 'nerve' troubles.

My poor Helene. She was unnerved by events in the household involving her father and his *ménage à trois* (the third was her aunt, a harpsichordist with a weak stomach; Arnold too was dyspeptic). She was even more alarmed when, in due course, he divorced the mother and married the aunt (only to divorce her in time and take a third consort). In her misery, Helene turned to me. I was her stave, her eyes and her ears, the wooden body which was less apt than hers to weaken. Our music filled the concert halls, drawing praise from even the coolest critics. It was she and I who saved the Dolmetsch concerts from utter drabness.

Nicholas

19

Those infamous viols. Solemnly scraping away, Arnold and his hermetic *ménage* would play like weird doctors performing rude surgery; cool in their sandals in the midst of the agony they created. Poor Rose, so reduced in circumstance; it hardly bore thinking about. The very image of Rose being played by Helene, the wilting flower, or Arnold, the mournful plucker, merely made one giggle. Yet one made allowances for women players. And one was not threatened, after all, by a relationship based not on good musicianship, but on a vague sense of sisterhood. Rose was Helene's prop. On the other hand, any musical comparison between himself and the small thing, Arnold, was an impertinence. Further, he had not imposed wicked stepmothers on his daughter; nor had he changed wives the way Arnold changed them, like instruments.

His own marriage he had considered a union of convenience; based on availability and timeliness. Perhaps, recovering from Sam and his American experience, he had sought someone secure and reliable, someone from his own culture whose behaviour he could predict and even control; someone too modest ever to pull a dramatic stunt like Hannah's. Someone who would love Rose.

Jean sat across the table from him in the Reading Room of the British Museum. He watched her, but she dissembled. He could see she was tall, and would have been striking if she didn't hunch inside herself. She sucked on the end of her pen and pulled her tangled hair further down her forehead, hiding her face. She dared not look directly at him. What did she have to be ashamed of? Nicholas thought of the viola d'amore with the scarf tied round her eyes: guilty of love and miserable with it.

Then what attracted him to her? It was like a weak progression, to go from Sam to this dishevelled, unsociable creature. Yet he felt drawn to her. Perhaps he saw his chance to make her over in his own image, as Sam had tried to do with him. He was aware of her surreptitious glance. He timed it right and caught her *in flagrante*. She became flustered, pushed and pulled simultaneously at her hair, blushed, mumbled something to the effect that it was terribly hot in there (it wasn't), grabbed her briefcase and fled, trailing a scarf which nearly tripped her up. Nicholas followed at a discreet interval.

He found her sitting outside on the kerb. Of all places. When he came up behind her, she started. Nicholas asked if she was all right, and she said fine, fine, he'd merely startled her. He enquired why she was sitting there, like an urchin. 'Just resting,' she stammered. 'I got out of breath from . . . from the stairs . . . oh, wait, there are no stairs, I mean, the Reading Room was so airless, I needed to get some air.' She grinned foolishly. Nicholas apologised for interrupting her work. 'Oh, that's all right . . . I mean you didn't, you didn't at all, I was just getting ready to leave. . . . In fact, I have to go right now.' Nicholas picked her up off the gutter and took her arm. He had meant to interrupt her.

She had recognised him, of course; that was what flustered her. She had heard him play on several occasions, owned his records. The viol was her favourite instrument. Did he know her work on the *Seaven Passionate Pavans*? No, why on earth should he, a great player like him? Whereas she, a mere scholar – no, her playing was hopeless – could do nothing else but lecture students, do useless research: another academic hack. Who cared, for example, about the *Virgo prudentissima* but for a handful of graduate students and a few of her (even more than she) desiccated colleagues?

One would never have known from her behaviour that she outranked him professionally. She rated her career as trivial compared with his. 'You're famous, talented . . . probably a genius . . . and rich, I mean I suppose you're rich . . . and handsome.' She swallowed the last word, but he heard her. 'I'm nothing.' She grinned; shot her hand through her hair like a shovel (a gesture she must have repeated millions of times throughout their marriage). 'It's true,' she insisted. It was disconcerting if so, yet it endeared her to him. He had never known anyone so self-effacing. He wanted to pick her up and dust her down; to straighten out the tangles in her hair. To put a proper smile on her face rather than that mad Cheshire cat grin. What better cure than Nicholas Jordan himself?

There was no question, this time, but of marriage. He wanted her secured for himself, and besides, he wanted to protect her and to improve her self-image. How better than to bestow the gift of his confidence, his benevolence, upon her? Oh, it must be marriage: the proper thing.

It would quite suit him too, he reckoned. After all, he was getting on for forty, had spent most of his time concertising abroad. She would fill the gap when he was at home, when things tended to be a bit empty. She would devote herself to his happiness, and, of course, to Rose's: they were the same thing. She would entertain their colleagues, organise their travels. She would be there when they needed her, though never intrude unbidden. In short, Jean would be the perfect wife for Rose and Nicholas.

He liked the idea of marrying a spinster: her independence, her reserve matching his own. They would be a compatible, if not an overly demonstrative, couple. Intimacy would not trouble them; passion would be bypassed – an unnecessary, uncivilised embarrassment. There would be no question of dependency: they would each get on with their lives and come together at elegant, agreed-upon (according to Nicholas's schedule) intervals. It was Nicholas's idea of conjugal harmony.

It amazed and, at first, delighted him that she expected so little from him, from life in general. She was basically undeserving; what little she got she was grateful for. Or so it appeared. A semiquaver of his affection threw her into a tizz. He first began to notice how she got herself into a muddle by not being able to say what she meant. When it was really bad, she stuttered. But it was usually something simple, like not wanting to go out to dinner, or not wanting a gift he proposed for her. 'Don't you like my taste?' He pretended to be offended, and she was mortified. She shook her head wildly, couldn't get the words out. She ended up twirling her fists round each other, as if winding (or rather further tangling) a skein of wool. Finally she lost her temper with herself – 'Oh God, what a balls-up' – and flashed her mad, helpless smile.

On their honeymoon, Nicholas played his part without haste or feverish passion, and with great dexterity. He aroused Jean's body by digital coaxes and teases, making it vibrate and hum. He calculated her responses, timed his moves perfectly. He allowed nothing – not even the tears coursing down her cheeks – to disrupt his concentration. Thinking of Rose, he rehearsed his repertoire of strokes for special occasions, of one- and two-fingered vibrato. He was as finely tuned as ever. Yet something was dreadfully wrong; even he could feel it. It was like commanding a well-drilled army: he took no responsibility for the troops. It was not music he played, not something fresh off the page, but a piece learned by rote.

He could not help thinking of young women like Sam, like some of his students, and was therefore quite shocked by his wife; actually a virgin at the age of thirty-four; totally passive, unwitting, clueless. Her tears unnerved him. He invited technical correction, but she thrashed her head from side to side. 'It's not technique.' Then what? 'It's music, Rose, the difference in approach.' Nicholas feigned bemusement. 'Forget it,' she said, having progressed quite quickly from diffidence to jealousy.

After a fortnight of this, he found himself rather less

charmed by her moral dilemmas, her tortuous inventions, her apologias. He missed Sam's explicit self-serving. At least it was honest; *out front*, as she would have said. He tried to leave the hotel room on his own, but Jean clung to him like a keyboard player with a bad case of nerves. The obsession with Rose was unnerving, too, for its acuity. Yes, it was true that Rose was always with them – with him. That was no madness. She had married them both – for better or worse.

Over a bottle of wine, she confided in him. She was not, she explained rather laboriously, a person who deserved – at any rate, she was not used to – such plenty. She had learned the lesson that unbeautiful, unconfident girls learn: they drink the dregs. She had aimed instead at a career. She became a modestly successful academic. She published well. She took pains to dress tolerably, became somewhat more self-possessed. (He should have known her when she was a teenager!) For ten years, she had had the respect and admiration, if not the sexual interest, of an all-male department. Then came the Women's Movement. Beside her new good-looking, vibrant, clever female colleagues (some even had husbands and children), she once again felt limited. For all that the cruel label had been disavowed, she became the department spinster.

Now Nicholas had given her the chance to disown her status, her bachelor tendencies: the chance to blossom. She meant to change, she vowed, to make up for what she called the dry years – to expand, to become more expressive (and more coherent?) – all the things she had envied in others. Now she had a husband – a magnificent, handsome, famous, talented husband – who would support her in her becoming.

Nicholas was alarmed: this was not what he wanted at all. He had had 'expressive' women, and look where that led him. No, best let the source of affectivity rest with him, for he had the means of controlling it, and of translating it into art.

He assured his wife of her current value, denied the attraction of an inflated version of herself. No, she must not change: he was quite emphatic. But she proceeded, good-humouredly at first; later less primly; finally, with grim determination. She would prove herself desirable; or Nicholas unfeeling.

Rose

19

'No wonder,' says Theophrastus, 'if love, having in itself all these three principles – grief, pleasure and enthusiasm – should be more prone than any other passion to vent itself in music.' In other words, Nicholas, love instructs music and music comprehends love; and so I knew that your human mate was right: you would, indeed, prove unfeeling.

Those who love, sing; those who cannot, speak. You spoke, through me – by small slides, avoiding the intervals and the leaps of expansive song. You were depressed, Nicholas, in your speechifying; you did not exult. You did not soar, you did not let yourself go. And I also was not sublime because I could not sing; for there was no love to teach me. Understanding speaks; only the passions sing. In Jean's company we were dull creatures, you and I.

I, too, thought her our perfect wife: uncritical, modest, loving – yet demanding little in return. She would complement my brilliance with her plainness; my high colour with her pallor; the conviction of my note with her wavering. (One could listen but briefly to such a *vox humana*.) She would serve her function well: our support – yours and mine, Nicholas. By nourishing you, she would feed me; by becoming your efficient housekeeper – thus lightening your burden – she would lift mine. We would be beyond care, you and I.

But, alas, she wanted recompense. She would become

part of us; failing this, she would come between us. She became clinging, cloying, indiscreet. Always she sat in the first row: you were the god, she the supplicant. Afterwards, she lay in wait for you – no one else could get near you. She took you home and conducted her own private interview. She wished to know *everything*: how it felt to be so carried away with passion – for the music and for me (perhaps she thought one day she would be its recipient? – foolish woman); how it felt to be so adored. When she asked if playing me excited you sexually, I knew, Nicholas, I knew: that underneath that simpering, sniggering exterior, there was an indecent streak, the heart of a *voyeur*, the mind of a prurient spinster, once and for ever. She was no longer humble, the convenience we imagined her, the little woman in the background. She tried to crawl inside you, to *become* you. This you could not tolerate; nor could I. Only I might do that.

She sat on the floor while we rehearsed, hugging her knees like a child, humming off-key. It was appalling. I remembered how she had said she wanted to blossom; was she trying to water herself, as it were, in our music? I could not bear the proximity of her, like an outsized flower, soaking us up. Nor could you.

She had reason, of course, seeing you with me, to feel excluded. In spite of her, your face became tinged with colour, your limbs were slack, your loins ungirded; my mellifluous voice was one with yours. Later, with her, you were stiff and silent. You lost your composure; you did not know how to behave. You were awkward without me. But she judged your condition stupidly, but those terrible human words: cold, passionless, heartless. Such people, I know, exist; I know them the moment they touch me. But not you, Nicholas. In our union, we throbbed with passion. You were not cold, I swear. You gave me so much, there was nothing left over.

Nicholas

20

Nothing left for anyone else. Jean, his wife, accused him of a stingy spirit, of shutting her out of his life, of giving more to his audiences, yet more to Rose. She found it demeaning to be forced into jealousy of Rose, having spent her life in envy of pretty females. Now her rival was an instrument: not only beautiful, but eternally so. She didn't care, she said, if he chased other women, but it was too undignified to be passed up for an instrument. Even she had more pride than that. She looked pathetic, the way she wrung her hands and twisted her lips, but the threat to Rose was all he heard.

Nicholas was unstirred except to anger. Her mistake was grave. The dumb instrument she tried to enemy was part of him; she would never succeed in separating them. If she tried, she would only drive him further away; if she forced him to choose between them, she was asking for sorrow. He reminded her of her own career, but she whined that marriage had spoiled it for her. Finally, thinking he might be spared, he suggested a child.

How had she interpreted his self-serving proposal? Possibly as a sign of affection; an invitation to closeness; an expression of his need. It was not. Perhaps she calculated: he had Rose; she would have a child. Or she may simply have wanted a warm being of her own to comfort; or comfort her. She may have hoped, as so many did, that the child would bring them together. An absurdity, of course.

For a time she seemed happy, or was at least distracted by the challenges and rewards of late motherhood. Nicholas, free to play Rose and to admire his offspring when it suited him, was also happy. But their domestic accord did not last.

Nicholas is in his studio, with Rose between his legs. Jean is in the nursery, where she holds the child similarly, as she teaches her to walk. At the dinner table, they share tales: Rose is out of temper; baby is teething. The balance is precarious and artificial; after a time they stop revealing to each other the intimate details of their respective beloveds. The separateness of their lives quite suits Nicholas; it provokes Jean.

She believed she was better off before marriage. She had her own life, her colleagues, friends who admired her. She rarely thought about what she was missing. Now – having quit her job – she was frustrated, reduced, step by downward spiral step, from scholar to nursemaid to beggar. She pleaded for his affection; begged for his attention and help. She got nothing. She insisted. She got less. Nicholas was a very famous man; he could afford not to respond to badgering.

Of course, the child made things worse. Nicholas became convinced that the baby changed her – hormones perhaps – she had been so docile before. Now she was weepy, had temper tantrums. Even her language deteriorated. 'I'm like the bloody messenger in Monteverdi: I don't count. Or the wet nurse.'

Perhaps he was reserved in his affections, but he was no monster. She created one. If he froze her blood, it was perhaps because she'd tried too hard. The more she tried to squeeze 'passion' out of him, the drier he became. Too dry perhaps. But her point – if she had one – was so overplayed that he could not listen. He had married an academic and wound up with an hysteric. It would not do.

After ten years, he left Jean and the child. How relieved he was to be living alone – with Rose – again! To have his own home, disposed as he wished it; his valuable time to himself; to have escaped their sticky touches and unmusical voices. His new music room was precisely as he'd planned it: the instruments, the statues in their niches, the chandelier, the paintings, the garden less geometrically precise than Versailles, but more domestically agreeable. In this there was comfort; as ever. As there was in Rose's voice.

He saw himself leaning an elbow lightly on the mantelpiece while a student played for him. When he is finished, he drops his arms, the bow trails on the floor; he awaits Nicholas's verdict. The anxious, exophthalmic stare begs a word of approval. Yes, he says, taking a deep breath. Where does one begin with these neophytes?

Making love (he begins) *is like playing music; playing music is like making love. If you want your instrument to sound beautiful, you must make her feel so. Look, open your eyes, appreciate her. Come, take her between your legs – no, not yet. Go to the other side of the room and observe her. Trace the swell of her body, imagine the smell of her wood. Now think of the sound she will make when you touch her. Once you can do this, you will not need me as your teacher. Her song must be in your head. Then you simply play. It is not a matter of technique; you must learn to love.*

'You are incapable of love,' Jean had lectured him. As she got older, she had become more sure of herself, more openly confrontational. What did she know of his capacities? She had used the wrong techniques to bring them forth: first she had effaced herself, then she had withered him with her effusions. She was at fault. What did she, with her graceless pushing and pulling, know of love's delicate touch?

'You must sit down, sayes Love, and taste my meat: So I did sit and eat.' Take a chair, then – but not a common chair; nothing must be common in the service of love. Now you are ready to embrace her; but do it with circumspection. Never like a sack of potatoes, nor like a cavewoman. Never grasp her by the middle of the fingerboard, disturbing her frets. Carry her with the left hand, at the base of the neck, just here, close to the body. Now she will tell you what to do. Listen to her. Learn to be humble before your instrument: it is the first lesson.

'What do you know about being humble?' By now she

was resentful and outspoken with it. 'I have spent years humbling myself before you, and where has it gotten me? Playing second fiddle to your bloody Rose. Go to her. Leave me alone.' He did so, but it was clearly not what she intended. Later she wept, was contrite, pestered him with embraces.

The embrace itself is both general and individual. We know the rules – grasp her firmly with the calves and knees so that no one can grab her from you; feet flat on the ground, the left foot a little more forward. Yet we make our own variations. There is more than one way to make love; the position must suit you both.

Music begins in the mind, but the body delivers it.

Now you are ready for the bow. The bow is the soul of the gamba; remember that when you make your first move. With what stroke will you animate her soul? A sweet, smart, clear stroke, or a harsh, scratching, scraping one? Will you delight her, tickle her, make her melt with desire, frustrate her . . .?

'Bravo, Nicholas, bravo. Tell us what you know about the soul, all about the soul, how expressive, how responsive you are to your instrument, how feeling a musician must be, how full of passion.'

Passion: such a troublesome, imprecise word. Music was fuelled by the passions, but Jean's modern version of *passion* was another matter. She had got them into a mess.

It had been, he saw, a matter of imbalance, each thrust to an extreme. But Jean's accusation of coldness held only in reference to her. It did not apply to his playing or his teaching: in these there was warmth, expansiveness. He looked to Rose to contradict her, to console him; to take away the torpid and impure vapours that dispirited him, and substitute the thin and agile ones which dispose one to joyous affections. Nicholas Jordan lacking passion? It was risible. Ask his audiences, his students.

Ask Rose.

Rose

20

Do not look to me for comfort, Nicholas. She was right: we lacked the baser emotions – desire and fear, anger and pity, hope and despair – these so-called passions, these simple, fleeting states of being human with which she judged you. It is no use denying it: we did not suffer them; we resonated to no one else's touch but one another's; we smiled coldly at their approaches. Like me, you were a decorative, empty body.

Only joined to me did you become inspired, and inspire others. Through me, you became passionate; and I, through you. With your bow you drew me out. You sang, seduced, made love. In my turn, I moved my hearers to joy or tears; I aroused sadness, I affected their spirits. We filled them with our ardour.

You were stifled in your marriage, Nicholas; I felt it. The atmosphere of jealousy and pique was deadening to the soul, the change of tune from huff to hurt unsettling. You were right to get away. I was glad for you – and myself. The only thing holding you was your daughter, whom you didn't want to lose. I did not blame you; how could I?

It was different with Dolmetsch and his daughter, Helene. Let me tell you about them. You remember Helene was my mistress. One day Helene received a court order for my return. Why? Because Arnold had been fined so heavily – of complicity in running a brothel (he owned the premises) – that he was reduced to bankruptcy. His instruments were attached and in due course sold by the Sir Joshua Reynolds Galleries. I repeat: *all* his instruments sold. Did that include me? Ah, Nicholas, you think of me still; it moves me to know it. The question beats at the very heart of my little opera.

Dolmetsch claimed that he never gave me to Helene, that I was merely on loan. The unfortunate girl faced him in court. With her great eyes on him, she swore that I was a gift from him in the year 1893, the same year he brought me from Paris. Dolmetsch denied it. Helene told how she and only she kept a key to my case. Dolmetsch insisted her key was only a duplicate. Helene called as witness one of Arnold's professional enemies, who told how Arnold had often spoken of 'Helene's gamba' and 'Helene's instrument'. It further hardened Dolmetsch's heart against her.

But the verdict was happily in our favour, and my mistress Helene was allowed to keep me. But her father could not forgive what he saw as her betrayal, nor could she forgive his denial. They were each unmovable. At first they quarrelled openly, but soon, and for twenty years thereafter, they did not speak: an estrangement which left my Helene outplayed. Some of the critics said her suffering added a spiritual beauty to her playing, but I cannot agree. Her stiffness, her tension, her misery produced in me a thin, enfeebled noise. Reflecting her pain, my richness and resonance were strangled. My voice was like the caterwaul of a rutting feline.

She was forced to organise her own concerts, which proved more difficult than she had anticipated. (Many, after all, attended the Dolmetsch concerts for her father's show; and perhaps, after all, for the *petits fours*.) She performed less and less in public, while her father played more and more. She shut herself in, was fearful and suspicious of the world. She behaved as though guilty of some unspecified criminal activity. She kept me hidden – her illicit hoard. She looked haunted, guilt-ridden. Her beauty turned to emaciation. Like a well-sucked reed, she became nearly transparent. The soft shoulder which I loved became harder than mine.

She became secretive, strange in her habits. She collected lacy underthings, which she folded away in tissue paper, for a mythical trousseau. Yet what hope was there or had there ever been of marriage? Only one suitor in the early years had ever shown himself: a poor novelist who wrote a most strange story with Helene as heroine in the thinnest of disguises. It is a ridiculous hodgepodge of fancy and musical misconception, worthy of a bad divertimento. In it, the heroine runs off to Paris, becomes a Wagnerian singer and marries a baronet with forty suits, slight hips and a golden moustache. (This her rebellion against a father who has trained her, tediously, in the rigours of fugueing.) But after sundry changes of heart, and a decent lapse, she is reunited with Papa. He forgives her, upon which she betakes herself to a nunnery in Wimbledon.

Does the mind not boggle at such a plot? And is it any wonder my Helene did not seriously entertain its perpetrator?

The real father, after twenty years, hearing that her heart condition had worsened, summoned her to him. She looked in the mirror, traced her wasted features. Did I cost her her looks, her success, her family, her life? Was I worth the sacrifice?

She goes to him dressed in dark grey. He is busy playing the tenor viol, rehearsing the family consort. They play Coperario's *Chi puo mirarvi*. He is dressed in breeches and high socks, his beard and woolly hair match Helene's frock. His latest wife sits with bow poised above her instrument, eyes glued to him. Helene sits listening in a corner with head bowed and hands folded politely, but the music escapes her. She hears only the glutinous bowings of the obedient wife. She thinks, *He has replaced me, his best player, why did he throw me away*? His perfidy paralyses her; a stroke knocks her sideways off her chair. Nor does his final cadence offer a resolution.

Nicholas

21

How extraordinary, thought Nicholas, to have had the vision to revive early music yet not the wit to preserve his own offspring. Simpson's phrase, 'indecent gesture' – which actually referred to poor bowing – presented itself. Yes, there was something indecent about treating one's daughter like that. And all because of an – he might say a mere – instrument.

Unless her success was the point. Perhaps he could tolerate it only in a precocious child. An adult who stole the attention of one's audience and wooed one's erstwhile faithful critics was an altogether less attractive proposition. Nicholas imagined him on stage as Helene played her virtuoso solo; nodding his head to the gigue or the variation, thinking, *This is my daughter, to whom I gave life, the one I taught to play. Those who compete with the Muses get turned into magpies. See how she sits here on stage, while I hover behind her. She is so full of the confidence I imbued her with, she plays the instrument I myself found in Paris, as if it were her very own . . .*

The reversal of roles. Today men played women, women played men. Nicholas imagined Dolmetsch dressed as Goneril, Helene as Lear, a *volte-face* no more outrageous than some of the characters who walked the streets of London or Amsterdam. Heartless Dolmetsch, dressed in a woman's gown and jewels, points at Helene, in an old man's robes, to be gone. She shies away from him, hurt, raging, distracted. She drags her instrument after her. Sing to me, fool, she says, but Rose, playing the fool, is lifeless and unvoiced. They might have been excellent, but now they are a poor pair.

Lucy and Rose: a fine pair indeed. Rose, the troublemaker, was looking distinctly upright and unapologetic; Lucy was formidable in her authentic dress: a believable daughter of the court. How ironic, he thought, that the liberated lady, his radical disciple, should look so at ease playing Princesse Henriette-Anne.

Nicholas watched and listened; for the first time in public, he acknowledged her. She was playing a little-known suite by Dollé. The audience, thinking she had finished after the gigue (there was a chaconne still to play), had begun to applaud. Lucy silenced them with a fierce look and a shake of her heavy, bewigged head; a familiar gesture. Had he not done the same thing twenty, thirty years ago? So many of her gestures now seemed like his; so much of her a part of him. Lucy, his student, his prize student.

His daughter.

Nicholas recalled her earliest years, how he had enjoyed the performances that marked her development – the crawling, walking, talking, dancing, singing. But even when she was very little, her primary aim seemed to be to displace him. He remembered coming back from a tour to find her waiting for him. It was as if he and Jean were already divorced, and this was one of his visits. It was all prearranged and formal: like a museum display. Lucy was on show, primly dressed. He sat and admired her while she played: a beautiful, mechanical doll. *Please do not handle the exhibition*. He noticed she had grabbed one of her dolls from behind and was holding it between her legs; she seemed to be sawing it in half across its belly. 'What on earth are you doing, Lucy?' he asked her. 'This Rose,' she lisped. 'I play her.'

He presumed, at first, that this was a way of getting his attention; but he was wrong: she wanted Rose. Unlike Dolmetsch, he never wanted to surrender her.

After the divorce, he made his house openly available to her: she was old enough to visit on her own. He invited her to have dinner with him, to go for walks in the country, to concerts. But there was only one thing she wanted to do: sit on the floor and listen while he practised. He would not have it. It reminded him of her mother; furthermore, it was distracting.

She listened outside the door. Soon she started making free with Rose when he wasn't there, at first simply miming his movements, but soon trying to play in earnest. He laughed when he thought it was a game, but when it got serious, he warned her off: she would get Rose sticky, drop her, break strings. But she did not stop.

Somehow – a miracle without his help – she taught herself to play. Over the years, she developed a most bizarre, limping style, which was not, however, without merit for a child. But so eccentric, so crude – his greatest fear was that someone would overhear her.

Someone did – a young French student, now quite famous. Nicholas tried to distract him by pointing out the marvellous 1690 lithograph of the French singer, Mlle Brigogne, he had recently picked up at Sotheby's. He was deeply embarrassed by his daughter's playing. 'It is not to be taken seriously,' he said. 'It is child's play.' He was more than embarrassed; angry. He wanted to make the young man wait while he punished her for disobeying him. He had warned her repeatedly not to play his best instrument; tried to discourage her from playing at all. But the impertinent student pursued the matter. 'Who is playing, please?' he asked. Nicholas grumbled, 'Don't pay attention, it's only my daughter.' 'But it's good,' he insisted. 'How old is she?' Nicholas was getting more and more annoyed with him. 'Twelve,' he said. 'But that's fantastic for a child of such an age.' Nicholas did not reply; he made it clear that he did not wish to discuss it further. The playing offended him. 'She has no musicality, no imagination. She is a very ordinary English child,' he said, rather more peremptorily than he meant to. But the boy was irrepressible. 'Do you teach her? When you teach her she will be wonderful . . .' He was smiling up at Nicholas, obviously trying to placate him. Nicholas said, 'No, I do not teach her, I have no intention of doing so. Please do not ask me again.'

Nicholas pictured himself opening the door without knocking. The girl looks up, frozen, bow in mid-air. The room is handsome and light, with Georgian alcoves containing nude statues and astragalled windows overlooking a formal garden. The floor is the original, wide bare wood boarding, exposed for better sound. The girl playing the gamba is tall for her age and blonde, like Nicholas, with smooth dark skin. She is lovely enough for a painting, with that anxious look: yes, a Vermeer. In another moment, the instrument is on its side on the floor and the girl is gone. It is as if she had never been there. The student tries to go after her, but Nicholas stops him: it's time for his lesson. 'I only wanted to tell her I liked her playing,' he says. Nicholas promises to tell her for him, but of course does not.

Yet he was no Forqueray. No one could accuse him of behaving like that to his own child. She had all the advantages, was free to play whatever instrument she chose. Nicholas had tried to encourage her to sing – such a pretty girl, it would be to her advantage – or to play the piano. It would not do to have the whole family playing baroque music. He had even tried to encourage her in a non-musical direction – something quite different, perhaps art or interior decoration; something suitable for a girl, something. . . . No, it was perfectly clear that he had tried his best to dissuade her. He did not want her playing gamba, like him.

Young Forqueray, young Helene, young Lucy; succeeding generations denied. Young Nicholas. Why? *I do wish you would stop. You're giving me a headache. I abhor that instrument.* How painful the words were now that he remembered them. His mother had stood with a limp hand across her forehead. 'God, I can't bear those boring, repetitious scales, can't you go out and play like other boys your age?' Then Forqueray, desperate to stop his son's talent, dragging him off to prison. Finally himself in the same pose as his mother, only more aggressive. 'Stop that, you're giving me a headache. That instrument is not for you. You haven't got what it takes.'

Why had he not displayed his own father's generosity; or Marais' or Couperin's, all-embracing men whose great ambition was to father whole dynasties of musicians? Men who did not understand mean-spirited jealousy. Men like Bach, succeeded by all those sons.

Ah, but even the undeserving fathers got punished; the sons took their revenge.

May 7, 1747. King Frederick is wetting his moustache and patting his curls. 'Oh dear, which flute shall I play tonight?' he frets, fingering his ivory, his amber, his ebony, his boxwood in turn, as if his kingdom would rise or fall on the decision. His chamber musicians – Quantz, Abel, Benda and Emmanuel Bach – are waiting to accompany him. He feels brilliant tonight; he will play at least three concerti. . . . But the chamberlain interrupts just as he is warming up. 'Gentlemen,' he sighs, 'there will be no concert tonight. Old Bach is come.'

Everyone knew the story of how he arrived in his dilapidated travelling coat; how Fritz never gave him time to change. How he led him from room to room, making him test the new Silbermann fortepianos. How he played a theme on his flute for Bach to improvise upon, and how that was the genesis of the *Offering*. But who knew the other part of the story, how Emmanuel and his ring of King's Musikanten slandered him after he left. *Come*, says Emmanuel, the traitorous son, *let us play something more spirited and charming. Let the King play; let Abel accompany him. Come, let us all play and forget the six-part labours of Bach. He is too serious. He gives us a headache*! Emmanuel leads the hilarity. Ashamed of his own father – poor dishevelled peasant, composer of fugues. *Fugues, hah! Who has use for these dry and dusty pieces of pedagogy? Oh, and his language – did you hear, gentlemen, how he went on and on apologising to His Highness? I did not know where to look.*

Nor I.

Nor I.

Nor I. Muttering under his breath. Your Royal Grace this, your Royal Presence that, and so on. And all over a frockcoat, imagine! Holding their sides and mocking him; pursing and smacking their lips and kneading their hands in imitation of him, or what they saw as him; tittering into their lace cuffs.

Such monstrous neglect. Bach never recovered from the rebuff. They never played his *Offering* – not even the trio sonata, one of the most heavenly pieces of music in the world. A few bars in and they broke off – laughing, groaning, making cheap remarks about 'the learned contrapuntalist'. Unplayable, they pronounced it; boring, deadly, hopeless – and went on to one of the King's own pieces of *Sturm und Drang*. That was more like it! They failed to hear – the irony – how much in their own style it was, and what it must have cost him to write it. He offered his genius in the service of their new vision and they spurned it. The *Offering* was a miracle, a revolution – and all they could do was laugh.

Lucy and her fellow musicians: did they laugh at Nicholas? What did they say? That he was passé, too? Like the critics who blamed him for 'lacking regularity in the beat'? They fancied themselves more refined, more scholarly, more authentic. He pleased no one at the end but Rose. Had he even pleased her?

Young Forqueray, young Lucy, young Emmanuel. They survived. No need to waste contrition on them. They had their revenge; they thrived, they turned tables on their fathers. Lucy had Rose, her youth, her audiences. She was the admired musician and sought-after teacher. Whereas Nicholas was barely alive; the reviled beseecher after favours. Let me play, please, just one piece. She reduced him to beggary.

Bach was also shut out. In *The Art of Fugue* he turned from experiment. He had learned better than to imitate the young; look what happened when he did. He had thought the *Offering* so marvellous, yet no one listened. They wanted old Bach to stay Old Bach. So he gave up and embraced death, and for his epitaph he wrote what he knew best, *The Art of Fugue*. Let the young men inherit, was its message. Or, as in Nicholas's case, the young woman.

Rose

21

Or in my case, the old woman. It is after Helene's death, and the Dolmetsch family, superstitious and also in need of money, have entered me for auction. I do not suffer. Though I mourn Helene, I am hopeful; I celebrate my freedom from the Dolmetsches, and I am rather inclined to a fine new master, one who savours life. I am sanguine, anticipatory. There are so many whose hobby it is – more tasteful than philately, and more lucrative – to acquire magnificent but 'outdated' instruments for purposes of study and amateur performances, who will surely want me. I imagine not a virtuoso, but one who is respectful and kind. I require simple adoration; I do not suspect an old woman.

Miss Dora Pether is a lady of means, a collector of instruments, and a violoncellist. (She plays a fine Petrus Guarnerius from the collection of the late Baron Knoop.) She has fast nipper knees and watery blue eyes under a seam of pale parted hair. Sitting semi-circle with her sisters, each in a long black frock, playing a furious but turgid, out-of-tune masterpiece of the previous century, she seems harmless enough. But she is not. She is the enemy in disguise. She is the raptor; I the wood-mouse.

She waves her bow – while her sisters beat their weapons against their instruments' breasts in a tremolo of thunder – and lo and behold I am magicked – transformed, transmuted, converted. My neck is broken and tilted further back. A higher bridge is inserted on my belly, causing a tense pain. My strings – a mere four – are as thick as horsewhips. I am divested of my frets and my ivory inlay.

But let me not continue the catalogue of atrocities. My ravishment and ruination is complete. I am become a cello.

Was it not ironic, Nicholas, that after surviving out the last century in original condition (if somewhat neglected in the museum), I was remodelled in this? Dolmetsch's efforts on behalf of 'old' music had revived the love of 'original' instruments. Yet there were still a few misguided souls, including la Pether, who had the temerity to rewrite history. To her my mutilation meant progress: the new is better than the old, English superior to foreign, bigger preferable to smaller, and, especially, loudest is best. She had me fully 'modernised', as one does houses today; in the process I was, of course, destroyed. It was a sin; a crime against history and music.

But the joke, if there was one, was on her. For all her efforts, the result was laughable. I could no more be a violoncello than a fagott, no matter how much reparation, realigning, replacing and reconstructing they did. I could grunt and growl through my four ropes, but I could never sing. I could not project my voice like her pompous little Guarnerius; could not make it flow, rich and thick, like the sweet Madeira she and her sisters were so fond of taking each afternoon. For I chose not to do so. I had the necessary equipment but not the inclination. Without frets I became gruff; with four, not seven, strings I lacked sympathetic vibrations, and without a pair of massive cello shoulders I was as weak and whingeing as the viola pomposa. The operation was a failure.

Nicholas

22

Nicholas was twelve when Rose came to him. That was how he had thought of it – as something determined, required. There was no element of the miraculous – of deliverance – about it; it was simply understood that one day she would be his. Nicholas knew nothing of the consequences for his father. He accepted Rose from him with an inclination of the head more felt than visible. He was not overawed by her, though she was bigger than he. He was uncaring of his peers' derision, considered his father's attempts at a ceremonious presentation (as if he were going off to war) as ludicrous. No, Nicholas's response was not effusive. It was only right that she be his. His world was, like a perfect circle, now closed.

Only in retrospect did Nicholas feel the event's significance. It was, if not miraculous, then decidedly coincidental: Harry Jordan's exit, Rose's delivery. At any rate, how extraordinary that his father should fugue directly on leaving Rose with him. Had he understood that to be the bargain, he might have behaved differently. Might he have tried to dissuade him? Perhaps not; perhaps his father's disappearance had been somehow a necessary part of the ritual, as in some fairy story, where one is given a simple choice: in this case, his father or Rose. Of course he had chosen Rose; would do so again.

Fifty years later it was his turn. Nicholas played the

deliverer, his father's part; Lucy received. It made perfect sense, was excellently timed, at the juncture of his retirement and the launching of her professional career.

He served tea, he was calm; he did not rattle the dishes. It was a sensible decision. While they drank, they signed the necessary papers; no money changed hands, no instrument passed from his hand to hers. Nicholas had planned nothing dramatic: no retirement cruise to the Aegean, no flit like his father's. He merely said, nodding in Rose's direction, 'So, now she is yours.' Lucy, looking rather uncomfortable, had asked if he was quite certain of what he was doing. She said she felt a bit of a thief. 'No, no,' he assured her. 'Go ahead . . . quite sure . . . only fair.' His prepared words had not come out as planned. He'd remembered his own father's tragi-comic speechifying and was too embarrassed.

But now, indeed, he thought it of her: a thief and a hypocrite. How often she had accused him of giving all his attention to Rose, saying Rose was all he'd ever wanted; Rose with her unknown history, her smile, her endlessly varying responses, her unrepeatable beauty; Rose whom he held in his arms. Now she held her; had coveted her all along.

The musician and his daughter. Nicholas read about them in his programme: *Lucy Jordan, daughter of the famous Nicholas Jordan, is well known for her continuo and solo bass gamba playing, both in Europe and the United States. Tonight she plays an original French instrument, formerly in her father's possession* . . . A seemingly *legato* transition, the detritus of family life brilliantly concealed, as it was between Forqueray and his son, Dolmetsch and his daughter, countless others. Which were the happy musical families?

Nicholas had been fond of Lucy as a baby. The variations of her movements delighted him. He surprised himself by wanting to spend time watching her, even cuddling her. He found himself twirling her round and throwing her up in the air – and was stricken by his own artlessness. But she loved fast motion, so he did it again; when he put her down she cried.

His involvement was cut short by Jean, who made it known, in her vague but manipulating way, that she felt put-out. Perhaps it was her way of getting even, for he had barred her from the closed unit that was Rose and he. Whenever Lucy put out her arms to him, Jean came running, deflecting her attention, cooing, 'Come to Mama. Mama loves you best.' Eventually, Nicholas supposed, Lucy believed it.

There were the years he hardly saw her, when he was on the international circuit: concerts in Australia, America, Japan, Canada. He had no time for little girls. After the divorce, she had come to his house to listen to him, pestering him for lessons. He had demurred.

Later, as a large, inelegant teenager, she seemed even less plausibly his. She became delinquent, she eluded him entirely. He dissociated himself, except financially, from her disastrous young life – abortions, drugs, suicide attempts – confident that Jean could cope, and that the child would survive without him. Jean thrived, after all, on tragedy; that way she could resent him all the more, and feel self-righteous in the bargain. But at the time, he had few regrets: he was, after all, a very busy man. To play well, one must protect oneself from stress and ugliness. The only thing one could not run away from was suicide.

Nicholas, finally afraid that Lucy would one day succeed in this, was forced to think of something. In extremis, he offered to teach her; he bought her her own instrument. But she was not, as he had expected, grateful. Instead she fairly erupted in misery, berating him for his timing. ('Why now?') She did battle with him, tried even in her temper to destroy his generous, if belated, gift. Would likely have destroyed him if she could.

They closed in on him, mother, daughter, therapist. He was forced to listen to their charges. From Lucy: 'How could you say I wasn't musical, when you never even gave me a chance?' And then, 'Why wouldn't you teach me earlier, when you knew I was dying for lessons?' – her face as compressed as the day she was born, her knuckles as white. (As a baby she'd been long and lean, with tiny replicas of his own fingers and toes; a frightening little miracle that wailed and flailed with unfathomable rage or longing – how could one tell?) 'Just because you're famous doesn't mean you can treat your own family like shit.' From Jean: corroboration and bitterness; the aside, 'He couldn't bear the idea that she might play as well as him.' And then her own not unweighty case of neglect.

The therapist chanted the litany of his crimes: not listening, not concentrating, not caring, not feeling, a case of ludicrously bad timing. Implausible crimes for a musician. 'Would you like to say something about this?' – perversely, she smiled. No, he wouldn't, (What, indeed, could he say?) The revelation of his inhumanity was effected, his failure at living in this world and out of it. Nicholas Jordan, the famous artist: now Nicholas Jordan, the famous monster.

Rose

22

Dear monster, how you play on my feelings. You rouse me to sadness; I would contradict you, be your armour. Embowered in your embrace, I would protect you from the world again. I would stop your lamenting, barricade you from a humbleness unnatural to you. I would restore you to your old self. Alone, alas, you are too touched by conscience. It hurts me to hear you.

Yet the tenor of their argument affected me too. We were in it together, you and I; the monster they accused had two heads. You were so lost in me that you failed to see them; you knew them not. A mere wife, a daughter – clumsy, cacophonous beings – how could they compete with me?

Yet I did not ask that you deprive them of your society. True, I demanded application and devotion: but not exclusivity. I did not make you my slave; I did not ask to be your fetish. I cannot accept blame for your withdrawal from the world. Perhaps you misunderstood. Of course I demanded your time, but I expected to share you. One expands from the centre, the circle enlarges and grows richer in its design, its melody and harmony taking in the world. And the world in turn feeds the centre.

For shame, Nicholas: you fed no one but yourself and me; the others starved. It was only the sight of Lucy's gashed wrists and the sound of the sirens that finally woke you out of your sweet *loure*. Well it might; you could ill afford another Hannah on your conscience. Your *femme* had tried everything, but it was you Lucy sought – or, failing you, me.

You congratulate yourself on your superiority to Dolmetsch, yet I wonder. He did not play his lute while Helene bled to death before his eyes. I do not excuse him – you were both equally guilty of the sin of pride – but at least he did not know what Helene suffered on the other side of London.

You knew, Nicholas, only you did not want to know. (Am I too facile, too *legato*?) You, the artiste, were beyond reach; you said she was only your daughter. Only. Is that where your artistry got you, beyond humanity; beyond your own flesh and blood? I led you away, and in that I share the burden.

But you denied her me; that I do not forgive. I thrive on attention, and not only yours. I loved the feel of her young limbs, her experimental fingers. Until you forbade her, she handled me with the greatest good will. Cast your mind back to how it was when you practised. How the little girl-child stood beside you with big eyes and ears. How was it you were not moved? She was no ordinary child, Lucy. She loved both of us, and yet you chose to ignore her. When you left the house without me, she practised imitation. She became you – and yet there was enough of her own style that I could not fail to respond. Such a lightness, such delicacy. It is true, she did not understand the subtleties of your approach, but it would not have overtaxed you to illuminate her. Rather, you were embarrassed. You apologised for her to your students. You punished her for touching me; once you slapped her – it hurt me too.

It did not become you. Why was it that you suffered those mediocre students; did not spank them or throw them out? Instead you took their money – cash preciously wrapped – and indulged their weakness for you. Many scarcely improved, whereas Lucy was, as you would say, a natural. She barely needed instruction; it was your encouragement, your closeness, she needed; your approbation she desired.

Now she is mine. Listen, Nicholas, to how she hugs my strings. I am her lifeblood, as once I was yours. She will not let go; she endows the pieces with soul, the chords are full, as you taught her (playing the gamba without chords is like playing the harpsichord with one hand, you said). Yes, she plays as you taught her, when you finally suffered her as your student. Of course she forced your hand by her operatic acts, yet how else was she to rouse your fatherly conscience? You see it now: she longed to restore the family triad, the basis of celestial harmony. In this she did not succeed.

It was good that you were forced to respond. My proud master on his hands and knees, weeping at her bedside. Bravo. One could say you too were saved that night. You gave before it was too late. Better than blood, you gave her what was most precious to you: in the end you gave her Me.

Nicholas

23

Nicholas gave Lucy Rose, but he withheld himself. He could not be father to his child, nor husband to his wife. It was a question of one's emotional repertoire: how to expand it? How does a Molière figure unlearn the effete gestures of a lifetime? How does one make changes that are fundamental, not merely stylistic? Perhaps it was better not to ask these questions. He was too old for public self-revelation; for a sudden burst of romanticism. It would be absurd, for example, to think of becoming suddenly swaggeringly demonstrative: of taking Lucy in his arms and begging forgiveness for past neglect, misjudgment; to think of promising – what? – more of himself. No, it was not his style; besides, what more had he to give? He balked; it was enough; now that she had Rose – his surrogate self – she in a sense had him. His warmth, his sweetness, his fire, his humour – let her listen: it was all there under her bow and fingers. Let her cock her ear to Rose's heart; his own was too weak to whistle. He had no more to offer the greedy girl.

He watched her. His daughter was built to perfection, on the grand seventeenth-century scale (like Rose: before *le grand goût* gave way to *le bon goût*). In her period gown, hair piled up, neck proud, she was the centrepiece of the stage. No more jeans, scruffy shirts; Lucy's adolescent wickedness, her delinquency, her frailty, were no more. She was a lady and a professional. She had grown up and, after all, his neglect had not damaged her; perhaps had even strengthened her.

She had finally condescended to study with him. They worked together almost daily for a year, and it transformed her. She became enlivened, approachable, responsible. She transferred her addictions to her studies, dedicated herself to learning everything he had to impart; to practising eight hours a day and more.

It transformed Nicholas too. He discovered her talent (as if it hadn't been there all the while), and found he too enjoyed their sessions together. Her efforts moved him, inspired him to invest more time in her. It pleased him to hear her repeat his phrases with dexterity and imagination; he felt comforted, after all, by the assurance of continuity. He thrived too on her appreciation: was finally proud of her.

Then, just as he had begun to depend on her, she announced she was going away to study at the Basle Conservatory. But why? Nicholas argued that a year was not long enough, he still had more to teach her, they were only getting started. He heard the greediness in his voice, but hoped Lucy didn't. It didn't matter what she heard, she said, 'I'm sorry, I just can't. I like our lessons too much.' Ah, this was not devastating, Nicholas was relieved. He laughed. 'But so do I; what may I ask is wrong with that?' Now her expression was determinedly serious. 'It's too dangerous.' He was becoming increasingly amused with his daughter. 'How dangerous?' She begged him not to laugh at her. Nicholas, enjoying her discomfiture, was magnanimous. 'Go on.' She explained that it was too seductive studying with him; one was tempted to copy his style – she must find her own. Besides, she wanted to study conducting. This he could not take seriously at all. She knew that he could teach her conducting as well as anyone, and as to style she well knew he much preferred originality to mimicry. The copyists infuriated him; hadn't she noticed? He was still feeling rather ebullient with conceit. She shook her head. No? No she hadn't noticed, or no she didn't care? She would not clarify herself, nor listen to further argument.

The stubborn girl was not to be convinced. Nicholas was to be denied.

On the night Lucy left for Basle, Nicholas sat down with Rose and a bottle of whisky. Tonight Rose was not enough for him. Life without Lucy was jejune and repetitive. His house, seen from the bottom of his glass, went from baroque to rococo, and nauseated him. The two hundred cantatas he had yet to record wearied him.

What had he not given her? What more would she get from that *faible* Frenchman, his opposite number in Basle? He was annoyed – very. What would have become of her without his masterful attentions? A drug addict, an unwed mother, a derelict? He had saved her – and now she had left him. Just like Abel and Emmanuel Bach. Poor Abel. Nicholas played one of his rather maudlin pieces. He pictured the fat man, sitting with broad thighs parted, smiling vacantly and humming to himself, taking little swigs from his hip flask during rests; improvising another sweet asinine adagio, his fingers too wormy for anything else. Nicholas's own fingers were loose but still in control. Abel bows and takes another drink; and another and another. He tells himself that he and his instrument are at the height of fashion and power; that he is no ungainly bear, exhibited and exposed by his friend Gainsborough in his very decline: in his shiny satin suit with those white fortepiano legs, with his dog and his faithful gamba. That brave, absurd face.

Nicholas too took repeated sips. He played the Abel rather well, he thought; the drunken slurs improved it no end. 'Of course, one feels foolish being left,' he said, conversing with the ghost of Abel, and drank to him. 'To poor old Abel. They left you too, didn't they? You supported Emmanuel for years and then he upped and left you for a pretty wife and a house in the suburbs. Well well, aren't we the pretty pair? Abel and Nicholas, the soppy leftovers of our time. Our respective times,' he corrected himself.

Lucy was no Abel. She gave no cause for derision; knew exactly what she was doing, and why. This music was her restoration, yet she was in command of it. Rose was her instrument, her tool, nothing more. She would never be slavish like Nicholas, nor a figure of fun like Abel. She would make her career playing, but she would have a life apart.

Nicholas recalled the day she came for Rose. (Finally, in spite of her defection, he had decided to give Rose to her; who else was there?) He had planned a simple handing-over ceremony, nothing so overdone as his father's. His dignity should be preserved. But the whole thing went topsy-turvy when Lucy turned up with a friend. Nicholas, furious, was more coolly polite than ever. 'Tea?' he offered the trousered individual, ignoring Lucy. 'Daddy' – she stuck her head between them – 'I'd like you to meet Sally, my lover. I met her in Basle. We're living together now; I wanted you to know. That's why she came with me today . . . it's important . . . I wanted her to share it.' Share? Share what: his daughter, his instrument? Had he heard correctly? Her lover? He took the hand and felt its weight: not a musician's. It sweated; or was that his own? A hand that caresses my daughter, he thought, and dropped it.

Nicholas was not to be thrown; he had survived difficulties before – played in excessive heat and cold, and near-empty auditoria (due to scheduling disasters or freak weather). But this situation required a kind of equanimity he did not possess. This Sally person's presence alone was an insult. The ceremony as planned was to have been between him and Lucy: a bit of private history, the handing down from one generation to another. But instead it was theirs – the two women's. The thieves.

How extraordinary it was, this 'women's movement'. Women together, raising their voices, demanding attention, determined to be noticed, to do things only men before them had ever done; resurrecting third-rate women composers, worse even than Abel. Women loving one another. He could not believe his Lucy – soloist, conductor, Rose's inheritor – was one of *those*. Smiling, sure of themselves. Rose made up the trinity: their mascot, their weird child.

Who could blame him for disowning Lucy after that? He instructed her not to visit him again. Let her keep Rose, but keep herself and her grotesque friend out of his sight. It was this kind of profligacy that gave the eighteenth century a bad name in the first place.

Now they were gone – both his daughters: incomplete without men to play upon them, to conduct them through life, to bring their musical power to fruition. He abhorred Lucy's perversion of the natural order. Rose he pitied. Poor Rose, he thought, how she must fail without me. What will become of her in that unsound *ménage*?

Rose

23

I am sorry to disappoint you, Nicholas, but truly I thrive in their *ménage*. It is full-bodied, soundful. I am a happy widow with a tune still on her lips. I am not alone: your Lucy loves me and I love her. She is not mine exclusively, but there are advantages even to that. I am not so depleted by her attentions. After all, I am not getting any younger.

So you are wrong, Nicholas. It is you who are misguided, who fail without us. How little you know of life beyond your own limbs – the once-strong, manly limbs that held me captive for half a century. Oh, I loved you – I was your *viola d'amore*, with a scarf across my eyes to signify my blindness, my head bowed in modesty and perhaps shame. But now I am unblinded; I hold up my head and smile.

It was wonderful with you; I was never bored. If I was sometimes afraid, as I was once of Forqueray (you too seemed wild and dangerous at times), you soothed me afterwards: you were always in control, you never hurt me. But you took your pleasure; riding me, you excited the very air around us until I shone with your sweat on my brow.

Lucy is cooler. She sits quietly composed, stroking me in rhythmical waves, gentling me into voice as only Marais was able to do. Then she smiles down on me, her hair brushing my cheek. She is not like my other masters; she has – how shall I put it? – greater humility. You imposed your will; she asks my permission. When I grant her wish, she is grateful for my response.

There are times when I miss you; when I excite myself with your memory, the recollection of our brave concord. I do not flatter myself that we achieved harmonic victory over falsity, folly, deeds of darkness, scenes of spoils; nor that we changed the world or diverted it from its evil course. But we made an alternative to its hysterical rhythms and painful discord. In bearing witness to the past – its darkness and light – I can safely say we brought moments of enlightenment.

But things have changed; you are wrong to pity me. This transition is no tragedy, for I am content with your Lucy. My Lucy. It is good to be played by a strong woman. I feared no mistress could master me, but I am proved wrong. I see that the women shall inherit; indeed, that they shall master their instruments and their men. They will even take one another as partners.

Then let me be their mascot. Let me enjoy the partnership of equals and not the domination of one upon another. Let me welcome this new passage, our sweet union: Lucy and mine.

So you stop and I go on. It is a moving forward and yet a starting over again, like the chaconne or the passacaglia, which is fixed in its harmonies and otherwise infinitely variable. The endpiece of our suite. Did you know, the *chacona mulata* was once a wild and sensuous dance from Mexico? We tempered it to suit our taste for order and restraint; by my time it was the noble dance of the grand finale. Yet in becoming tame it became more magnificent; as Racine's passions grew hotter within their Alexandrine confines. But I am partial. I am French. It suits me. I am in love with a form which never ends and is always beginning again.

Repetition; constant repetition, as inexorable as the movement of the ocean, yet each wave different from the last. The ocean and time move on and no two tones, though they be the same, ever sound the same. We change, our notes change; the emphasis, the length, accompanying harmonies, rhythms – all vary from couplet to couplet. Even the rests are various.

There is a special pleasure in it. The tension builds from the recurring, endlessly recurring bass. We are comforted, we know what to expect and yet the transformation amazes us and makes us smile. Will it come again? . . . we wait . . . we hold our breath . . . ah, *quelle surprise*! Like sunshine on a dark day. Yet it is sinister too, that addictive, obsessive, never-endingness. Stop; go on; stop; go on; let it finish! Yet it haunts. Listen, it is coming again . . . now . . . you cover your ears – no more! – yet you listen more intently than ever, on the edge of your seat, and a shiver finds its way down your spine.

Nothing can stop it, not revolution nor earthquake. Your pulse quickens – it cannot go on, yet it must. It may never end, spinning off beyond its thirty-two couplets into the pure essence of the musical elements.

When it stops, you nearly tumble out of your seat.

Nicholas

24

Nicholas leaned forward in his seat and lowered his head between his legs. He held his chest, and shut his eyes before a seemingly inconsequential vision of himself playing, and a woman kneeling at his feet: God and his child. Now he was the child. He was afraid, not of death – his heart had stopped long enough to remind him of it – but of his remnant of life without Rose. He was the supplicant. Don't let me go, he intoned, you are my warmth and my reassurance. We are connected by a magic circle: the sound comes out of my body and enters yours and then returns to me; you are the continuation of me. You cannot cut me off.

But Rose finally was not to be trusted. She appeared to him changed: the prominent grain on her chest reversed direction; the flame-shaped *f* holes took on a reckless abandon; the modest smile turned to a leer; the unreproducible red varnish burst into flame as if she'd leapt from hell; her voice became a whine. She would never be his again.

He could not listen any more. He managed to get to his feet and push past others in his row. Let them stare at him, whisper, purse their lips; it did not matter now. Oh the vanity of his art. A lifetime with Rose reduced to a paltry affair: a bit of gentle wooing, controlled charm, a gradual warming to one's subject, a discreet explosion and, not long after, the inevitable cadence. Perhaps a bitter-sweet *petite reprise*. And then on to the next piece and the next and the next. Women and music. *My dear, there will never be another like you. Cheeribye for now.*

He had trusted her; she had been in his power. For all her wilful ways, he had thought her more malleable than his other loves. How much safer to indulge this passion: she asked no questions, demanded nothing he could not give, and offered perfect responsiveness. So he believed. He in turn had given freely of himself, pouring his feelings into her as he had not done, to their utter frustration, with mortal females. She knew better than any of them how to draw him out; through her he sang, cried, whimpered, bellowed, moaned, whispered the secrets of his innermost soul, and died in agony and joy. But afterwards he became frigid again. Another Graswinkel, God help him. Perhaps he deserved her infidelity.

Air; he had to get some air. Leave the hall, make his way outside. Breathe slow, measured breaths. Think of the sarabande.

He thought of Lucy's first lesson; how frustrated he'd been by her coldness. How to get her to let go, play a little dangerously? Without thinking he'd said, '. . . this passage must be *orgasmic*,' and she'd looked shocked and embarrassed. Such words did not belong in a lesson of music. Cover their virgins' ears.

There will never be another like you, Master, never . . . Foolish Nicholas, consigned to a history of past masters. Plain Nicholas Jordan, hot-blooded and charismatic only when his Rose was with him; without her dry and cold as an old bone. A great musician but an insufficient father: the final, simplistic analysis. He stared at a floodlit statue of a once-great god. Is that the epitaph Lucy and her lady friend would carve for him?

He thought of the hundreds of letters declaring love, men and women alike offering him their services in capacities from nanny to maidservant to mistress, just to be near him; of the armfuls of roses from anonymous admirers; of accolades from reviewers. Surprising, in fact, that such an anomalous activity should have been so well received. (Not that there were magnums of champagne or black orchids or any of the lavish glamour of the opera.) His concerts had attracted small and exclusive audiences with an ear for detail and nuance and a taste for reviving lost magnificence. Many were young musicians: recent infatuated converts from modern instruments, still half in love with their vibrato and their propsticks.

He was the exception in a nation of amateurs. He had taught them so much: even in England they were forced eventually to recognise his supremacy; to acknowledge him, as they had long before in Europe and America. But heroes get knocked off their pedestals. Nicholas shivered; he would have to go back in soon. He was calmer now. He did not want, after all, to miss the *pièce de résistance*: the opera-ballet, *Pygmalion*.

Change was in the air. They had begun to question him, prickling and bristling at the slightest deviation from what they called *authentic performance practice*. The way they spouted those packaged phrases. Every performance must be correct from a 'purist' (whatever that might mean) point of view. Did they not know with what variety and international haphazardness instruments and musicians came together? Italian violins, German flutes, wrong ornaments – it hardly mattered, so long as there was conviction. His last concert: a band of pedants waited to pounce with their points of order. *Excuse me, Mr Jordan, I see you don't use mean-tone tuning; why is that? Mr Jordan, you were using your French instrument to accompany Italian songs; surely a cello would be more appropriate* . . . How tired he was of their questions; how bored. They with their 'authentic' instruments bought at auctions and restored to spanking original condition, or copied scientifically by computerised photographic methods down to the last dogfish scale. But did they make music? No, the lot of them.

Nicholas, as in the beginning, made his way through the Hall of Mirrors, and saw himself repeated, *ad nauseum*.

They'd tried to emulate and depose him at the same time: they were wary of stepping into his place, yet excited at the thought they would have the next turn. His style, they complained, was too individual, too eccentric, to be exemplary. What did they mean? That he could excite an audience to laughter and tears, and they could not. Too many had tried to imitate him and failed; now they would turn the world against him by slurs on his character. They could not, after all, fault his playing. One way or another they would set themselves up in his place. It was the way with each new generation. They take your genius and push you out.

Yes, these days one was apt to be criticised from both sides. If the purist fanatics didn't get one, the new converts would. The latter had invited him to conduct *Messiah* as a party piece at the Royal Circus in Belgium. When he'd refused, telling them it should be performed only in church, they put it about that he was too old and stuffy to take seriously. The new backlash, his colleagues called it. Just because they owned cheap copies, they thought they could play in the old heavy-breathing, flank-gripping ways. No, it would not do. Nicholas took his seat again, still wagging his head, in time for the Rameau.

Rose

24

We did not push you out, Nicky. You forget: you chose to retire, even before it was necessary. Your time was not yet come, but at the first sign of failure you panicked, and put me from you. It was the performance of a lifetime, your handing over ceremony. Hypocritical Nicholas, you gave me to Lucy, and hated her for taking me. Such generosity. And then you resented, to put it lightly, her female lover. Why, so long as she loves and loving, loves both of us? Male or female, young or old, would you sooner see her a tragic spinster like my poor Helene? Look at your daughter, Nicholas: Lucy, my mistress. Look carefully; what do you see? Blooming health, innocence, joy, precision, hope for the future coupled with love and respect for the past. Do not destroy these before you die. Accept her. Put no conditions on your love. Let her go; and do the same for me.

Transitions. From subject to bridge, major to minor, fast to slow; junctures where one 'gives' or goes on deliberately in time. Time – I need more time to develop my passage. When one is normally bounded by strictness, a moment of abandon, or a moment's hesitation, is most eloquent. I savour the unwritten voyage; with no notes charting my way, I am free. *Though* only briefly, we leave behind the composer, not his conventions. We find our own way, ornamenting as we go; improvising, bridging, fugueing, touching, running with virtuosity through our cadenza to the trill; until we find our way back to the written score.

Painful transitions. The words slide downwards as naturally as the *port de voix*. Yet must it be so? You look uncertain, Nicholas; perhaps contrite, I cannot be sure. You fidget still; there is an emptiness about you between the knees. I feel myself there yet, though I rest quietly in Lucy's embrace (the extra padding on the gripping part of the knee is surprisingly comfortable). But then I am experienced in adjusting to new bodies. So many pairs of knees down through the centuries, so many embraces. Yours was unique while it lasted, Nicholas. I shall not soon forget.

Stay those lonely fingers. Listen while I tell about *Pygmalion*, my favourite *acte de ballet*. As you know, it is based on a myth from the *Metamorphoses* of Ovid. It relates the story of the sculptor who, disillusioned by women, carves himself a statue out of ivory. She is his ideal; he falls in love with her. (Originally sculptor and statue joined together in an act which Ovid described as 'abominable love'; Rameau's version is more polite.) Amor brings the statue to life. Only an excellent sculptor like Pygmalion, he explains, could ever deserve such a miracle. He promises eternal happiness as his reward. Amor calls in the Graces to proclaim the power of love. *L'Amour triomphe, annoncez sa victoire*! A rousing air.

The lights are hot. They make me lose my temper, my flanks go hot and swell. But Lucy is as cool and graceful as the statue. *O ciel*! sings Pygmalion. He is enchanted; when the statue sings of her adoration he is exalted. The Graces teach her the Sarabande, a dance of great skill in balance and mental concentration. But see how she wobbles in the early hours of life, only gradually gaining assurance and poise. And now: is she not beautiful, Nicholas, dancing the Sarabande all by herself?

Pygmalion is beside himself with joy and love. He sings to the people, the chorus echoes him, and the people dance round the statue. And now he sings a song of praise to Amor who, with his divine fire, has brought the object of his love to life. Finally we play – while they dance – the Tambourin.

All restraint is thrown to the wind. *Gai*; not as Lucy would use it, but as Rameau wrote it. Is it not joyful?

But see, Nicholas, how the statue holds out her arms to you. She smiles, invites you from us all; look, she entreats you – do not turn away – come up with us on stage. Play one last piece for us, for your audience. Do not pretend ignorance or modesty; it is too late for that.

Nicholas

25

No, I cannot play, I am an old man. Nicholas felt weak; it was all too much for him. Where were they leading him, through what labyrinth? He could not play for this audience, not now; it was too late. His fingers were too stiff, he was unpractised. What inept scratchings would he produce? He was afraid of embarrassing his daughter, of disappointing Rose; of becoming a figure of fun: an Abel. Let them be, he thought, with their new life, with their new variations and interpretations; he would not stand in their way.

The statue held out her arms to him; so did Lucy. Rose smiled. People in the audience turned to stare, bemused, expectant. He tried to pretend he did not know what they wanted of him. They began to applaud. He was profoundly uncomfortable, yet now he could not refuse them. It was their last chance; his too. He acknowledged the praise, stood up. His row made way for him.

He managed a spring in his step. That was always easy for a performance; it was afterwards that one collapsed with fatigue. He leapt up to the platform as if young again, Rose once again his.

Lucy handed him Rose and stepped aside; she sat not far from him. He received her offering, bowed to his audience, to Lucy, then sat down to play.

Rose. How warm she felt. Familiar. He secured her

between his legs. Yet his muscles quivered, ached. Such an unnatural position. Never mind, it would come back. But what should he play? What could he add to such a feast of music? His fingers faltered even as he tried to tune. There was silence, as the audience indulged his hesitant foolishness. He was tempted to change his mind, to stop before it was too late. Why did they want him? Out of pity, curiosity, condescension? No, they wanted him to be as reliable as ever, with a carnation in his buttonhole, his hair silver, his blue eyes. Not old, just a bit tired; more romantic than ever. Could they not see his shaking limbs? Rose felt them, but it seemed not to matter this time.

He fondled her old head, traced the scar that had been his fault, that marred her beauty. He stroked the back of her neck with his thumb, begging for time. Were they getting restless? He still did not know what to play. Never mind, his pulse was slowing, a familiar warmth filled him. His fingers took to the frets. Even if not perfect, he knew it would be all right. Rose would help him; and Lucy at his side. His beautiful daughters. Hush – he held up his hand, he was ready. He would play, and *La Statue* should sing: Henry Purcell. He balanced the bow and grasped the precious neck. His last encore.

Rose

25

Ah, Nicholas, how good is your touch: I am home, your faithful Rose. I am carried back to Henry Purcell's time, which is perfect time; in death as in life, in pulse with the world. I am tossed by billowing clouds, the intervals of joy bounce my strings, like dolphins playing on the waves. *And again. And again and again and again.* Your bumptious florid song raises us up, and we may never, never sink to earth again. *And again I say rejoice.*

But I fall. Deeper and deeper in sorrow I sink, to the bottom-most notes that I know, for all the lost loves of this world and for ours too. *O God, thou hast cast us out and scattered us abroad.* Let me weep; oh let me weep and sigh my soul away, plunging a diminished fifth to the depths of my range.

No more. The matchless man would have me happy once again: *Tread down our enemies and forget sorrow.* From here and there he summons up the instruments of joy to accompany his heavenly chorus, bids them tune their voices and celebrate. Come, they sing: *Sound the trumpet. . . . Strike the viol.* We sing in full harmonious lays, another and another: odes, anthems, songs and grounds. I am stirred to the rhythms of your pleasure and my own.

Listen, the British Orpheus tells it all, how music eases pain, how it makes the whip drop from the dread Alecto's hand, the snakes drop from her head. Beguiled by me, even you, Nicholas, can be persuaded to smile before you let me go for ever.

Together we celebrate. My time is come round again, after two hundred years of neglect. And what relief, not to be endured by audiences in respect for my age and fragility; not to be regretted and pitied for my past achievements, a beauty which had become passé; no more the desiccated one, abandoned for the lubricious cello. I am revived, this is my renaissance. I live again; I am looked upon with admiration and enthusiasm; I am attuned to. The whole world talks of me – intones, lectures, demonstrates: the great viol, the noble viol, the expressive and passionate bass gamba. They drink to me, they write learned articles and theses concerning my best features and characteristics; they organise courses and master classes on how to play upon me, and they feature me in international festivals.

I am uniqueness and beauty personified in an age of uniformity and ugliness. The cacophony of the streets follows people indoors, oozes through their windows and trails down the backs of their necks. In the quiet of the night they creep downstairs and play a record to soothe their jangling spirits. They listen to your fingers pressing against my gut, the tension-free bow pushing and pulling across me, each position creating a new surprise. They see how corrupted they have become by their culture and its technology, the mechanicalness and the speed of their lives. We slow them down: Listen, we say, imagine yourself on a quiet beach, only the sound of the waves as continuo against the treble of stones and shells mingling. Bend to look and what do you find? Each stone different, a miracle of colour and shape and texture. So it is with my voice: clear and ringing, hoarse, tremulous, translucent, whispering, always changing; the same notes and yet not the same, the same form and yet not the same. Listen to how I sob, I rumble with anger, I mount the scale of violence before I break off again into sweet harmony. Gentle and soothing, tart and strident is my voice (as one of Lucy's feminist friends raising hers to the crowd) – it expresses all times, straddling the centuries as you – master for the last time – straddle me. I am the emissary of past beauty, of polished discourse, of ornament, wit and the graces. I bear witness to the trials and upheavals which threatened me with extinction. Yet I survive.

Ah, the *Pompe funèbre* of Couperin: your own good night; our final encore. It is like replaying our life together – I almost cannot manage, do you hear me falter? I wind down, prepare to give you up, and then . . . 'No,' I cry out, 'not yet, I cannot.' The theme returns, solemn and dark but sweet nevertheless, this reminder of our parting. Once again I resist, make a detour from our stately procession in mourning crêpe. But it is no use: this time must really be the end. How sweet it is, finally.

I smile. We are consummate together, Nicholas; transported from care, from knowledge. Yet I cannot protect you for ever. I cannot cure the colds or the sorrows of our listeners, nor the starvation, torture or homelessness of your fellow human beings. All I can do, in my light and dancing voice, is to soothe your mortal wounds. I am the lovely simpleton at the funeral who, in the face of death, smiles and sings in a perfectly tuned voice more movingly than any pompous disquisition. Nor can I cure your anguish at losing me.

New beginnings take strength from old endings. Now that is a wise saying, and cadentially useful. Forgive me, one is tempted to be pompous when one has lived as long as I have and heard all I have heard. There is no point in prolonging the end overmuch as the Romantics did, with their trumpets and their kettledrums and their endless dominant-tonic flip-flops while the audience rolls its eyeballs and looks to its watches – they have trains and tubes to catch, cars to rescue. Will it never end?

There are so many ways of ending; how shall I do it, Nicholas? Shall I leave you sitting here on stage while Lucy whisks me away with a nod in your direction? The final cadence, as you know, can be authentic, perfect or imperfect; masculine or feminine. One repeats a formula, and yet the end is always unique; for nothing stays the same.

I might be tempted to end on a tragic note, thinking of how things are not likely to change after you are gone; how I shall continue to be mocked and ridiculed and accused of frivolity and élitism in the face of poverty, crime, wars, nuclear disasters. How shall I defend myself against future 'improvements' or 'modernisation'? Each one that I went through has killed me a little. I die a little each day, each time I am played. It cannot be helped. Nothing lasts for ever, not even your Rose.

You know I am bound by convention to make my endings sweet: the *Tierce de Picardie*. Then what is left? To embrace for the last time, to hand me back to Lucy, with a bow and a gracious smile. This time you do it with love. That is good. As for me, it is not so difficult to let me go. Think of me as living only for the moment; moments that have a sense of time, that will never come back. They might be called moments of grace. But you cannot force these moments and you cannot hold them in your hand. Be grateful for the adventure and say goodbye.

Petite Reprise

Listen, Nicholas, while I sing to you. Listen to the music that fills my chest and blossoms forth from my rose hole. Rose of the responsive bosom. The music flutters about inside me; the breasts of the tiny birds inlaid on my fingerboard rise and fall with the strains of our song. Close your eyes and let me caress you for the last time. Listen to my voice, which resembles the human in all its inflexions; in its accents expressive of joy, sadness, gaiety, sweetness, breathiness, languor, excitement and fury; and in its vitality, its tenderness, its consolation, its support. If instruments are prized in proportion as they imitate the voice, then the prize is surely mine: clean and piercing in the treble, caressing in the tenor, ravishing and golden in the bass. The most alluring voice in all Europe, in the most resonant body.